Beyond the Western Margin

Mark Morgan

Published in Melbourne, Australia by Bible Tales Online.
www.BibleTales.online

Beyond the Western Margin

ISBN (eBook): 978-1-925587-29-6
ISBN (Paperback): 978-1-925587-28-9

Last modified: 27 May 2024.

Cover photo by Cathy Morgan (2021).

To my ever-patient wife, Ruth.

Contents

Foreword

It was November 2021, and I was taking the NaNoWriMo challenge for the fifth time. For those who don't know, to "win" at NaNoWriMo, one must write a 50,000 word novel in a month. November was speeding by, my daily required word count was ballooning, and my heroes were making little progress. Would I finish?

This is often my story of self-inflicted stress that is NaNoWriMo.

I did finish, and also eventually completed the extra chapters needed to guide the story to its conclusion.

While the plot was prompted by the COVID-19 pandemic and my experience of closed borders, lockdowns, masks and social-distancing, the situation presented in the story is just one of an infinite number of possible short-term futures. I hope that readers can simply enjoy the story without suspecting me of either attempting to be a prophet or of criticising governments for mishandling the pandemic! Neither was my intention.

This story and all of the characters are fictional; any similarity with any existing people or names is purely coincidental. However, it is set in many real locations in the state of Victoria in south-eastern Australia. The existence of a bad guy trying to take over Halls Gap and the Grampians National Park is simply part of the story and not intended to reflect badly on the pleasant town of Halls Gap, where the author has spent many happy days with his family.

Particular thanks go to Ruth, my wife, who always helps me find time to write, patiently reads what I write, and humours me when I spent inordinate amounts of time on research into minute details.

Extra information about the book, including high resolution maps and photos, are available on the Bible Tales website as listed below. Use the links on the left or the QR codes on the right.

"Beyond the Western Margin" page
https://www.bibletales.online/beyond-the-western-margin/

Map of the World and Australia
https://www.bibletales.online/beyond-the-western-margin/#MapOfAustralia

Map of Victoria
https://www.bibletales.online/beyond-the-western-margin/#MapOfVictoria

Map of Northern Grampians
https://www.bibletales.online/beyond-the-western-margin/#MapOfNorthernGrampians

No manuscript is ever without errors, but early readers have helped eliminate many typos, bad grammar and uncomfortable usage. Cathy, my oldest daughter, has tirelessly undertaken the thankless task of proof reading the entire manuscript more than once. Thanks, Cathy.

I have a request to make of you, dear reader: if you find any errors; typos, spelling errors, poor grammar, or any other fault, please let me know.

Mark Morgan
May 2024

Map of Australia

Dan and his family live in Australia in the southern hemisphere where summer fills December, January and February and winter lasts from June to August.

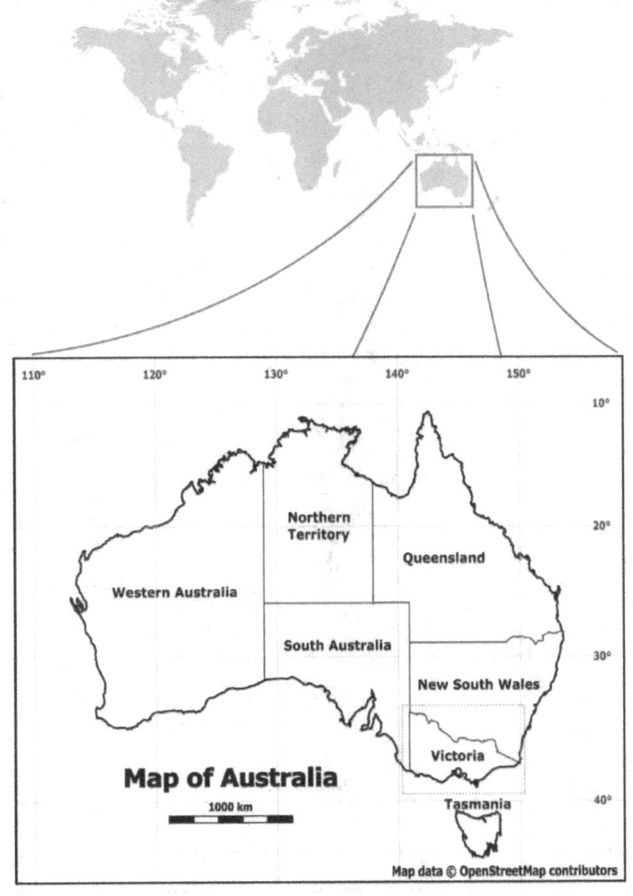

Map of Victoria

In the southeast corner of Australia lies the state of Victoria, the smallest of the mainland states.

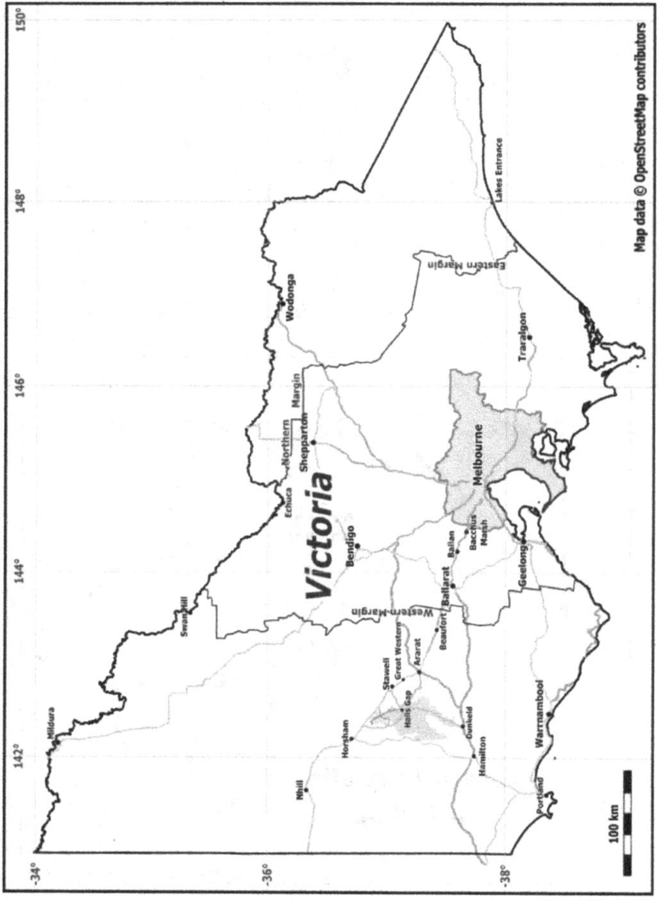

Glossary

4WD – four-wheel drive vehicle.

4WD track – dirt road not suitable for two-wheel drive cars or those with little ground clearance.

Bitumen – road surface typically used in Australia, also known as asphalt or tar macadam.

Chook – hen.

Crim – criminal.

Crook – criminal.

Dirt road – see gravel road.

Freeway – high-quality major highway allowing high-speed travel.

Gravel road – formed and graded road, surfaced with loose gravel. Common in country areas of Australia. Also known as an unmade road.

National Park – state government-run public open space.

Petrol – petroleum, called gas or gasoline in some countries.

Petrol station – sells fuel and other conveniences. Called a gas station or filling station in some countries.

Service station – see petrol station.

Service centre – collection of service stations, fast-food outlets and convenience stores on a major highway or freeway.

Servo – see petrol station.

Uni – university.

Chapter 1

Disturbing News

"They're locking us up tomorrow. Time to head for the hills!"

No answer.

The young man shrugged his shoulders and sighed, then turned, closed the door and made his way to the kitchen.

He helped himself to a slice of cake from the pantry and took it into the lounge room, where he slouched in an armchair and began eating. Dan Turner was 17 years old and had finished school that very day. Just one hour ago, he had put down his pen and filed out of the school hall with the rest of the students, walking out to freedom. His last exam was finished; no more school – ever!

When he woke in the morning, a dream of months of freedom stretching almost endlessly ahead of him had eased his doubts about that last exam.

Now the exam was over – and it hadn't been too bad – but his dream had been shattered.

Dan had met his friends on the courts outside the hall where knots of students were reviewing the exam and discussing the future. After a few minutes, an impromptu game of basketball – or was it football? – began, using someone's now-superannuated textbook. Dan grabbed the battered book and was threading his way towards the basket, ready to put it through the hoop, when he bumped Osmond Ortrick. It was really only a slight brush, but Osmond was the son of the Premier of Victoria and considered himself a touch above his fellow students, and his person hallowed ground.

"You idiot," he snarled, staggering a little.

Dan finished the lay-up and turned around. "Sorry," he said. "I just couldn't resist putting the Ball through the hoop." J. J. Ball was the author of the despised textbook whose influence in their lives was now a thing of the past.

"Well, make the most of your freedom," Osmond replied sardonically. "It won't last long!"

The look on his face caught Dan's attention. Ordinarily, he would have ignored Osmond and dismissed his words as classic Osmond-speak: sneering and supercilious. But this felt different somehow.

"What do you mean?" he asked.

"Another lockdown starts tomorrow, Danny."

"The name's Dan – as you know," he replied. "But how come? We've got the virus licked, haven't we?"

Looking mysterious, Osmond launched into what felt like a prepared speech, raising his voice enough to be heard by a wider audience on the court. He enjoyed speaking and was looking forward to the campus politics of university. "The overall community response to the virus has been successful in minimising societal damage, but certain aspects of everyday life have been compromised to the extent that modification to the common functional behaviour of ordinary citizens must be introduced in the interests of improved societal development and environmental protection. At times, freedom of movement and communication are the most dangerous features of a democratic society, particularly when the overall safety of the community is at risk."

"Umm... what is all that gobbledygook meant to mean, Osmond?"

"My father is signing papers today for the introduction of indefinite travel restrictions and extended health-related rules."

"That's *more* like English. So we'll have to stay home most of the time again, check in everywhere and wear masks?"

"It's going to be a lot more than just masks and checkins, Danny. Don't you follow politics? Don't you know that the opposition is deceitfully blocking important new legislation? They're aiming for anarchy: resisting the responsible progressive direction of the government. They're trying to stop the government governing. And they'll ruin the state unless the government publishes these new health orders right away. "

"But if we've got the virus more or less under control, where's the need for more health orders?"

"Ah," said Osmond, looking conspiratorial. He put his index finger in front of his lips briefly, leaned forward a little and spoke quietly, with the timing of a consummate actor. The growing crowd of students around him moved even closer – as he intended that they should. "Sometimes the appearance of events on the surface is not the true perspective," he said. "There are... movements... at large in our society. Dangerous, underground movements that want to subvert our government's courageous victory over the virus. They want to enforce their regressive minority opinions on the majority and take away our hard-won freedoms."

"So your Dad will fight for our freedom with another lockdown?"

Some of the other kids laughed, but Osmond was not amused.

"You ignorant so-and-so! Better some short-term suffering than the destruction of everything the government has fought for."

"I thought you said *permanent* travel restrictions."

"No, I said 'indefinite'."

"And the difference is...?"

"The end date will be set at an appropriate time."

Dan snorted. He left the conversation and rejoined his friends. Slam-dunking old Ball had lost its attraction now that his vision for the holidays might prove a mirage.

☙

By the time Dan finished his cake, he was feeling deeply frustrated. All of his plans for holidays – time with friends, vacation employment – all were in jeopardy. Was there anything he could do about it? Should he head out to the margins? As the idea took root in his mind, new possibilities began to fill his thoughts. Surely these meaningless restrictions wouldn't be enforced so rigidly near the margins? With a rebellious leap of thought, he wondered if perhaps he should just drop everything and go out *beyond* the margins. He knew of the dangers reported by news services, but his family had been out there many times in the past, back before the margins were drawn. Surely it couldn't be so very dangerous now?

As he mulled over this question, he heard the garage door opening. Mum must be home. He wondered if she had heard anything about new restrictions.

Tanya Turner unlocked the door from the garage and entered the lounge room. "You're there, Dan. That's good. I'm glad you're safe."

"Why wouldn't I be safe, Mum?"

"Oh, everywhere seems to be getting more dangerous. A nurse from our paediatric ward was robbed when she went out to her car after the afternoon shift last night, and another nurse was attacked last week. Your Dad and I are getting worried about me working there – and about Belinda going to school on public transport, too."

"I guess so. A few kids from school have got in trouble on the way home recently. Osmond blames it all on the opposition and talks about 'mysterious movements' that keep trying to undermine his Dad's government."

"Well, I don't know about that, but life is much less safe than it was. If the virus doesn't get you, some hoodlum will. Our neighbours on both sides have been burgled in the last three months, and Mrs Throgmorton down the street was assaulted on her way home from work too. It's terrible. We might need to have a curfew just to keep everyone safe!"

"Osmond would agree with you there. After the exam, he was saying..."

"Oh, Dan – your exam!" said his mother, putting her hand on his arm. "I'd forgotten it because I was so worried about all the problems. How did it go?"

"So-so. It wasn't too bad."

"That's your last exam! Congratulations! My son has finished school." She patted his arm proudly. "Now you've just got to wait for the results, and then it's on to uni next year."

"They said this morning that the results will be delayed. Something to do with delays in postage and breakdowns in communication with the markers."

"Yes, I heard that on the news, but they didn't mention any new date for when the results will arrive. Did they give you one?"

"No. They just said it would definitely be before the end of January," said Dan, disgustedly. "January! Would you believe it?"

"That's a long delay. It's even later than it was when I did Year 12!"

"A lot of things have been going backwards recently, Mum. I even heard that there are bushrangers out near the margins. There haven't been bushrangers in Victoria for more than a hundred years!"

"I think we're even starting to get them in the city. Lots of people won't go out at night now."

"From what Osmond was saying, they might not be *allowed* to go out at night after tomorrow."

"What was he saying, Dan?"

"He said the government's introducing permanent travel limits. Perhaps extended lockdowns. He described them as health orders, but then he blamed them on opponents of the government."

"Travel limits? But we were planning to go on holiday next week!"

"Yes," said Dan, glumly. "We might not be allowed to go. Should I just run away tonight, Mum?"

"No, son, I don't think so," said Tanya, looking worried. "We'll have to talk about this tonight as a family. Perhaps we'll get more information on the news."

Dan went to his room. He had planned to fly his drone over the golf course that afternoon, looking for lost golf balls and discs in the rough and the lake, but now he needed to think. Osmond was a loud-mouth, for sure, but he often heard news before anyone else. Dan chewed his lip. If there really was going to be a lockdown in Melbourne, should he make a run for it before it started? There was sure to be plenty of work in the country. After all, the reason the government drew the margins in the first place was to define an area that was small enough to maintain properly, but big enough to support the population.

Osmond's father often used the phrase "a border of mutual support" in his press conferences. Honestly, Dan didn't think it meant much, but it had a ring to it and rolled nicely off the tongue. In the years since the start of the pandemic, the economic effects of frequent lockdowns and the sudden reduction in population had been felt all around the world, and Australia had suffered badly. Self-imposed national isolation had initially saved many lives, but hadn't helped much in the long run as new variants swept through, one after another, seemingly unhindered by the various vaccines that had saved so many lives at first. There had even been a time of optimism when the pandemic had been declared over and recovery was on everybody's mind.

The next wave had taken everyone by surprise – killing many. Desperate lockdowns and panic followed, destroying the livelihood of many who survived. Huge numbers of businesses went broke and unemployment rose quickly. Generous social help was provided, but it had to be funded through massive government debt across the country. When international demand faltered as other countries struggled with their own problems, managing the debt became almost impossible.

The de-federation of Australia could be said to have begun with border closures at the height of the pandemic, but the breakdown of national ties re-emerged as economic difficulties grew after the pandemic returned, reinvigorated. Each state government did its best to keep money within the state, and Australia as a single united country disintegrated. The states emerged from 125 years of subordinated slumber into a new era of re-discovered local power. For a time, the borders were even more tightly policed than ever, but as the impossibility of supporting the vast inland areas of Australia became obvious, each state began to pull back even from its own borders. No longer was there an endless drive to expand and grow; instead, governments were forced to recognise the need to maintain only what they could afford, and abandon the rest.

The smaller states – Tasmania and Victoria – suffered least from this, having the smallest road and rail networks. Yet even so, the burgeoning costs of labour were quickly using up any available cash as the economy was forced to revert to older methods of operation. Communication networks were deteriorating and the bullish advance of electronics into every area of life had been compelled to retreat.

In Victoria, the outlook was very gloomy.

Dan's family had been caught up in all of this like everybody else, but they were a little more isolated than many. Originally from Adelaide, the family had moved to Melbourne when Dan was seven, not long before the pandemic began. Most of their relatives still lived in Adelaide, but they had not been able to visit them or meet them for several years. Schedule conflicts during the short-lived lifting of the declaration of a pandemic had cost them the opportunity for shared holidays, although Dan's family had visited the Grampians by themselves.

Over the past year, the progressive degradation of internet connections had even made it difficult for Dan to maintain his close friendship with Dave, the cousin nearest his own age.

If Dan fled the city, could he make his way to Adelaide? Now that access to most social media was so unreliable, he wasn't even sure he could discuss it with Dave. It was almost two months since they'd last managed a brief flurry of messages.

If only he could arrange to meet Dave halfway, perhaps in the glorious Grampians! But the deadline for making a decision was tomorrow.

Chapter 2

Dinner Time

"Carrie said she was followed as she went home last night," said Belinda.

"Who by, dear?" asked Tanya.

"Some guy in dark glasses and a black coat."

"He was probably just walking down the road," said Dan.

"No, he wasn't," insisted Belinda. "Carrie said she tried walking faster but he walked faster too. Then when she walked around the block to get away from him, he followed her all the way around."

"Did she get home safely?" asked Nathan, Dan and Belinda's father.

"Yes. After going around the block, she started running and got inside as quickly as she could."

"I'm glad of that," said Tanya. "What's the city coming to? I'm starting to feel unsafe just going outside!"

"No doubt our premier's plan will fix it," said Dan, sarcastically. "Osmond says he's locking us down again tomorrow night. Curfews and other travel restrictions, too. Can we listen to the news and see if he's right?"

The family had just finished their evening meal, so Nathan turned on the news. They were astonished by what they heard. Osmond was indeed right.

Strict travel restrictions were to come into force across the state from *midnight the following day*. Mr Ortrick said that a new wave of infections was spreading across the city and that limiting the movement of people was the only way to get it under control. Travel in and out of Melbourne would be forbidden without a permit which would carry an administrative fee to cover costs. A night-time curfew would keep people in their homes between ten o'clock at night and five in the morning. For weary citizens used to lockdowns and restrictions, neither these rules nor the limits on the numbers of people who could meet together were anything new, but the introduction of conscription and school-based cadet training was a complete surprise. With his typical gently aggressive delivery, Mr Ortrick warned his audience that there were dangers to the state that would require the support of all loyal Victorians against attacks from beyond the margins. Shadowy forces were also at work within the state already, making a strong and immediate response essential.

"Whew!" said Dan when the speech was over. "So much for going to uni. I thought conscription was a thing of the past."

"Let's listen to the reporters' questions," said Tanya.

It was soon clear that some of the reporters had been primed about the changes – and that only selected questions would be answered. Mr Ortrick only seemed to see reporters who had previously shown themselves supportive of the government.

After a while, Dan's father turned it off, saying, "I think that's enough. We're getting pats on the back, not information."

"Some of those questions were the sorts of things Osmond spouts," said Dan.

"Well, son, what do you think of the news?" asked Nathan.

"It messes up all my plans, and it doesn't make sense. Osmond's Dad just seems to want to lock us up."

"He probably thinks he has good reason for it, but I have to agree – that's what it sounds like."

"Is there anything we can do?" asked Belinda.

"What do you mean?" asked her mother.

"Can we get away from all these restrictions?"

"We've had lockdowns before. They all come to an end."

"True," said Nathan, "but did you notice that the premier didn't put any time limit on *these* restrictions? He didn't even say what changes to the situation would allow the government to relax the rules."

"He doesn't want to relax the rules," said Dan, bitterly.

"Danny-boy is right," said Belinda.

"We should head for the hills," said Dan.

"Where?" asked Tanya.

"Out to the margins. Go for that holiday we planned, and maybe go out even further."

"You mean *beyond* the margins?"

"Yes. The new rules are ridiculous."

"Well, Dan," said his father, "you know that they drew the margins because the state can't afford to maintain all the existing infrastructure and services so far away from Melbourne: roads, rail, government services, policing, defence and so on. The borders were carefully chosen to enable the state to survive despite the pandemic. We have access to *most* of the natural resources in the state and the best farmland, not to mention the biggest population centres. The less populated areas have been shut off, left to fail or survive on their own."

"And they've cut off all the most interesting parts of the state!" said Dan.

"All the beautiful places too, all the nice little towns," agreed Belinda.

"Well, the government says most of the people who used to live beyond the margins have abandoned their homes and moved inside. News reports say that the land beyond the margins is mostly empty," her father responded.

"But what about bushrangers?" asked Dan. "Kids at school are always talking about NK2 and Captain Starship."

"NK2?" queried his father.

"Ned Kelly 2.0."

"I've heard of him," said Belinda. "Is he an improved version of Ned? More like Robin Hood?"

"More likely he's just some no-hoper trading on someone else's infamy," said Dan.

"Anyway, the fact is that the government says the areas beyond the margins are dangerous," interposed Nathan firmly.

"The western margin is a bit beyond Ballarat, isn't it?" asked Dan.

"Yes," said Nathan, "it crosses the Western Freeway just beyond Lake Burrumbeet."

"Are places like the Grampians really dangerous?" asked Belinda. She had a habit of opening her eyes very wide when asking about something she couldn't really imagine.

"Why don't we go and find out?" asked Dan, blurting out the idea he'd been working up to all afternoon. "I don't believe the reports."

"You don't *want* to believe them, Dan," answered Nathan.

Tanya was sitting quietly but now her brows knitted. She put her hand on her husband's arm and spoke: "I think Dan might be on the right track, love."

Her husband looked at her in surprise. "Are you sure, dear?"

"Well, we were going to camp beside Lake Burrumbeet next week, but if we wait until then, we can't go."

"The lake is inside the margin, Tanya. Dan is talking about going *beyond* the western margin. We don't know what it's like out there."

"But if we don't go now, Nathan, we may never be able to go. You said yourself that the Premier didn't put any limits on these restrictions. If the past is anything to go by, they'll get tighter, not looser."

"True. I just want to make sure that we don't do anything too hastily."

"If we don't do it hastily, we won't be able to do it at all," said Dan.

"Let's get on with planning what to do," said Belinda. "There's nothing much keeping us here, is there? – that is, unless we don't leave before tomorrow night."

"What about Derek?" asked Dan, slyly.

"Don't talk to me about Derek. He has no brains."

"What did he do to upset you?"

"He tells blonde jokes."

"So does Mum. And she's blonde too!"

"He made me laugh while Carrie was getting annoyed with him, so then she got annoyed at me too."

"But Carrie's not blonde! Why would she care?"

"She was worried for me. And then Derek told a redhead joke and I laughed at that too, so Carrie got even more annoyed."

"I don't understand," said Dan.

"No. You'd get on well with Derek, Danny-boy."

"That'll do, children," said their mother. "Let's have a family meeting: make some decisions and get on with planning. We haven't got long."

❧

They were all in the lounge room, Nathan in his reclining chair and Tanya in hers. Dan was lounging on the couch, while Belinda sat cross-legged on the floor.

The family meeting was still in progress, but many decisions had already been made. Dan was puzzled, though: Nathan seemed to be disputing each decision, and Dan couldn't understand why.

"Why do you keep trying to convince us to stay here and lose our freedom, Dad?" he asked at last.

"I'm not trying to get us to stay. I just want you all to understand what the problems are. If we go away, how long do we stay away? What will you do about university? And what about Belinda's schooling? What will happen to our house while we are away? Can we afford to live out there?"

"University doesn't matter any more. After all, they're talking about conscription! And Belinda's schooling is just as bad as mine was. You're always criticising the teachers."

Belinda was happy to dismiss school too. Her altercation with Derek seemed to have been the last straw.

"Nathan, you should tell the children what's happening about the house. After all, you've already started arranging it."

"I just want them to learn to think through the issues, dear."

Dan sat up. "What's this about the house?"

"You know how the government made non-citizens pay an extra tax to own houses here? Well, that's been widened to include us."

"But we're citizens, aren't we?" asked Dan.

"Of Australia, yes. But we've only been in Victoria for ten years, and apparently that's not enough for the government. From next month, if we want to keep this house we'll have to pay a monthly fee to the government because we're 'foreigners'."

"Huh?"

"And it'll add up to more than we can afford. Particularly if I lose my job."

"I thought your job was secure."

"It was. But with the employment problems and changes to citizenship rules, it's not secure anymore. My boss is saying that the Head of Department is putting pressure on him to get rid of all foreigners and only employ Victorians."

"But surely Australians who live in Victoria are Victorians, aren't they?"

"Not any more. Victorians are now people *born* in Victoria. Everyone else is either a threat or a potential source of income. They told me I could *buy* citizenship, but the cost was almost as much as the house tax and it would only cover me. The rest of you would still be called foreigners, and I'm sure it's only a matter of time before access to universities and hospitals goes the same way. I didn't want to tell you until I'd heard your decisions about heading out, but we might not have any choice in the end anyway."

"Dad's right, kids," said Tanya. "You know I work as a volunteer, but the head nurse has been hinting that I won't be needed soon. The health department is cutting staff and closing wards because they're running out of money. With various services cut, lots of us volunteers won't be needed any more either."

"Why would anyone stay here then?" asked Dan. "Let's head for the hills!"

"That's fine," said Nathan quietly, "but how do we afford it?"

"We've got all the equipment we need, Dad," said Dan. "Camper-trailer, tents, four-wheel drive, even solar panels and large water tanks in case we have problems. You've already been collecting food for our holiday. Out beyond the margins, we won't have tax collectors and premiers who want to lock us up!"

"Hmm," said Nathan. "I'm not sure what we'll find out there. But I am convinced that we'll have to go *somewhere*, anyway. Maybe things will be better near the margins."

"Nobody has said which direction we should head," said Tanya.

"Aren't we going to Lake Burrumbeet first?" asked Belinda in dismay. "That's where we were going for our holiday."

"It's closer to Adelaide, too," said Tanya. "We wouldn't be foreigners if we went there!"

"I wouldn't be so sure," said Nathan, darkly. "Don't forget, we've been away for ten years. We might be foreigners there too."

"Let's go out beyond the western margin," said Dan. "Why not go to the Grampians?"

Chapter 3

Decision

A knock on the door interrupted the family meeting. Nathan quickly explained that he would be busy for an hour or two then went to answer the door. He welcomed the visitor quietly, then disappeared with him into his study.

Almost two hours later, the study door opened, and shortly after that the front door opened and closed.

Dan, busy in his room, resisted the temptation to poke his head out and watch the visitor depart. Over the last two hours he had been asking himself what to take. Pocket-fillers: phone, keys, wallet and so on; that much was easy. Other essentials too: laptop, sunnies, books, sports equipment, drone. He pulled out the family's list of things to take on holidays and ran his eyes down it. All sorts of clothes, toiletries, sleeping bag, blankets, chair, camera. He didn't normally bother with a camera anymore – his phone was good enough – but they might be away for some time, so perhaps he should take both. Surveying the growing pile on the bedroom floor, he suddenly asked himself: would they be coming back *at all*? And if not, what should he do with his stuff? And what about the house? He was mulling over this startling thought when his father walked in, trying to hide a smile.

"Hey, Dad, are we coming back?"

"Yes – at least, I expect so. But let's go back into the lounge room and talk about it with Mum and Belinda."

They reconvened in the lounge room, and Dan thought Dad was looking unusually animated. Mum looked at Dad, raising her eyebrows, and he nodded briefly. It was clear that there was some secret business going on between his parents.

"What's the secret, Dad?" blurted out Dan.

"We'll get to that, Danny-boy."

More proof that Dad was distracted: only Belinda called him "Danny-boy".

Dad sank into his chair and smugly surveyed his audience.

"Any second thoughts about leaving?" he asked.

"How long are we going for, Dad?" asked Belinda. "Mum said I had to ask *you*."

"Only after you'd already asked *me* a hundred times!" smiled Tanya.

"How long do you want to go for?" asked Nathan.

"I don't know. When you went to talk to that man, I suddenly started to think of all the things I've been taking for granted about next year: Year 11, my friends, sport, and lots of other things."

"Would you prefer not to go at all? What about Derek?" teased Dan.

"I told you what I thought of Derek! Of course I want to go, but have we decided where to go?"

"Not really," said Nathan. "But I need to give you some news. That man was a colleague of mine from work. He's been asking me for some time about buying our house. Your mother and I have considered leaving the city because of the pandemic, but it's hard to know where to go. Ownership will soon be too expensive for us as "foreigners", and rental is becoming harder too. The new taxes tipped the balance: we decided to sell the house and rent it back until things became clearer. Tonight was settlement time. We've sold the house, kids – with a few special conditions. And after our discussions earlier, we aren't going to rent it back, either."

"What happens about school next year?" asked Belinda, eyes wide. "That's less than three months away."

"Then we don't have to worry about it for a while, do we?" said Tanya.

"No, but..."

"And anyway, we don't know what conditions will be like by then, either here or out in the country."

"Let's get going west and worry about next year next year," said Dan.

"OK, but..."

"You won't even have to get upset by Derek's jokes!"

"True, but..."

"Why do you keep saying 'but'?"

"Because you never let me finish."

"Well, finish then."

"What shall I do with my old teddy?"

"You still have that bedraggled thing sitting at the end of your bed, do you?"

"Yes, that's why I'm so emotionally well-adjusted. Unlike you."

"Yeah, right. But I was wondering, Dad: if we've sold the house, what do we do with all of our stuff?"

"I said there were some special conditions," answered Nathan. "We can leave our stuff in the three rooms at the back of the house for up to twelve months before we need to come back and take it away."

"Oh, good," said Tanya. "I'm glad he agreed to that."

"Well, he doesn't need all the rooms at the moment – the house is just for him and his wife."

Whatever else happened, Dan didn't want the plan for a grand escape to degrade into a mere month or two's holiday near Ballarat! If they did that, Sis would get all soft about Derek again and want to get back to Melbourne.

"Dad, when do we leave and where do we go?"

"Okay, you want a decision, so here it is, Dan: we leave tomorrow, and we're going beyond the western margin."

Dan was surprised to see Mum and Belinda smiling. He himself celebrated with a whoop.

"How long for?" he asked, breathlessly.

"At least three months. And if we need to start schooling Belinda, we'll do so. Somehow."

"Hooray!" cheered Dan.

"Now everyone, stop and listen," said Nathan. "We can leave 'house' stuff in the back three rooms and outside stuff in the shed, so everything we're leaving behind needs to be in one of those places before we go."

"I suppose we have to leave soon enough to reach the margin before midnight tomorrow night," said Dan.

"You've got it," said his father.

"And we've got to get the car and the camper-trailer packed too," said Belinda. Dan was sure that if her eyes opened any wider, they'd fall out.

"And the garage emptied," he added, starting to realise the size of the job they'd taken on.

"And be ready to leave by noon," said Nathan.

"Noon?" said Tanya. "Uh-oh."

"I'm glad we cleared out the rumpus room a few weeks ago," said Belinda.

"Hey!" said Dan, accusingly. "You planned that, didn't you, Dad? You knew."

"Well, I didn't *know* at the time, but it seemed like a wise thing to do."

"Oh, okay. I suppose so."

"Now, everyone, that means we leave in about thirteen hours. We need to keep a few hours spare to decide what to do when we get to the margin. Okay?"

"Yes!" chorused Dan and Belinda.

"Let's hop to it, then."

Chapter 4

Leaving

In the end, they left at two o'clock the next afternoon – an achievement which pleased Nathan and Tanya, although they didn't admit it.

The previous night, Nathan and Dan had quickly fitted pad bolts on the doors of the three rooms in which their goods were to be stored, including Dan's and Belinda's bedrooms.

Of course, this meant that Dan and Belinda had to immediately make some difficult decisions: what should they take, and what should they leave? Once their rooms were packed full of furniture and other things being left behind, they wouldn't be able to change their minds.

As Dan and Belinda tackled their bedrooms, Nathan and Tanya started packing the camper-trailer and the four-wheel drive. Fortunately, they were used to packing for longer journeys, as the family had several times taken month-long holidays in the camper-trailer.

Work was progressing well, but it was getting late. Sometime after midnight, Tanya found Belinda blundering around in exhausted confusion, and sent her to the now-empty lounge room to get some sleep while Nathan and Dan began moving the furniture from the rest of the house into the back rooms. It was hard work, and a few corners were knocked in their hurry.

Dan had been determined to stay up until the packing was finished, but sometime after two o'clock, Tanya overrode his insistence that he was not tired and sent him to sleep in an empty room. Despite the hard floor, he was asleep within moments, and the rest of the house was packed up around him without disturbing him.

Neither Nathan nor Tanya slept that night, and as soon as Dan and Belinda each woke from their excited sleep, they were back at work again.

Wall hangings, pictures, furniture, bookcases, beds, kitchenware, spare clothing, the fridge-freezer, microwave and even the piano were stashed inside those three rooms, and by the end, they all understood just how many possessions filled their house. And now they were leaving them, probably for three to six months.

At eleven o'clock, with the packing at last completed, Nathan and Tanya told Dan and Belinda that they had exactly one hour to say their goodbyes to any friends they could visit in that time. They must be back by noon. The pair hurried off on their bikes, and Nathan and Tanya did their own visiting: farewelling friends and doing their best to arrange the cancellation of utilities and subscriptions. It was a frantic time, and many friends had to be asked to pass on messages to others.

When the hour came to an end, they all met back at the house. Nathan was proud of his family for successfully meeting such a tight schedule. As he walked down the hall, the wall clock struck twelve.

"The clock!" he said. "I'd forgotten it!" He quickly took it down and stored it in Dan's old room.

Next, the family started cleaning the house ready for the new owners. True, it would not meet Tanya's strict standards, but there was no time for more.

Once the empty rooms had all been cleaned, it was time to lock up all the outdoor equipment in the shed.

Tanya also parked her little runabout a few centimetres from the garage wall, as agreed with the new owners. Nathan locked its doors and disconnected the battery. Tanya patted the car and walked away without looking back.

Dan took one last look in his bedroom, filled now to the ceiling with all sorts of things considered non-essential. A bookcase stood near the doorway, hundreds of books on its shelves. Should he take any of them? His eyes fell on the Bible he had been given at Sunday School three years before and he picked it up. He had a Bible on his phone, but a paper book was different. He thought for a few moments, then took it out to the car.

There was very little room left for people in the four-wheel drive. The storage area was crammed full, as were the roof box and the right-hand rear seat — it was easier to stack things against a closed door than in the middle between two seats. Every available nook and cranny was stuffed with "essential" things, although Nathan and Tanya had each removed quite a few items quietly stashed away by Dan and Belinda.

"Come on, kids," their father had said once, frustrated. "We'll need these solar panels *every day*, but your game of

Monopoly won't be used once in six months – and if you ever do use it, you'll spend the whole time arguing!"

Belinda's teddy, however, had slipped through the net, and so had Dan's slingshot. Perhaps the family would need him to go hunting sometime....

Astonished neighbours were farewelled briefly, with one being asked to pass on to the new owner a package containing keys and a few scrawled notes. Nathan locked the front door and the family piled into the four-wheel drive. Packing up an entire house in such a short time was an amazing achievement, but now it was time to leave. Dan and Belinda exchanged excited smiles as the overloaded vehicle rolled out of the driveway.

Within minutes they had filled the fuel tank at the nearest service station and withdrawn as much cash as possible from the bank nearby. It was a beautiful mid-November day with all the warmth of late spring, and the mood in the car was light-hearted as they drove through the city. In little over an hour they had joined the Western Freeway. Although they had been familiar with this road in the past, there had been no opportunity for travel in the last few years and Nathan was surprised how much it had deteriorated. No longer was it a high-quality two-lane road with extra emergency stopping lanes in each direction. Instead, the left-hand lane was covered with frequent deep potholes and the emergency lanes were littered with debris: shredded tyres, broken goods that had tumbled from trucks or trailers, and even the occasional car – normally reduced to a burnt-out shell. The right-hand lane was the only lane good enough to use, and even it was poor.

Fortunately, there were very few cars on the once-busy road, and they saw none of the large trucks that had frequented it in the past.

I wonder what the road will be like beyond Bacchus Marsh, worried Nathan. *This journey might not be as easy as I thought.*

☙

Nathan's concerns were well-founded. The steep sections beyond Bacchus Marsh were in even worse condition. The few smaller trucks that climbed the hills were travelling slowly and there were few opportunities to overtake on the degraded road. It was evident that there had been no road maintenance for several years. The once quick and easy journey to Ballarat would be much harder now. The 110 km/hr speed limit signs were still mockingly in place, although some in the more badly damaged sections of road bore graffiti that emphasised how unattainable the limits had become.

After two long hours on the "freeway", they finally reached the turn-off to Ballarat and drove down into the town. They planned to get as much fuel as they could carry, just in case it was not available further out. The service areas at Ballan had been empty, boarded up and covered with graffiti, a situation that caused Nathan and Tanya to exchange worried glances. If fuel could not be found in Ballarat, they would have to reassess their plans. They were all on edge as they approached the first petrol station in Ballarat, and the boards nailed over the windows of the shop were not encouraging. The "Pump Closed" signs hanging from each fuel pump were the final discouragement, before Belinda suddenly saw a sign and called out excitedly, "It says: 'Petrol 2km', with an arrow in the direction we're going!"

They drove on, but the next station was also closed. However, it had another helpful sign: "3km ahead for petrol/diesel".

By this time, the mood in the car was sinking, and sighs greeted the sight of the sign.

"Should we stop and ask someone?" asked Tanya.

"Let's try the three kilometres first, then if that one's closed too, we'll try to find someone to ask. It's not as if there are lots of people around, anyway. I've never seen the streets of Ballarat so quiet."

Three kilometres further on, there was still no sign of any petrol station, and another two kilometres passed without them seeing another soul. Suddenly Dan shouted excitedly, "There's a servo up ahead!"

"And it looks as if a car is going in there," added Belinda.

They drove into the service station and looked around. The car in front of them had stopped at a pump and an attendant was putting the nozzle into the petrol tank. He turned around and waved the family to another pump labelled "Diesel".

"Wow!" muttered Nathan. "Look at the price!"

Dan climbed out and unscrewed the diesel tank cap. As he did so, the attendant called out, "I'll serve you in a minute when I've finished filling this one."

Dan took the hint, stood back and waited. Nathan climbed out too, commenting, "That's the way it used to work, you know. Before they introduced self-service, a real human filled your tank for you! That was a few years before I was born, though. I've never seen it before."

"Why would they do it now?"

"You could always ask."

The attendant finished filling the tank he was working on and hung up the nozzle. The driver paid in cash and drove off.

"Looks like he only takes cash," said Dan.

"Yes," answered the attendant, hearing him as he walked over. "We don't take credit any more, and we offer full service because I find that the pumps keep working longer if I use them myself. It's so hard to get anything fixed nowadays.

Full service can also be a bit of a selling point when it's cold and windy, which isn't unusual in Ballarat."

"We're from Melbourne," said Nathan, "and I can't help noticing that the price is pretty steep."

"You're right. Petrol is hard to get – and expensive. We don't sell as much as we used to, either, which is why so many of the service stations have closed down. Business is tough."

"What's it like further out?"

"Oh, about the same as around here or worse, I believe. The smaller towns are struggling more."

"What about beyond the margin?"

"I don't have any cause to go out there – not looking for a reason either! Sometimes customers *claim* to live away out there, and I believe convoys go out at times to collect resources we need here inside the margins, but overall, from what I hear, it's pretty wild." The attendant looked pointedly at their overloaded vehicle with the camper-trailer and its bicycle holder with four bikes. "I've got no plans to go out *there* for a holiday."

"How many visitors do you get from Melbourne?"

"Very few, recently, and with the new rules I expect there'll be even fewer. How ridiculous, limiting travel to 25 kilometres out here in the country! Don't they understand that Australia's a big place?"

The pump clicked off and the attendant removed the nozzle from the tank. Nathan asked him to fill the extra tank they carried on the pack-rack too, but he looked doubtful. "I'm running a bit short of diesel and don't want to take it away from my trusty customers. Look, I'll half-fill it. That's the best I can do. You might be able to get more further on, but don't be surprised if their prices make mine look cheap!"

Tanya and Belinda had climbed out of the car to stretch their legs and were wandering away along the footpath. The attendant noticed them as he finished half-filling the extra tank and said quickly, "Hey, don't let your ladies go off by themselves. It's getting late in the day and there are some dubious characters around – even here in Ballarat."

Dan hurried after them as Nathan paid with some of their precious Victorian money. Money in banks wasn't much use any more, now that electronic payments were a thing of the past. Cash was all that mattered. He thanked the attendant, climbed into the car, and drove after the others, wondering what they should do next. The afternoon was drawing on and they hadn't even reached the margin yet. The sun would set in just three hours and there was too much uncertainty about the roads to risk travelling very far before stopping for the night.

Nathan pulled up beside the three and waited for them to climb in. Suddenly, he saw a group of five sullen-looking youths come out of a park that bordered the road 50 metres ahead. Something about them looked threatening and Nathan snapped, "Get in quickly!" He got ready to jump out of the car if necessary.

Hearing the urgency in his voice, Tanya was inside with the door closed and locked before the group started to run towards them. Nathan could see that they all carried short, heavy sticks. Belinda was quickly seated, too, but since Dan had to get in through the same door, he was still climbing in as the thugs approached frighteningly quickly. Suddenly, a police siren sounded briefly and the young men paused metres from the family's car, looking back over their shoulders to where a police car, lights flashing, was stopping in the middle of the road.

Two police officers climbed out of the car, leaving two more inside.

"Hey, fellas," said the closer officer, "out for a run, are you?"

He made no mention of the makeshift clubs they carried.

"Yeah, officer," answered one. "Been exercising in the park, just jogging home now."

"Well, don't forget that from tomorrow you'll only be allowed in the park between noon and 3pm. New government regulations and health orders from midnight."

"We'll remember, officer."

"Well, you can head home now. First, though, let me warn you lads that with those new regulations, I can also decide that those 'exercise sticks' you're carrying could be used as weapons. That might get you a one-way trip to the new Melbourne detention centre, so let's leave them at home, shall we?"

"Okay." The young men shambled off down the path.

The police officers approached the family car and Nathan wound down his window. "Thanks, officers. I guess you came in the nick of time."

"Yes. Those kids have started causing a lot of trouble lately. I hope they'll listen to my warnings. And what about you, sir? Remember that from tomorrow, the travel limit across the entire state of Victoria is 25 kilometres per day."

"But not beyond the margins?"

"No, sir. We have no jurisdiction beyond the margins. But I strongly recommend that you stay within the margins. Those kids are nothing compared with what you'll meet beyond the margins."

"How many people are left out west?"

"It's hard to know. We meet some people like yourselves who want to go out there. They don't all listen to our advice, and some come back with their tails between their legs, telling horror stories of bushrangers, armed robberies, terrible roads and autocratic local governments." He paused, then looked Nathan in the eye. "Most don't come back at all."

"So from tomorrow we can travel up to 25 kilometres per day within the margins?"

"Yes, and for the next month we won't have to ask for your home address if you have a camper-trailer attached. After that, you'll need a permit to travel more than 25 kilometres from your home address."

"How long will these restrictions last? Surely they can't last forever?"

"Maybe not, but we've been told that even if they get the new wave of the virus under control, these limits will still last for at least six months after that."

"Six months! We were planning to get back to Melbourne before then. What would we have to do?"

"You might have to stay in Ballarat for a few months."

"Wow! We didn't realise that when we came," said Tanya, worried.

"And we couldn't get back tonight if we wanted to," said Dan.

"They really don't want us travelling, do they?" Nathan said to the officer.

"They're just trying to keep everyone safe, sir," said the officer, heartily. "Think of those hoodlums and be grateful that we'll have extra powers tomorrow to keep 'em under control!"

"Well, thank you, officer."

"You're welcome, but don't forget about the health orders tomorrow."

"We won't."

"After all, that's why we're leaving!" said Dan under his breath.

They drove on, discussing what they should do.

"Should we stay inside the margin tonight?" asked Tanya.

"Yes!" said Belinda. "Those hoodlums were scary. I don't want to arrive anywhere after dark."

"Just *driving* in the dark might be difficult, based on what we've seen of the roads so far," said Dan.

"It might be best to stay at the caravan park next to Lake Burrumbeet tonight," said Nathan. "That'll put us within 25 kilometres of the margin, ready to cross early tomorrow morning. That'll give us our best chance of arriving in daylight even if the roads are bad."

"Arrive *where* though?" asked Tanya. "That policeman made it sound dangerous out beyond the margins."

"But it sounds dangerous inside too," argued Belinda.

"I think we'll be safer outside," said Dan, hopefully.

"Maybe we can get more information from people in the caravan park," said Nathan.

They drove along the Avenue of Honour, finding the road in surprisingly good condition.

"Not many trucks come along here, I guess," said Nathan. "It's almost a dead end now – it pretty much only leads to the margin."

"I'm trying to check how far the camping ground is from the margin, but my phone doesn't have any coverage," grumbled Dan. " 'No signal,' it says."

"Hmm. I'm sure we've had coverage here in the past," mused Nathan.

"Yes, I remember sitting beside the lake talking to Dave," said Dan.

"We're getting close to the margin," said Tanya. "Maybe that's it."

They drove into the familiar caravan park, but how different it was! Instead of a bustling campground with tidy roads and neatly mown surrounds, it was mostly empty. The roads were half-covered with leaves and small branches, and the grass was only mowed where people were camping and around some permanent living areas.

"Whew!" said Belinda. "What's happened here?"

They drove to the office but found it empty, with a sign on the window: "Pick a mown site on the hill. We'll come around in the evening."

On inspection, they found plenty of empty sites, but only a few had been mown in the last couple of weeks. They chose one a little down the hill towards the lake, overlooking the boat ramp.

"Something makes me want to check out the facilities before we set up for the night," said Tanya.

"Agreed," said her husband.

Their investigations didn't turn up any good news. The facilities were all locked, with new entry codes. Signs advised that electricity was only available for an hour at midday and that the solar hot water system was no longer boosted with electricity, so the water temperature would vary from day to day. Hot water was available on a first-come, first-served basis. Powered sites no longer provided power. Water was available, but it was recommended that it be boiled.

"Not good, but not too bad," said Nathan philosophically when the full extent of the decline in conditions became clear. "We're going to have to get used to changes soon, so we might as well start now."

Having decided to stay, they quickly set up the camper trailer, with the annex for Belinda, and a tent for Dan. As they added the finishing touches and the sun set across the lake in flaming splendour, a man approached. He was not the owner they had known in the past.

"Welcome to Lake Burrumbeet Caravan Park. I'm Ed. You want to stay for the night?" The man was short and stocky, with wiry grey hair. He carried a hat in his right hand and a pen behind his ear.

The price he demanded was much higher than they had paid at their last visit, despite the reduced services. Nathan rolled his eyes, but paid without complaint.

"If you don't mind me asking, what are your plans?" asked Ed. "We might be able to help. We see a lot of things here by the lake."

"We're hoping to find somewhere to stay, out beyond the western margin," said Nathan.

"Plenty of people make their way across the margin here – in and out. The bush around the lake, particularly the pine plantations, provides a lot of cover. That's one of the reasons why the authorities turned off the mobile coverage here – annoying though that is. You're probably best not to walk around the lake from dusk onwards."

"Thanks for the warning. We'd planned to camp here for a few weeks, but now we've decided to cross the margin for a while instead."

Tanya and Belinda were in the annex, chatting as they set everything up for the night, so they didn't hear this, but Dan heard it as he set up the bedding in his tent and was puzzled. His father seemed to be suggesting that they'd come for a short holiday. Maybe Dad was starting to have second thoughts?

The fact was that Nathan Turner was being cautious.

"Well, I'm sure you already know about the new rules coming in at midnight," said Ed. "You can't leave the caravan park after midnight, because they're introducing a night curfew from 10pm until 5am. Of course, you won't have to worry about the distance limits beyond the margin. When are you leaving? I should warn you, it's best not to be out too early."

"Why?"

"The bushrangers cross the margins at night, they say, but sometimes we hear people on the move at dusk and for two or three hours after dawn. You know, if I were you, I wouldn't leave before eight or nine."

"That sounds serious! Well, it takes us an hour or two to pack up, so we won't be leaving too early."

Dan, now sitting on his bed at the entrance to his tent, saw a curious look flit across Ed's face in the gathering gloom – a look of triumph?

CR

When Ed left after a few more minutes' chatting, Dan and Nathan looked at each other. Nathan had also noticed the strange look on Ed's face.

"What do you reckon about Ed?" asked Nathan.

"Dodgy," said Dan.

Nathan nodded and pursed his lips. "I think we might leave early tomorrow. I wonder when it gets light?"

"Let's ask Belinda," said Dan.

When consulted, Belinda said that the sunrise in Ballarat would be about five minutes later than in Melbourne. It should start getting light at about 5:30am.

"That sounds like a good time to get up then," said Nathan. "We're certainly not waiting until 8 or 9 o'clock!"

"In which case, let's have dinner and get to bed," said Tanya. "We're all exhausted. It's been a long couple of days."

"And kids," said Nathan seriously, "when we get up in the morning, *be as quiet as possible*. It may be important."

Chapter 5

Crossing the Margin

The family had plenty of practice at packing up in a hurry, but they excelled themselves that morning.

Dan's phone alarm sounded softly at 5:30, waking him instantly from a deep sleep. It was time to get up. Adventure beckoned and Dan was excited.

Today was going to be a great day!

Before the sun rose a little after 6 o'clock, Dan had packed up his tent and bedding and stashed them in the roof box. By that time, the others were up too, and they worked rapidly together to pack up the kitchen goods, table, chairs and fridge.

As they were dismantling the annex and folding up the camper-trailer, Ed approached, looking agitated.

"You folks are up early," he said, trying to sound light and airy.

"Yes, it's been a lovely sunrise, hasn't it?" said Nathan.

"Oh, yes, indeedy," said Ed, "but the night was even nicer. Bright moonlight most of the night, then an hour of utter darkness before dawn." He rubbed his hands together looking pleased and Dan wondered why he should be so pleased by utter darkness. "Wonderful. I suppose you're going for an early morning walk? It's really nice beside the lake before breakfast."

"Hmm, we might do that once we've finished packing up."

"It's best to head south along the shore. Keep away from the bush on the north shore."

"Okay. Thanks for the warning."

Ed, taking Nathan's non-committal words as confirmation that they would go for a walk, looked pleased.

Ed strode away and the Turners quickly finished their packing. As they drove off the site, Ed hurried towards them.

"What are you doing?" he asked, wringing his hands. "Aren't you going for a walk?"

"No. We decided to leave now to get the most time for travel."

"But I warned you about leaving early...."

"We'll take our chances."

ℭ

Nathan drove, as he normally did when they used the big four-wheel drive. He drove carefully but quickly, and they soon rejoined the Western Freeway. There were no vehicles in sight as they made their way towards the hill that rose at the western end of the lake. This was the western margin, and, as far as Osmond's father was concerned, the end of civilisation – the border of Victoria. Beyond the margin was, legally at least, beyond his purview.

A substantial barrier straddled the road, flashing lights surmounting its crest. As the Turners slowed to a halt, an armed man approached them from a solid-looking bunker. From what he could see through a window, Dan decided there were at least three more armed men inside the bunker, ready to deal with any trouble-makers.

"You've reached the western margin, stranger. What's your business?"

"We want to go beyond the margin. We're heading for the Grampians."

"Holiday or permanent emigration?"

"Does it matter?"

"Yes, the tax rates are different."

"Tax?"

"Of course. Remember, it was the State of Victoria that built the roads you're going to drive on, and it's Victoria that will miss out on your taxes while you're away. Either way you owe us money, but the rates are different."

"What's the difference?"

"We charge per day for holidays, based on our estimate of lost revenue from goods and services taxes, income taxes, fuel taxes, the new Health and Welfare tax and the Pandemic Mitigation tax, as well as a couple of minor fees. For permanent emigration, we charge a flat Margin Migration fee, plus a deposit that you can reclaim if you ever return. For you four, the levy for a vacation would be...." He held up his folder, ran his eyes down the page, then pointed to a line and read out an extraordinarily large amount. "That's per day, of course. For permanent emigration... let's see." Consulting his folder again, he quoted an utterly unbelievable amount.

Nathan's mouth fell open. He couldn't help it. With such charges, they'd never even get past this ridiculous toll booth, whichever option they selected.

"Are those charges for real?" he gasped.

"Of course," said the officer smoothly, somehow managing to sound hurt.

"But those charges amount to more than I earned in the last year. Does anyone ever pay these taxes? If they do, they must be bank robbers or embezzlers!"

"Oh, come now, sir. These taxes are perfectly reasonable. Just think how much tax the state will lose when you leave. It's only common sense for the government to collect it from you now."

"Does anyone get past you without paying any tax?"

"I hope not, but some foreigners only pay a nominal amount."

"Foreigners?"

"People from out of state. The government believes the state is better off without them, so we don't charge them much to leave. Of course, if they come back later, they have to pay higher entry fees."

"Out of state? We're from out of state. What's the fee for foreigners?"

The officer named a third amount which, while still astronomical, was at least within the realms of possibility.

"Wow! If that's a nominal fee, I'd love to be able to charge you a high fee for interviewing me! I'd never need to work again."

"Come on, sir, be reasonable..."

"What evidence do you need that we're 'foreigners', as you call it?"

"We just write down your details, and if you ever come back we charge you an entry fee that makes the fees you've been complaining about look like petty cash. Show me your driver's licence."

Nathan handed over his licence and the man copied the details into his folder.

"How will you be paying the fee? We take gold or VicDollars."

"VicDollars," said Nathan, bitterly. "With your promise of ridiculous charges, we're not likely to come back, so we won't need them any more."

"Most people do come back, sir – and then they wish they'd paid the original fees. Many end up indentured to the government for years."

"I reckon we'll go anyway," said Nathan, aggrieved. He looked questioningly around at the others, who each gave a little nod. He turned confidently back to the officer and said, "Yes, we're really looking forward to getting out of here."

Ↄ̸

Nathan rummaged under the dashboard and pulled out a soft material bag that was obviously heavy. Climbing out of the car, he followed the officer inside the building. The rest of the family sat waiting in the car, wondering what effect these extortionate taxes would have on their future plans. After a few minutes, they began to notice the stillness and the complete absence of traffic. The gentle whisper of the occasional breeze and the frequent birdsong drew attention to the lack of human clamour. Their own voices sounded unreasonably loud, and they soon lapsed into silence.

Gradually, however, a distant sound of engines began to encroach on the silence. Curious, Dan climbed out of the car, walked to the back and scanned the horizon. Several kilometres away, at the other end of the lake, he could see many trucks travelling together, several topped with flashing lights. What was this unexpected intrusion? As they slowly approached, a faint disquiet, even a hint of fear, crept over him. He had heard too many reports of danger recently, often centred around the very margin where they were standing.

As the trucks drew closer, he saw that they were led by a four-wheel drive with flashing lights on its roof, while a similar vehicle brought up the rear. Presumably all of these vehicles were travelling together in convoy.

Belinda climbed out of the car and joined Dan, and together they watched the approaching convoy.

The leading four-wheel drive drove up the hill towards them as Nathan walked out of the customs post. Dan could see that it was no ordinary four-wheel drive. Gun-muzzles protruded from openings in the dark-tinted windows of the rear doors and the wagon section of the vehicle, and the words "Escort vehicle" were painted on its side. The vehicle pulled up beside them and a uniformed man opened the front passenger door, greeting Dan with an airy, "G'day, mate."

Dan answered in kind, and soon the air was vibrating with the deep rumble of large diesel engines and the release of compressed air as many trucks rolled to a halt. Looking along the line, he saw petrol and diesel tankers, empty cattle and grain trucks, and even a large tow-truck. In the middle of the convoy, he recognised an armoured security truck, an increasingly familiar sight near banks in the city. A mobile mechanical maintenance vehicle was there too, and Dan guessed its job was to keep the trucks running. But what was the convoy for?

"Forty-one," said Belinda, contentedly.

"Forty-one what?" asked Dan.

"Vehicles in the convoy, of course."

"I wonder where they're going?"

By that time, Nathan was chatting to the officer from the leading four-wheel drive. Dan walked across to see what he could learn.

"We run these convoys every few weeks," the officer was saying, "taking supplies up to some of the small towns that are still in operation. Places like Ararat and Stawell. Then we bring back goods that we need in the state."

"I thought the idea of the margins was to cut off the areas the state didn't need any more?"

"That's what the politicians say, and that's why most people don't know about these convoys. But trade goes on. The margins aren't as impervious as you might think."

"And are the areas beyond as dangerous as we hear?"

"Yes and no. We've got three armed and armoured vehicles with us: ours at the front, another at the back, and the big one in the middle. We've needed them all at times, but mostly we don't have any trouble. The crims go for the fuel on the way up and the gold on the way back."

"Gold?"

"Yes, there's still a gold mine in Stawell. To be honest, it's the main reason the convoys happen at all. Now that our economy isn't digitally-based any more, we need gold. There are gold mines within the margins – in Bendigo and Ballarat – but we need more. It suits the people beyond the margin too: they get fuel and other things they need. I reckon it's setting up Stawell to become the main centre in the west."

"And the crims? Who keeps them under control?"

"There's law and order in the bigger towns, but outside of them... let's just say there aren't policemen patrolling the roads!"

"Is it safe for us to drive to Stawell?"

"The most dangerous area is between here and Beaufort. Bushrangers – looking for rich pickings from people who've just moved outside the margins. Your bikes and camper-trailer would be a dead giveaway."

"What would you do in our situation?"

"If I were you, I'd travel with our convoy, at least until we get past Beaufort. Stay close behind our rear-guard and you should be okay."

"That sounds good. We'll pull off to the side while you drive through."

"Okay. We'll deal with the paperwork and then get moving. The roads aren't what they used to be."

Nathan, Dan and Belinda climbed back into the car and the officer from the customs post opened the gate for them. Nathan drove through slowly, then pulled over while the convoy dealt with the bureaucracy. As they sat waiting, Belinda suddenly said, "Hey, I just realised. We've crossed the border! We're beyond the western margin!"

Chapter 6

Convoy

The convoy was given permission to cross the margin much more quickly than the Turner family had been. After just a few minutes, the customs officer opened the gate and they prepared to move on.

One by one, the trucks passed the Turners until finally the last four-wheel drive rolled past. Nathan pulled back on to the road and followed close behind.

Little by little their speed increased as the convoy picked its way along what had once been one of the best country roads in Victoria but was now a crumbling, unmaintained strip of mingled bitumen and potholes. Travel wasn't too bad at that speed, but it was clear that the journey would take at least twice as long as it would have done in the freeway's heyday.

After a few kilometres, brake lights lit up the back of the vehicles in front of them and the convoy slowed to a stop. CB radios in each vehicle allowed them to communicate, and it wasn't long before one of the officers in the four-wheel drive in front of the Turners poked out his head and shouted to them: "There's a tree across our carriageway. The clean-up team will handle it, but stay in your car – it could be a trap."

They followed his advice. For a few moments, nothing stirred, but suddenly Dan heard a short burst of a siren from the front of the convoy, echoed immediately by the four-wheel drive just in front of them.

"What's going on?" asked Nathan.

"Sounds like a warning," breathed Dan.

"I can't see anything. Wait.... There's a truck coming the other way, over on the other carriageway."

Craning his head to see past the vehicles in front, Dan finally saw a dump truck lumbering along the other carriageway at speed, a four-wheel drive close behind. Standing in the back of the truck were ten or fifteen men, each holding a rifle pointed up to the sky. Dan had a clear view of their jeering faces as they swept past.

"What was that about?" asked Tanya, worriedly.

"Was that the trap they were suggesting?" asked Belinda.

"What would have happened if we'd been travelling by ourselves?" asked Nathan quietly.

No-one answered. It wasn't hard to imagine what would have happened if they hadn't been delayed at the margin and so had been travelling alone when they reached this fallen tree.

"Phew," said Dan. "This place really is dangerous!"

"I think we'd better stay with the convoy, at least for the time being," commented Tanya.

Soon they heard the sound of a powerful chainsaw in front of them, and it wasn't long before the convoy began to move again. As they drove past the remains of the fallen tree, which had been cut into pieces and dragged off the road, Dan called out, "Look at that stump. The tree didn't just fall: it was cut down!"

"I wonder if Ed is involved in any of this?" mused Nathan.

Thankfully, there were no more nasty surprises as they passed through Beaufort – which looked surprisingly dilapidated – and made their way towards Ararat.

♋

The family had planned to take the Halls Gap road from Ararat, but after the incident with the tree, they were rethinking this.

It sounded like the town of Stawell might be a safe place to stay, but they still wanted to get to the Grampians if they could.

"Let's just follow the road from Ararat to Halls Gap as we planned," said Dan. "Sure, none of the roads have been in great condition, but none have been impassable."

"What about bushrangers?" asked Belinda, eyes wide.

"I doubt there'd be enough traffic to make it worth their while," said Dan.

"Don't forget, it's only one lane each way," warned Nathan. "If trees have fallen down, we won't be able to drive around them the way we have in places with this convoy."

"You mean, we could go around a corner and find an enormous tree across the road right in front of us?" asked Belinda.

"We wouldn't be going fast enough for that to matter," said Dan, scornfully.

"You're right," said Nathan, "but our little chainsaw isn't powerful enough to cut up big trees. If we met any, we'd have to go all the way back to Ararat."

"It seems to me that the wisest thing to do is to stay with the convoy as far as we can," said Tanya. "We know they keep the roads clear all the way to Stawell, so we won't need to worry about clearing it ourselves."

"I s'pose so," said Dan, disappointed. He wanted to get away from the convoy – it felt like training wheels on a bike! They were out beyond the margins, yet even here they had people holding their hands and looking after them.

❦

At Ararat, the convoy stopped for half an hour while a diesel tanker and a petrol tanker visited the two petrol stations left in town. They couldn't provide them with all the fuel they wanted, but there would be enough to meet many of the town's needs.

While the convoy waited, the Turners left briefly to check the start of the Halls Gap road, since Nathan hoped to learn more about the condition of other country roads. As they drove out of the town and up towards the cutting, they found a large tree lying across the road. Not far beyond that lay another tree, and a third lay partly across the road further up where it rounded a bend. Many of the branches appeared to have been trimmed and car tracks led around one end of each tree, but in places the tracks led off the bitumen.

"It doesn't look good, Dan," said Nathan.

"No – it could take us a long time to get there," Dan admitted. "I suppose the highway is the best way to go."

They turned around, Nathan demonstrating his skill in backing a trailer, and returned to where the convoy was still waiting for the tankers to return. The roads were quiet, but otherwise the town looked little different from when the Turners had last seen it – in stark contrast to Beaufort, which had felt more like a ghost town.

The morning was warming up. Most of the truck drivers had left their cabs and were sitting under trees beside the road. A van had stopped near the convoy, selling snacks to any who could afford the steep prices.

Nathan and Dan walked across, hoping to find some answers to their questions, but the van driver was too busy to stop and talk. Some old-timers, however, were sitting outside the bowling club, and Nathan approached them.

"How's life in Ararat these days?" he asked.

"Nothing much has changed," said one old man, "except that those hauto-crats" – he pronounced it as two distinct words – "in Melbourne don't tell us what to do anymore. We're doin' fine with the convoys comin' through. And the town's freer-er than it's ever been."

"To be honest, Jake's right," said another. "True, the roads aren't so good, and I'm not sure how things will be in ten years' time, but at the moment we're pretty happy. There's food and money enough; work for anyone who wants to work; and many of the troublemakers have run away to the city. Other hardworking folks from further out have come to take their place, including some doctors and nurses."

"Yer right, Sid," said Jake; "yer right."

"Have you heard what things are like in the Grampians?" asked Nathan.

"Well, there's no park rangers, I know *that*," said Jake.

"Is Halls Gap okay?" asked Nathan.

"Nope – from what we hear, it's been taken over by a bunch of cattle rustlers and tin-pot dictators," said Jake.

"You should stay here in Ararat," said Sid. "Things are good here."

"We even have a school for the young 'uns," added Jake.

"What about Stawell?"

"My daughter lives in Stawell," said Sid. "She says the town's growing – bigger than Ararat now. Melbourne's so desperate for gold that they provide everything Stawell needs. She says the gold mine has begun to produce gold from a new reef they found last year. Maybe the convoy you're with will take back a bigger load of gold. Of course, the amount of gold shipped is all top secret, just like the convoy timetables."

" 'Top secret!' " laughed Jake, mockingly. "That armoured truck is bigger'n any they've sent before. More armed guards inside it, too."

"You're right, Jake," agreed Sid. "And if they won't open the doors in the middle of Ararat, they must already have something valuable inside."

"Ah," said Nathan admiringly, "that's a clever observation. I hadn't noticed that."

"Oh, I used to work for the State Bank in the old days, back when we had armoured trucks carrying cash all over the state. Now we're going back to that."

"Yeah, so much for progress!" said Jake. "They said we didn't need the old ways, but now they're the only ways that work! These new-fangled mobile phones don't work no more. It's 'no coverage' here, 'no coverage' there, so now we're worse off'n we were with the old phones. In the shops, the young girls are learnin' to read price labels again now the fancy computer networks don't work."

"The supermarkets even had to raid the smaller shops to get their old cash registers," interjected Sid.

"We older folk're quite happy with it," Jake concluded; "but the young 'uns are findin' it tough."

The old men's smiles made it clear that they didn't mind technology stepping back to the times of their youth, but Nathan couldn't help wondering if the backtracking would stop there.

"They're having to learn skills nobody thought we'd ever need again," said Sid. "But they're country people – they'll cope okay. We always do."

Nathan answered, "I'm afraid we're not country people – at least, we weren't until now."

"So you're not part of the convoy?" asked Jake.

"No, we've burned our bridges in the city. We probably can't afford to re-enter, and they call us foreigners anyway. We'll be looking for somewhere to stay in the Grampians."

"Welcome to the country then, young man, and your family too," said Sid with a toothy smile. Then he stopped smiling and leaned forward seriously. "But if you want some advice, mister, don't go near Halls Gap."

"Sid's right," said Jake. "City slickers've taken it over. Tryin' to run it like *Melbourne*, they are." The old man spat out the name as if it tasted bad. "Taxes and charges for everythin'. Reg'lations everywhere. Helpin' the crooks and pickin' on the workers. Keep away, I say!"

"We'd have to go further north-west, then. What are conditions like there?"

"Sorry," said Jake, shaking his head, "cain't help you."

"Nor can I," added Sid, "but I'm sure this is a great time to start living in the country. And your son will have the best possible opportunity to make a life in the loveliest place on God's earth."

At that moment, Tanya came over with some snacks for Nathan and Dan. Greeting the locals with a smile, she offered them some too and they helped themselves with matching smiles.

Seeing the tankers returning, the Turners soon said their goodbyes and left to return to their car. Sid said in parting: "If you need any help in Stawell, ask around for Linda Holland – she's my daughter. Her husband Terry works at the bank. They help everyone. Tell them I sent you, and they'll do even more – guaranteed." He beamed and added, "And thanks, missus, those meringues were delicious."

⊂⊃

The convoy proceeded cautiously to Stawell with only a couple of stops to remove fallen trees that blocked parts of the road. They met few vehicles, but from what they could see, it appeared that nearby farmers were still farming and tending their vineyards.

This area seemed less altered than the region near the margin. Wine production seemed to be continuing and the homes all appeared to be lived in.

"It's good to see that the country isn't completely deserted," said Nathan.

"Or abandoned to bushrangers," added Tanya.

"Is that what's happened to Beaufort?" asked Dan.

"Possibly," said Nathan.

"I always liked Beaufort," said Belinda, "but all the lovely homes looked empty and uncared-for."

"Maybe it's part of a ring of ruin around the margin," said Dan. "Hey, I like that expression, 'a ring of ruin'!"

"It's close enough to the margins that people could easily move inside if they wanted to – maybe most of them did," said Tanya.

"And that could lead to having more crims around than ordinary citizens," observed Dan; "particularly if they're preying on new arrivals."

"It's always hard to predict how major changes will play out," said Nathan. "Often things don't work as we might expect."

"Dad's back to his favourite sayings about unexpected consequences," said Dan.

"True," laughed Nathan.

The convoy made its way down the long hill into Stawell and stopped, the trucks spread out along the highway.

Nathan pulled in behind the four-wheel drive that brought up the rear.

As he did so, Belinda said, "Wow! Look at the price of diesel! I remember thinking the price in Melbourne was high – was that really only yesterday?"

"We'll have to get used to using the car less, that's for sure," said Nathan. He climbed out and approached the four-wheel drive in front of them.

"Thanks for letting us travel with you," he said to the driver.

"You're welcome," the driver replied. "Just don't tell Or-trick or he'll find some way to charge you for it!"

Nathan laughed. "It's been an eventful day, but thanks to the convoy, we're here safely."

"Well, if you ever want to go back, you're welcome to travel with us, particularly between Beaufort and the margin!"

Chapter 7

Stawell

The Turners left the convoy and drove up to the town centre. Finding a place to park north of Main Street was easier than ever – even with the camper-trailer attached.

"Let's do some research," said Nathan. Their experience with the chatty old men in Ararat had convinced him that ordinary people would provide helpful information.

"I'll go and look at the supermarket," said Tanya.

"Let's go in pairs and meet back here at 12:30," suggested Nathan. "We don't know much about the security situation here."

"Okay," said Tanya. "You come with me, Belinda. We'll have a look at the stock and prices, and see if we can find out anything about the Grampians."

"Good. Dan and I will go along Main Street – see what shops are open, what's available and how much it costs. We'll also try to find some locals to talk to."

Nathan and Dan walked down the narrow lane to Main Street. At first glance, the street looked the same as it used to, except that there was more foot traffic. Presumably the high price of fuel had convinced more people to walk if they lived nearby, or perhaps to car-pool if they lived out of town.

"Fewer empty shops than I remember," said Nathan.

"Yes," agreed Dan.

"I suppose the town needs to sell a wider range of goods now that shopping trips to Ballarat or Melbourne aren't an option."

"Maybe Sid was right: Stawell is growing."

This time there were no old men sitting on seats in the sun, but the shopkeepers seemed happy to see prospective customers and were eager to help. Spotting a general goods and hardware store, Dan suggested that they go in.

"Welcome!" said the shopkeeper as they entered. "Are you from out of town or escaping from Melbourne?"

"We left Melbourne yesterday and crossed the margin this morning."

"And now you're trying to find answers, right?"

"I suppose so. How did you guess?"

"Oh, everyone who comes up from Melbourne has heard horror stories of how bad everything is beyond the margins, so when they see the main street looking perfectly normal, they want to know what's going on."

"How bad is everything around here?"

"As far as I'm concerned, it's not bad at all. We've been left alone to get on with life. No condescending city types. No absentee government rules. No interference from people who don't know what we need in the country. Just country people who know what's going on, or people like you who enjoy the country and want to make it their home."

"What about the price of goods?"

"Some goods are more expensive, but others are cheaper. Mostly it depends on where they come from. Locally-made things are generally cheaper."

"What about law and order?"

"We still have police in the town."

"But in the Grampians, say, you're on your own?"

"Pretty much."

"What's happened to the national park?"

"When the government cut off the funding, most of the staff went back to Melbourne. The offices were abandoned, and most of the equipment as well. A group of locals and trouble-makers took it all over, and now they think they're the lawful controllers of the national park. They charge fees for using the Halls Gap road, and I hear they lock up anyone who does anything they don't like."

"Do they control the whole national park?"

"Not yet – that'd be too much work for them! They claim control and charge for anything they can, but they don't provide anything for the fees."

"So we could get into the national park through Roses Gap?"

"Oh yes; just make sure you go along the Roses Gap Road. Don't go too close to Halls Gap."

"Is the Roses Gap Road in good condition?"

"I haven't been along it for two or three years, but I know people around here still visit Beehive Falls."

𝜕

After some more looking around and chatting to shopkeepers, Nathan and Dan returned to the car at 12:30. Not finding Tanya and Belinda, they went into the supermarket and looked around, but saw no sign of them. Nathan even described them to the staff at the checkouts, but nobody had seen them.

Nathan and Dan looked at each other in concern. It seemed that Tanya and Belinda had never even made it into the supermarket.

"Let's go back outside," said Dan. "Maybe they were there but we missed them."

"I'm sure they weren't in the carpark," said Nathan. "Could they have met someone and gone somewhere with them?"

"It doesn't seem likely, but let's see if there's anyone we can ask."

Looking around, they noticed a young lad, about Dan's age, collecting trolleys, and made their way over to him.

"Have you seen a blonde woman and a 15-year-old blonde girl?" asked Nathan. "They would have been in the carpark about half or three-quarters of an hour ago."

"No, I was inside, re-stocking the shelves then. Sorry."

"Would anybody else have been in the carpark then?"

"Only customers."

They looked around again, but there was no-one else to ask.

"What do we do now?" asked Dan.

"I guess we'll have to go to the police," said Nathan. He called out to the young lad, "Is there a police station around here?"

"Yes, it's down on Patrick Street. Follow Main Street along to the islands at the top end, then turn right. It's on the left."

By this time, Nathan and Dan were worried. Tanya and Belinda wouldn't have just wandered off somewhere without letting them know!

They made their way back to Main Street and were looking carefully around when Dan called out excitedly, "There they are!"

Tanya and Belinda were walking towards them on the other side of the street with a middle-aged woman who seemed slightly familiar to Dan, although he couldn't work out why. Belinda waved and ran across the street to meet them.

"Sorry we weren't at the supermarket. We only went away with Linda for a few minutes, but then we got caught up with her husband at the bank."

"Linda? Linda who?" asked Nathan, blankly.

"Linda Holland, the daughter of that old man we met in Ararat."

"Oh, yes. I remember. How did you meet her?"

"We were walking towards the supermarket and saw her packing shopping into her car. Both Mum and I thought she looked familiar, but couldn't think who she was. We were looking at her – not staring, of course – when she saw us and said 'Hello'. Mum said we'd both thought she looked familiar but couldn't place her, so then we asked questions back and forth until we worked out that it's because she looks a lot like her father, Sid."

By the time Belinda had finished her explanation, Tanya and Linda had crossed the street.

"Here are my husband Nathan, and my son Dan," said Tanya. "Nathan and Dan, this is Linda Holland, Sid's daughter."

They exchanged greetings and Tanya continued, "Nathan, Linda knows a couple who own a camp along the Roses Gap Road.... Oh, it's probably best if she tells you about it."

"Well, our friends Steve and Sylvia own the Roses Gap Camp," said Linda. "Their facilities are used by schools and other organisations, but business hasn't been good for them over the last few years, what with lockdowns, closed borders and now the margins. They dismissed their staff and struggled on by themselves, but then discovered that Sylvia has cancer! The doctors arranged for her to go across the margin in one of the convoys to get treatment in Melbourne. They had to just lock up the place and leave."

"Oh, what a tragedy!" said Nathan.

"Yes. They didn't have time to organise anyone to look after the camp. In fact, they didn't even have time to contact the groups that already had bookings, so they asked Terry and me to let them all know that their camps were cancelled, unless by some miracle we could find someone to run the camp for them."

"Have you had any success?"

"No. As their bank manager, Terry knows a bit about their finances, and if we can't get anyone to run the camps, then... well, I suppose they'll go broke like so many others have in this pandemic."

"It's a pretty specialised sort of job. And it sounds as if they were struggling anyway."

"That's true, but it's hard to see people lose out when they've worked so hard."

"Nathan," said Tanya, "couldn't we do something to help? After all, we don't have any definite plans, and we've helped with running and catering for church youth camps before. We even know the Grampians pretty well."

"Yes, but..."

"And I'm a nurse, so I could look after most of the medical problems we might have."

"True, but..."

"You make sure all the equipment in the university lab keeps working, so I'm sure you could keep this place going!"

"Perhaps, but..."

"And they have high ropes courses and things like that," chimed in Linda. "Your kids would love that!"

"Yes, but..."

"Why do you keep saying 'but', Dad?" asked Dan. "It sounds like a great opportunity."

"I keep saying 'but' because there's far too much we *don't* know. We don't know the place, the equipment, who would be coming for camps, how many would come, or what they've been promised for their camps. Without knowing a whole lot more, there's no way we could satisfy the campers. The owners would be better off *without* our help than to have everything go wrong and upset all the campers!"

"Terry answered some of those questions," said Tanya. "Why not come and talk to him now? I started out just as dubious as you are, but I'm starting to feel that this opportunity may be better than anything we had planned."

Nathan stood looking at her for a few moments, then he sighed. "Maybe you're right, but I don't want to accept a job and make a mess of it. If they wanted me to run a university lab, that'd be different, but a camping facility?"

"I don't want to push you into something you're not happy with," said Linda, "but this would be a great help not only for Steve and Sylvia but also for the schools and companies who're looking forward to the marvellous camps they've provided in the past. We don't know you, it's true, but if you're the sort of people who stop and chat to my old Dad, that's a good sign. If you love the Grampians, that's another good sign. And if you've helped to run church camps, I call that a great sign. Come and talk to Terry!"

Map of the Northern Grampians

This map is available online. Use the QR code or visit
https://www.bibletales.online/beyond-the-western-margin/

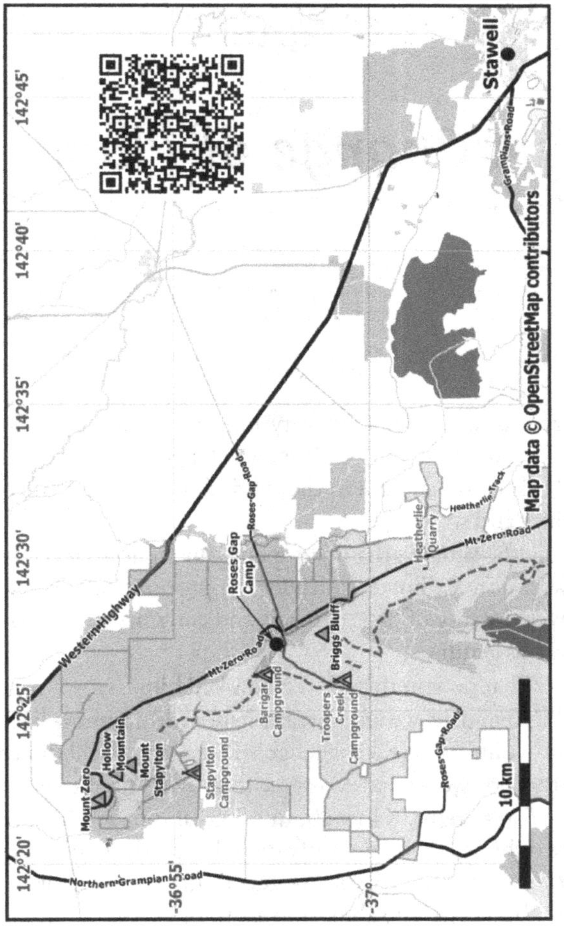

Chapter 8

A Change of Plans

Terry was the epitome of everything a bank manager should be. The moment you met him, you felt you could trust him. He looked you straight in the eye and projected a sense of reliability and steadiness.

By the time Nathan had spent half an hour at the bank, he was more willing to consider the proposition. Terry had answered many of his questions and convinced him that the need was genuine.

"What do you think?" Terry asked him.

"Obviously, we didn't come here to do anything like this, but it would be a real challenge. Tanya and I will discuss it, but the kids would have to agree too. We'd need their help."

"You're right. How about we go and have a look at the place right now? My deputy can look after the bank – I don't have any customer appointments. Linda and I will bring our four-wheel drive and show you around."

"Shall we, Tanya?"

"Sounds good."

"Kids?"

"Yes!" chorused Dan and Belinda.

The Turners left Stawell with very different expectations from those they'd arrived with mere hours before. They filled up the car's tank again – Nathan wincing at the price – and then followed Terry and Linda northwest along the Western Highway. Fallen trees that would not impede traffic seemed to have been left where they fell, but where necessary, trunks and branches had been cut up and dragged out of the way. Smaller branches were scattered all over the shoulders of the road and dead leaves formed an attractive carpet wherever wheels did not run.

"Where does the Roses Gap Road go off, Belinda?" asked Nathan.

"After the 253 kilometre post," she answered. "Maybe it should be beyond the 254 kilometre post, but I think that one was missing." The family often made use of Belinda's particular interest in distances and signposts: she not only noticed them but remembered them, especially those near the Grampians. She said that it helped her to visualise the map in her head.

They passed the 253 kilometre post and soon afterwards followed Terry and Linda in turning left onto Roses Gap Road. This road was considerably narrower and more seriously affected by fallen trees and minor flood damage near blocked culverts.

"If we want people to come along this road, we might have to start clearing some of the culverts ourselves," said Nathan.

"An activity for the campers," laughed Dan.

"That might not be as silly as it sounds," said Nathan.

"Thanks," said Dan, sardonically.

"Oh, sorry, Dan," said Nathan. "I wasn't sneering. It's just that all my life the idea of private citizens clearing culverts on a public road would have been ridiculous. But now it's not: it's just practical. And having campers help and then spread the idea might be good all round."

"These pandemics have caused lots of changes in society," said Tanya. "Some are definitely improvements."

"You know, we only left home yesterday, and then today we left civilisation," mused Nathan. "We're driving along an awful road that might lead nowhere, following people we hadn't even met two hours ago. All to take over a job we're completely unequipped to handle, running a camp we've never seen, owned by a missing couple we've never met – in fact, we don't even know their surname!"

"It's 'Jones'," said Dan. "It was on the folder Terry showed you with information about the camp."

"Ah," said Nathan, lapsing into silence. His oratory hadn't received the response he felt it deserved.

"Oh dear," said Tanya. "Look at that!"

A massive tree lay across the road, completely blocking it. Near the base it was more than a metre in diameter, far too big to remove without special equipment. Wheel tracks led off the road and squeezed through between the unearthed roots of the fallen giant and a smaller, but still substantial tree. Nathan cautiously followed the tracks using four-wheel drive mode, glad to have good clearance beneath both car and camper-trailer.

"We'll need to get rid of that tree," he observed.

Back on the road again, they eventually passed the Beehive Falls parking area and came to the entrance of the Roses Gap Camp. A lonely-looking sign stood in the middle of the gravel driveway announcing that the camp was closed, but

Terry and Linda skirted the sign and drove on. Nathan followed them around a corner to a long low building, where they parked near a sign which said "Office".

"Let's have a scout around," said Terry, leading the Turners around the site. Cabins were arranged in neat rows with nearby amenities blocks. Two mess halls stood back to back with a kitchen in between, where meals were crafted to feed hungry campers. Purpose-built sporting activities were scattered around and an almost circular lake lay near a quiet creek, still flowing freely after a wet spring.

They stopped by the lake to enjoy the view. "What do you think of it?" Terry asked Belinda.

"It's idyllic," said Belinda. "This area is wetter than most places we've seen in the Grampians."

"True. There are a couple of good creeks here, and some springs as well. If you look down at this place from Briggs Bluff – that's the steep mountain behind us – you'll see just how green it is compared with the areas around it."

"Is the camp part of the national park?" asked Dan.

"No. It's private property or else the camp wouldn't exist. They never allowed camps like this in the park. Although they did allow some serviced camp areas for hikers on the Grampians Peaks Trail."

"That passes near here, doesn't it?"

"Yes, it's just up the valley." Terry pointed to a dirt track that disappeared among the trees. "That track leads to one of the campsites." He stopped and looked thoughtful. "Hmm, I wonder why the gate is open. Steve and Sylvia recently started keeping it locked, to keep troublemakers out. I'd better have a look later."

"Good idea," said Nathan.

"Anyway, apart from that, there's nothing obviously wrong. Let's go back to the office and get some keys and show you more of the place."

Two hours later they had finished their tour and Dan and Belinda were completely sold on the idea. True, the camp had not been used for a large number of campers for some time, and it would take plenty of work to get it ready to do so again, but none of it looked too difficult. The comfortable games room, outdoor sports settings and other entertainment options convinced them that staying here would be even better than their rosiest dreams of life beyond the western margin! They had expected to lose the basic amenities they were used to: running water, unlimited power and a large living space. Instead, they saw a huge area that would mostly be available for their exclusive use.

Nathan and Tanya, however, were still asking questions, so Dan and Belinda wandered off to explore.

"Tell us again how many camps are already booked, and how far in advance? How much income will they generate?" Tanya and Nathan were satisfied with the facilities, and now Nathan was moving on to the business end – which Tanya was more than happy to leave to him!

Terry and Linda worked through Nathan's questions while Tanya thought over the situation. Terry and Linda's friendliness and openness appealed to her, and their willingness to spend so much time helping their friends impressed her. These were friends worth having. She had only two remaining questions, but Nathan must have read her mind. He asked them first.

"How long a commitment would you need from us? And what happens if we do our best but just can't satisfy the campers?"

"We'd need you to commit to at least three months managing the camp," said Terry. "That would cover the three camps already booked: the smallish business camp at the start of December, and two larger school camps, one at the end of January and the other in the middle of February. You've only got 18 days before the training camp for the mine, and you'd need to clear the road before then. After that, the other projects we've mentioned should keep you busy until the school camps come. You'll need to become familiar with the way Steve and Sylvia run camps, and the money side as well: fees, answering enquiries, marketing and so on. We know you don't have direct experience with that, but it sounds like you have enough to start with, and we're convinced you can make a go of it. When we offered to show it to you we felt pretty desperate, but now we're confident, aren't we, Linda?"

"Yes, we are," answered Linda, smiling at Nathan and Tanya. "We wouldn't ask if we didn't think you'd succeed."

"And Sid will be pleased that he was the one who directed you to us," said Terry.

Linda smiled in agreement, then added, "You know, Terry, I've been wondering how we could help the Turners learn about the sports equipment and the national park sites the campers normally visit. It occurred to me that we could provide a past employee."

"You mean Alex?" asked Terry.

"Yes. He's not really enjoying the work in the bank. He'd be glad to get back here."

"Good idea," said Terry. "We could cover the cost of wages. He'd be a real help."

"Who's Alex?" asked Tanya.

"Our son," said Linda. "He's 23 years old."

"He worked for Steve and Sylvia," explained Terry, "but when things went bad, they couldn't afford to keep him on, so he's been working at the bank since then. He's a good worker, but he doesn't enjoy indoor work. He's properly qualified for supervising outdoor adventure activities."

"Of course, nobody cares much about qualifications now," admitted Linda. "Anyone could do it and nobody would complain."

"Unless something went wrong!" said Terry.

"I can imagine that," said Tanya. "With the nursing shortages during the pandemic, they've been willing to use just about anyone who can stand up! Nobody cares much about qualifications until something goes wrong."

"Having someone who knows how the place works would be a great help," admitted Nathan. "We're all willing to work hard, but genuine knowledge is hard to beat at times!"

ℂℛ

As Dan wandered around the campsite, he saw the track leading to the Grampians Peaks Trail, and decided to explore. As he passed the gate, he saw pieces of a padlock lying on the ground – obviously cut with bolt cutters. Steve and Sylvia hadn't left the gate open at all: someone had broken in. He'd report that later.

In the warmth of the afternoon, he appreciated the shade of the trees that grew beside the track. After a few hundred metres, he walked through another open gate and came to a place where the valley angled to the left. A sign by the side of the track directed south-bound walkers on the Grampians Peaks Trail to follow a trail that slowly climbed to the ridge running parallel to the Roses Gap Road. The four-wheel drive track, however, ended at a footbridge that crossed the creek where another sign indicated that it led to Barigar camp on the other side of the valley.

Should he return to the campsite? The adults had sounded as if they intended to talk business all afternoon. If he went back now he'd have to sit for hours listening to the minute details adults seemed to consider so fascinating!

Deciding instead to have a look at Barigar camp, he crossed the bridge and continued along the track. As he passed through a dense stand of wattles, a sudden heavy thump sounded a few metres away, followed by more thumps moving quickly away from him for a few seconds before stopping. He recognised it as the sound of a kangaroo or wallaby. Creeping into the trees, he peered around and soon spotted a wallaby, its dark, furry form standing a little over waist-height, black eyes looking directly at Dan.

Dan stood perfectly still, speaking quietly to calm the animal while he studied its dense reddish brown fur and distinctive shape. It stared back at him for a few seconds, then turned and hopped away, disappearing quickly into the bush.

Meeting a wallaby made the bush even more interesting and the campsite another step closer to ideal.

At Barigar camp he explored the main building and the several raised areas for pitching tents. There was no-one there, but it looked like a nice place to camp. He wondered how much the Grampians Peaks Trail was used now that the national park was no longer operated by the government.

By then it was getting late and he set off back to the campsite. As he passed the place where the walking trail left the vehicle track, he heard some quiet scratching sounds in the bushes just off the track, along with a curious sort of rubbing or rattling noise, something like a straw broom being shaken. He thought he recognised the noise and guessed that its author would only be a few metres away. Pushing gently through the bushes beside the track, he found that he was right. There, its pointed snout rooting around in the soil, was an echidna, hunting for ants. The sound he'd heard was caused by its sharp spines rubbing together. Despite his attempts to be quiet, the little animal heard him and quickly burrowed its head into the ground, presenting nothing but a spiky ball for any predator to attack. Dan watched for a few moments, then remembered to keep moving. His parents might be missing him.

Hurrying back to the campsite, he went straight to the office area to find the others. As he approached, Belinda called out, "Here he is."

The four adults came out of the office.

"Where have you been?" asked Tanya.

"I just went looking for the Grampians Peaks Trail."

"What took you so long?" asked Belinda.

"I found the Grampians Peaks Trail and went to Barigar Camp. There was no-one there, but I saw a wallaby and an echidna."

"Oh, I like echidnas," said Belinda. "Do you know what *I* saw?"

"No – what?"

"A snake!"

"What, in the camp area?"

"Yes, over near the lake. It was only a little one, but I don't like snakes."

"What sort was it?"

"How would I know? Snakes are horrible. I didn't hang around working out what brand it was!"

"Well, now that's settled," said Nathan, laughing, "let's go back into the office and tell you kids what we've agreed on."

"Linda and I will head back to Stawell now," said Terry, holding up his hand in farewell. "See you all tomorrow."

"Good-bye," said Dan. "Oh, I almost forgot. You know how the gate was open on that track? The padlock's been cut off with bolt cutters. Somebody's been up to no good!"

CR

Nathan and Tanya led Dan and Belinda into the office. The room was light and airy and the sun shone warmly through the window. Outside, several cabins and bunkhouses stood out against the backdrop of the encircling bush. The family hadn't expected any of this when they left Melbourne in such a hurry! It seemed well worth the effort.

"Okay, kids," started Nathan, "we've agreed with Terry and Linda to manage the camp for at least the next three months. During that time, there are three camps booked and we'll have to run them, doing whatever it takes to keep the campers happy. Tomorrow, Alex Holland will join us here to teach us about the campsite. We'll probably have to arrange for some extra staff, too, when the bigger camps are running. Anything else, Tanya?"

"Just that this is a good opportunity for us. We didn't anticipate that huge fee for crossing the margin, and it left us with less money than we expected. Managing this campsite gives us free food and lodging – plus payment for every camp we run. That's much better than we expected."

"We'll review the situation again in the middle of February," said Nathan. "And Steve and Sylvia might be back from Melbourne by then."

"In the meantime, we'll be very busy," continued Tanya, "but we'll also have plenty of opportunities to enjoy the beauty of the Grampians as we planned."

"Do you really think we can make the camps successful, Mum?" asked Belinda, eyes wide.

"Of course we can," said Dan, scornfully.

"We'll do our best and we'll do it in good faith," answered Tanya. "We can't do more than that."

"We've never met Steve and Sylvia, but there's no doubt that they need our help," said Nathan.

Tanya looked at Dan and Belinda seriously. "A lot will depend on you two working hard with a good grace. Will you commit to that?"

"I will," said Dan. "Sure, I'd like to help those people, but I'm also looking forward to staying here. There's sport, plenty of different equipment, fixing problems, learning all sorts of new stuff – all in my favourite place."

"Me too," said Belinda. "There'll be lots of new things to learn. Would I be able to learn about arranging supplies and running a big kitchen?"

"Yes, and I think you'd enjoy learning some of the accounting side of it too, Belinda," said Tanya.

"Accounting?" exclaimed Dan, horrified. "I avoided that at school. Give me practical things to do, not counting money!"

"Money is very practical," laughed Nathan, "although I tend to agree that I'm more interested in things that move. Speaking of which, one of the first things we need to do is to get that huge tree off the road. It has to be gone before the first camp in three weeks."

"How do we do that?" asked Dan.

"I've got some ideas we can start working on when we go into Stawell tomorrow to sign the campsite papers."

"Can't we just email the papers?"

"Have you looked at your mobile signal recently, Danny-boy?" asked Belinda, sweetly.

"No," admitted Dan. He took out his phone and checked. There was no signal at all. "What do we do about phone calls?"

"Terry and Linda say there's no mobile coverage outside the towns. All the other towers have been turned off – apparently they cost too much to run."

"So we're going to be out here with no coverage for three months?" asked Dan in disgust.

"Yep," answered Nathan.

"And there's no other way to get internet access? I know it's been pretty bad at home lately, but do we really have to survive with none at all?"

"Yep," repeated Nathan, smiling.

"But what do we do?"

"Pack away our phones and get busy," laughed Tanya. "It'll be good for all of us."

"Sometimes I can do without things that are 'good for me'," muttered Dan.

"What about electricity?" asked Belinda.

"There are lots of solar panels out the back," said Nathan. "You saw them, didn't you? They provide all the power the camp needs. There's even enough power to provide air conditioning in many of the rooms. Plus there are batteries which collect spare power during the day to use at night."

"And water?" asked Dan.

"They collect water from all the roofs and store it in tanks. In good years, that provides enough water, but apparently in drought years they get water tankers too. There are water filters for treating drinking water."

"Sounds like they've thought of everything," said Dan.

"Pretty much, including quite a few things you haven't asked about yet, but we'll talk about them some other time."

"It's amazing for such an out-of-the-way place as this."

"True. But remember, all this infrastructure must have cost a huge amount of money to build. The owners don't want to lose it all because of a health problem."

"And that's where we come in."

"Yep!"

Chapter 9

Confrontation

Dan woke up slowly. The small bedroom that was to be his for the next three months was quite dark, thanks to thick curtains that covered the large window. Despite the dark, his phone told him that it was almost eight o'clock in the morning. He stretched luxuriantly, relaxed and comfortable.

He was beyond the western margin and safely settled in the Grampians. The city's restrictions seemed distant, and the prospect of an unlimited holiday stretched out before him. Of course, it wouldn't be all holiday, but for the moment it felt like it.

No more school! No more health orders or movement constraints! Just freedom and peace.

Yesterday had been a very long day, and he'd been far too tired to organise his room when he finally made his way to bed. Revelling in the new day once more, he smiled to himself and looked around the room. It wouldn't take long to set it up just as he wanted it.

After a few minutes' pleasant day-dreaming, he was just considering getting up when he heard Dad and Mum moving quietly in the corridor. When Belinda followed a few moments later, he bounced out of bed. There shouldn't be anyone around except family, so he found his way to the kitchen in his pyjamas. Their living quarters were connected to the office building but separated from it by a lockable door. Four single bedrooms and a double bedroom led off the corridor, while a kitchen and a combined dining room and lounge were located at the far end.

Mum and Belinda were standing at the dining room window watching a kookaburra sitting in a tree and laughing at the world.

"Here's the sleepy-head," said Belinda.

"I've been awake for *ages*, Belinda Lucinda," said Dan, loftily, "but I've been *thinking*, not just running around like a chook with no head as some people do."

"I can just imagine your thoughts," laughed Belinda. "All one letter: z... z... z...."

The kookaburra chose that particular moment to laugh.

"Oh, listen to the kookaburra!" said Dan. "He appreciates your humour – you two must be on the same intellectual level."

"Let's go and have breakfast," said Tanya, pleased at the relaxed note in Dan's voice. He had worked hard in Year 12, and his temper had become a little frayed towards the end. Most of the time Dan and Belinda got on very well together, and starting the morning with light-hearted banter was a good sign. She looked at Nathan and smiled, knowing that he had been worried that the kids would be upset about having to work hard. She had reassured him that Dan and Belinda would be so pleased to be out in the wilds that there would be few problems.

☙

Nathan screwed up his nose as he struggled to finish a bowl of ageing cereal drowned in pineapple juice, both found in the almost-bare pantry. They made a formidable mixture. "We must go shopping this morning," he said. "Some fried eggs and toast would be nice tomorrow morning."

"We can go shopping after we see Terry at the bank," said Tanya. "We're meeting him at eleven o'clock, aren't we?"

"Yes, and Alex should be there too."

"I'm looking forward to meeting him," said Dan. "He's done a lot of rock climbing, hasn't he?"

"I believe so. Linda said he loves physical activity, and isn't afraid of hard work."

"Ah," said Dan, straight-faced, "another person like me. I *thought* he sounded good."

"You!" scoffed Belinda. "You can't even *spell* hard work, let alone do it!"

"But at least I'm not afraid of it... watching it, that is!"

"This will be serious hard work, Dan," said Nathan. "I'm sure you'll help as much as you can, but I don't want to overload you."

"I'm honestly looking forward to it, Dad. How are we going to move that tree?"

"We'll stop and have a look on the way out, but I was doing some quick calculations last night, and that tree must weigh at least 20 tonnes."

"Don't worry, Belinda will pick it up for us with one hand. She's been working on her strength to improve her netball."

"Thanks, Danny-boy, but I think 20 tonnes is beyond me – even with both hands."

"Could we cut it into pieces?" asked Dan.

"I think we'll have to, but we don't have the right equipment. We'll need to get someone out from Stawell to cut it into sections so we can move them off the road."

Breakfast over, Nathan and Dan were about to go out and familiarise themselves with the solar panels when suddenly they heard a vehicle on the driveway.

Hurrying through the office building, they found a white four-wheel drive stopped near their car. A man was stepping down from the running board as they approached.

Nathan greeted him. "G'day, I'm Nathan Turner."

"I'm Brad, the mayor of Halls Gap. What are you doing here?"

"We're managing the camp for Steve and Sylvia."

"Who are they?"

"They're the owners. They've been here for a few years. Don't you know them?"

"I might have met them sometime, but I heard they'd left; gone to the city or something."

"Yes, they've gone to Melbourne. Sylvia's not well."

"We heard the place was empty."

Dan had already decided that he didn't like this mayor. His voice was cold – the sort of voice Dan imagined a snake might have – reminding Dan of the reports they'd heard about the people who'd taken over Halls Gap. He hoped his father wouldn't give this man too much information.

"No, it's not," said Nathan firmly. "We're managing the place and the campsite is well and truly in business. In fact, we've got several camps booked for the next few months." Changing the subject, Nathan asked, "How are things going in Halls Gap?"

"We're running the place much better than the government did. We all live there – we're the right people to look after the National Park."

"Well, the good thing about wild areas is that they don't need much looking after. As long as we leave them alone, they generally do okay."

"Up to a point, perhaps – but don't forget the roads and buildings, fire tracks and walking tracks, water supply dams and piping. Infrastructure needs maintenance, so when people visit the area, we have to charge fees to cover those costs."

"I suppose that means you're able to maintain the roads better than they're being maintained around here."

"Yes, we'll be able to do just that."

" '*Be* able to'?"

"Yes. Once we have enough funds, we'll be able to maintain the roads."

"How much have you collected so far?"

"Let's put it this way: we're getting there. Eventually we'll have enough not only to restore the National Park to its former glory but to improve it. At the moment, we only collect entry fees from people who go near Halls Gap, but we plan to expand the collection model right across the park."

"But no maintenance yet?"

"Not yet... but we'll get there. As I say, we're doing a better job of running the park than the politicians and rangers were! We've got collection booths on a few roads already, and they're all manned 24 hours a day. And we're extending that to the other entry points of the park. We plan to relocate small cabins beside the roads, with solar panels so that they're environmentally friendly and self-sustaining."

"So you're using the fees people pay to put up more booths for charging fees?"

"Look, mate, you're running a camp here. You understand that sometimes there are upfront costs even for collecting money. And it's not as if we've collected a Timbuktu-full of gold here!"

"So you're bringing in cabins from Stawell, are you?"

"No, we're relocating existing cabins. The drop in tourist numbers has meant that there are surplus cabins around. People have just abandoned them."

"I see. So that's what you were looking for here, was it? Cabins you could, ah, 'relocate' to collect your entry fees?"

"Now look here, everyone told me that this place had been abandoned."

"You obviously need to ask people who know what they're talking about."

"Don't you get smart with me, mate!"

"As far as I can tell, Brad, you came here to check what was available so that you could send your men to steal as many cabins as possible for your revenue collection business – and probably all of the solar panels as well. You need to understand that this camp is private property belonging to Steve and Sylvia Jones and you have no right to enter it."

"What right do *you* have to be here then?" challenged the man.

"If you want to check that we have permission to be here and authority to manage this camp, contact Terry Holland, the bank manager in Stawell. He's Steve and Sylvia's agent while they're away. I'm sure he'll be interested to hear of your plans."

The man looked surprised to hear Terry's name, and his tone changed.

"Now come on, don't go causing trouble," he whined. "We weren't going to steal anything, we just aimed to put unwanted equipment to good use. There's so much around here that isn't being utilised to its full potential. We need to work together in these difficult times, not go around looking for fights."

"I'm happy to avoid fights, but this camp is still in business and you can't just come around and take anything you want. That's stealing. What's the rest of your name, Brad?"

"I'm Brad Jessop, and this is all a misunderstanding. Now that I know you're here, I'll let you get on with your work. Cheers."

Brad climbed back into his car and drove off. Nathan was pleased to see that he was looking at least a little taken aback.

"I'm glad we were here when he came!" said Dan.

"Yes," agreed Nathan. "Otherwise I suspect there would have been all sorts of things missing when we got back."

"I don't suppose he could have put any cabins on his roof racks, but he might have helped himself to a few solar panels!"

"We don't want to go anywhere near Halls Gap, that's for sure. Collecting money from naive travellers to pay for maintenance they never do! Disgusting."

"Yes."

"Let's go and chain the camper-trailer to a tree – with two chains," said Nathan, grimly. "And Dan, don't tell Belinda about this. Not yet, anyway."

"Okay."

Chapter 10

Alex

Terry Holland was outraged to hear of Brad Jessop's claims.

" 'Mayor'!" he snorted. "Halls Gap isn't a separate council area, so it doesn't have a mayor. He has no authority to collect anything. They're just a gang of upmarket bushrangers."

"In the olden days, many bushrangers called themselves 'Captain'," said Nathan. "This one's calling himself 'Mayor'."

"Do you think you scared him off?"

"Yes, I do. Actually, it was your name that seemed to have the biggest effect. Does that group have any dealings with the bank?"

"Some of the individuals do. Maybe they think I'll refuse to let them withdraw their money if they cause trouble."

"But who would have authority to decide that?"

"The way things are at the moment, I could do it myself, but I don't like running things that way. I'll talk to the council and the police. I know quite a few people are concerned about that outfit, but I don't know of any formal complaints. Apparently their cash collectors wear uniforms that look a lot like the park rangers' uniforms. They may even be using uniforms the National Parks people left behind."

"That's sneaky. Now, where are these forms you wanted us to sign? We'll stay for three months and see how things go. If Steve and Sylvia are back by then and don't need us any more, that's fine. If they still want us, we'll talk about it then. Sometime, Dan should go to uni and Belinda should go back to school. But for now, they'll learn more useful things here than they would at school or uni."

"We don't have a uni here," said Terry, "but we do have a school Belinda could attend."

"That could be a good solution, but for the time being it can wait. Don't go looking for trouble, I say. Each day has enough trouble of its own."

"True. Jesus said that, didn't he?"

"Yes, I believe so, and I've always found that it's true."

"Same here. Here are the forms we discussed. Have a read and make sure we all have the same expectations. I know Steve and Sylvia would hate you to feel pushed into signing up for something you don't really want. They love Roses Gap – and I reckon you'll love it too when you've stayed there for a few weeks."

"I think we already do."

Nathan and Tanya read and signed their papers, while Dan and Belinda signed papers giving them permission to stay on the site and operate the camp equipment as representatives of camp management. They would all be genuine employees during camps.

Once the forms were signed, Nathan asked Terry if there were any tree experts in Stawell who could cut up the huge tree blocking the Roses Gap Road. "Once it's cut into small enough pieces, we can get it off the road ourselves," he said, "but we can't do the whole job."

"All the arborists are very busy now," answered Terry. "In the past, a lot of tree removal work was done by companies from Ballarat, particularly the bigger jobs. Now that they can't get here any more, the locals have to do it all. I think most of them would be glad to cut up the tree if they could leave you to remove the pieces and tidy up the road."

"Do you know of anyone with a big enough chainsaw to cut that trunk? I measured it on the way here and it's up to 1,100 millimetres in diameter. It's massive."

"It is. And getting it off the road will still be an enormous job even after it's cut into sections, but I don't think you can leave it there. If you do, there's a good chance quite a few of the campers won't turn up. When they see that tree, they'll turn around and go home."

"That's right, and Dan's looking forward to getting rid of it."

"I'm sure Alex will enjoy it too. He should be here in a few minutes."

Business over, Tanya and Belinda headed for the supermarket to restock the pantry.

Dan stayed with Nathan, hoping to meet Alex, already somewhat of a hero in his mind. Anyone who could lead the sporting activities he had read about in the camp literature must be worthy of admiration. Dan was over the moon, thinking of all he could learn from such a great man.

Soon, a small young man with short dark hair entered the bank. His movements were quick and confident and he looked cheerful. "Hi, Dad," he called. "Are these the new managers?" When Terry nodded, Alex said to Nathan and Dan, "I'm Alex and I'm very glad to meet you. You've rescued me from spending the rest of my life working in a bank!"

Terry laughed and said, "If you listen to Alex, you'll think we've kept him locked up in the bank every night to make sure he didn't escape. In fact, he volunteered to work here – and he works hard. But he doesn't enjoy it as much as working at Roses Gap Camp."

"Have you cleared any trees at the camp?" asked Nathan.

"Small trees from time to time, but Dad mentioned a much bigger tree on the road. I've never handled anything like that. We'll need to get a professional to cut it up for us. I know a bloke who works with tree lopping and removal, using those really big chainsaws. He's always busy, but I think he'd be happy to help if we can handle the disposal. Shall I ask him?"

"Yes, please."

"I'll try ringing him now. If that doesn't work, I'll have to go to his offices and leave a note. It's kind of a pain not having a reliable mobile phone network."

Alex tried several times, but the phone system wouldn't cooperate, so he left for the arborist's office, agreeing to make his way to Roses Gap Camp that afternoon.

Soon afterwards, the Turners hurried back to the camp with their shopping, hoping to keep the frozen goods frozen.

⭕

Having found the arborist and made arrangements, Alex packed what he needed into his car, squeezed his bike in the back and drove towards Roses Gap.

As he was driving past the Beehive Falls car park, he noticed a four-wheel drive parked there. A man stood at the start of the walking track, hammering in a star-picket with a sign fixed to it. All he could make out as he drove past were the words "Walking Fee". He stopped as quickly as he could and reversed to the parking area. Climbing quickly out of the car, he walked towards the man with the hammer.

"Hey, what's going on here?" he called.

"We're putting up signs to notify walkers of the new fees."

"Fees? Who said there should be fees?" Alex was not tall, but he exuded confidence.

"The National Park Management Committee has set new fees for walks in the park. Soon we'll be selling National Park passes and putting honesty boxes at the start of various walking tracks."

"National Park Management Committee? There's no such thing – at least, not with any authority." Alex spoke coldly, dismissively. The whole setup sounded like a rip-off.

It was then that Alex noticed the second man. He had been lounging against the bonnet of the four-wheel drive, but now he stood, highlighting his tall, powerful build and vaguely threatening demeanour. He pointed his finger at Alex. "Come on, kid, the committee is the natural successor to Parks Victoria. We care for the park, and care costs money. People who love the park will be glad to pay fees to make sure it's properly cared for."

"Have any of the committee even *looked* at this path to decide what maintenance is required?"

"Look here, shrimp," answered the threatening man with a sneer, "who do you think you are? The committee sets the rules here, not you. We know what work needs to be done."

"So who's looked at this track then?" repeated Alex.

"Brad looked at it this morning," answered the man with the hammer.

"I suppose he stood where you are, looked up the track and decided it needed fixing?" retorted Alex.

"Now you be careful, kid," said the man, pointing his hammer at Alex almost as if it were a gun. "Don't call the mayor a thief or you might find that *you'll* have to answer for breaking the law."

"Breaking the law!" scoffed Alex. "There's no law making Brad Jessop mayor of anywhere."

The tall man walked threateningly towards Alex, reaching into a deep pocket as he did so. Alex felt genuine fear for the first time.

"We haven't used our new jail yet," put in the man with the hammer quickly, looking uneasy. "He could be the first inmate."

"We don't need to bother with that, Darren," said the other man. "Let's just touch him up a little – teach him a bit of respect." He pulled a large adjustable wrench out of his pocket. "Come on, Darren, you get him from that side, I'll get him from this."

"Let's just take him back to Halls Gap. They can lock him up there," whined Darren. "I don't want to get involved in beating people up."

"Oh no, Darren, of course not. You're a wuss. Remember, we're the law around here! We can't let runts like this get away with stuff like that. If you won't help, then at least make sure he doesn't get away. I'll do the rest myself." Once again, he advanced threateningly on Alex, who quickly turned and stepped back to keep his car between him and the nameless thug with the wrench.

"Don't forget there are genuine police in Stawell," he said, a little breathlessly.

"Who's going to tell them?" asked Darren with a sneer.

"My Dad knows I'm here and he'll report it if I disappear. Someone will come out looking for me and your signs will give you away."

"Who's your Dad?"

"Terry Holland, the bank manager."

"Hey, Craig, we better be careful. Don't forget our bank accounts."

"Shut up, Darren!" said Craig, looking furious.

"I reckon we should leave this kid alone."

"Oh, alright." He stuffed the wrench back into his pocket, then pointed at Alex again. "You can go this time, kid, but understand this: the committee makes the rules around here, and if anyone causes trouble, we know how to deal with them. Don't forget." He gave his finger a final shake and turned away dismissively. "Have you finished with that sign yet, Darren?"

"Yes, I'd just finished when Mr. Smart Alec turned up."

"Let's go."

He turned away and climbed into the four-wheel drive. Darren followed and they drove away. Alex stood and watched, glad to have escaped without injury. Nevertheless, he couldn't leave the sign there. Hearing Darren and Craig turn onto the road towards Halls Gap, he walked across and tugged at it. Darren hadn't done his job very well, and after jiggling the picket backwards and forwards for a minute, Alex was able to pull it up and throw it into the shrubbery behind the fence.

"Fees!" he said to himself in disgust. "Extortion, more like. No money anyone pays those crooks will ever get used to pay for maintenance, that's for sure."

Chapter 11

Starting to Plan

When Alex reached the camp, he parked near the office building and climbed out, still feeling a little shaky after his confrontation with the two thugs.

Nathan came over and invited him in. "We're just about to start a late lunch, Alex. Would you like to join us?"

"I'd love to, Mr. Turner, but before we go in, I need to warn you about Brad Jessop and his gang."

"Just call me Nathan, Alex."

"Okay, Nathan. I've just come from the Beehive Falls carpark where I met a couple of fellas putting up a sign about fees for using the walking track. I asked them what they were doing and in the discussion that followed, I said they had no right to do it. They didn't like that."

"I'm not surprised. Did they do anything?"

"One of them wanted to drag me off to jail in Halls Gap, the other wanted to beat me up with a wrench. Fortunately I managed to convince them they'd be getting themselves in trouble either way, so they left. Then I pulled up their sign."

"So I was wrong to think I'd scared Brad and his cronies away," said Nathan, thoughtfully, then described his morning confrontation with Brad Jessop.

"Hmm," responded Alex. "They haven't wasted any time, have they?"

"Do you think the council or the police will do anything about your Dad's report?"

"I don't know. I guess the council might consider pretending to be mayor a serious offence – especially if he's collecting fees *they* feel entitled to."

"How dangerous do you think these two were?"

"Very – at least one of them, anyway. It was pretty scary. The only thing that stopped them beating me up was the fact that they have accounts with Dad's bank and were worried about his reaction."

"I'm glad it stopped them!"

"Me too," smiled Alex. "But if the police don't act quickly, I reckon they'll soon have barriers across every road, collecting money from everyone. Plus they'll be charging fees for using the walking tracks, and anything else they can bully people into paying for."

"You're probably right," sighed Nathan. "I was hoping to get on with work here tomorrow morning, but maybe I should go and talk to your Dad again."

"Tomorrow's Saturday, so it can probably wait until Monday. I can't imagine Brad Jessop working hard on the weekend."

"Saturday? I guess I've been too busy to notice the days of the week! I'll talk to Tanya about it later. Let's go in for lunch."

During lunch, the Turners started getting acquainted with Alex, and they liked what they saw. Sitting around the meal table, Alex reported his progress with the arborist and they discussed their plans.

"It's two weeks until the first camp begins," said Nathan.

" 'Two weeks'?" asked Belinda, precise as always when it came to numbers. "Today's Friday and the camp starts on a Monday, right? Isn't that seventeen days?"

"You're right, and that extra three days might be important," agreed Nathan.

"How many people are coming?" asked Dan.

"Exactly thirty," said Tanya. "Mostly men, but a few women too, so we'll need facilities for both."

"Since it's a training camp," continued Nathan, "the mine staff will run the morning and evening activities themselves. We'll be organising the afternoon activities, but they've already agreed with Steve and Sylvia what those activities will be."

"That's good – at least we know what we're aiming for," said Dan.

"True, but there are still lots of other arrangements to discuss with the Training Coordinator at the mine," said Nathan.

"We need to confirm the menu," said Tanya. "We'll have to avoid the allergies reported in the initial booking. Then a week before, we'll confirm the number attending and check on payment, and lots of other administrative things. We'll be busy alright, but at least a lot of it has already been organised."

"Which cabins will be used?" asked Belinda.

"It's a bit like running a small city, isn't it?" commented Dan. "We've got to make sure everything is in good condition and working well: the roads, signs, housing, electricity, heating, cooling, water, food and so much more."

"But the camp has been well designed and built," observed Nathan, "so most of the work will just be checking that everything works as expected. It'll get much harder if we come across any problems."

"There's all the sports equipment too," said Alex. "I'll have to check the records. I expect Steve and Sylvia will have kept them up to date, but if not, I'll have to inspect *everything*."

"There's also the dining room, games rooms, activities hall, and so on," said Nathan.

"At the start I didn't understand why you said there was such a lot to do, Dad. Now I see!" said Belinda.

"We'll divvy up the jobs, then each do the work to which we're best suited. I'll look after the utilities and bathroom facilities. Tanya, you're checking the cabins, halls, kitchens and so on, aren't you?"

"Yes, and Dan and Belinda, you'll help each of us at different times. That way, you can learn about all the jobs needed in a camp like this. To some extent, we'll all be learning together!"

"I'm sure we'll have to spend money fixing or replacing things," added Nathan, "and then Belinda can indulge her interest in accounting."

"And I could help Alex check the sports equipment," offered Dan. "If he needs help, that is."

"If your parents can spare you, I'm sure you'd be a great help," said Alex.

"Yes, that'd be good," said Nathan. "Dan can learn about both the equipment and the record-keeping."

CR

The rest of the afternoon flew by, and dinner was delayed until it was too dark to work outside.

With only 30 people attending, the first camp would not require all the facilities, so to minimise the preparation required, Nathan and Tanya started by deciding which cabins and other buildings to use. The other buildings would remain locked until afterwards.

That done, Tanya began inspecting the chosen cabins, while Nathan went to check the water tanks. He removed the cover that protected the piping, valves and pump on the first tank. What he found worried him, so he checked the second. It was just as bad.

Hurrying towards the sports equipment shed where Alex and Dan were spreading everything out for inspection, he called, "Hey, Alex! Can you come and look at this, please?"

They returned to the first water tank, and Nathan pointed to the uncovered pipework. The electrical wires supplying the pump had been cut and the pump was missing.

"We need this tank to supply water to the main kitchen," said Nathan. "Would Steve and Sylvia have left the tank like this, Alex? The valves are closed so the water hasn't been lost, but with no pump, we've got no pressure. I opened the bypass and turned on a tap in the kitchen, but it's hopeless. Not only that, but this tank over here..." He led them to a nearby tank where the cover also lay to one side, and Alex and Dan saw that this pump was also missing. "It's just the same," finished Nathan.

"Steve and Sylvia wouldn't leave things like that," said Alex. "I guess this morning wasn't the first time Brad Jessop or his cronies have been here."

Nathan sighed. "That's what I was wondering. We thought we were so fortunate being here when they first came, but it looks as if they've visited before. What else could they have taken?"

"Good question."

"Well, we were trying to minimise the amount of work required before the first camp starts, but now we'll have to do a full stocktake straight away."

"At least for the equipment in the open," said Dan.

"What do you mean?" asked Nathan.

"The buildings were all locked. All the padlocks around the site are intact except for that one on the track."

"I guess you're right," agreed Nathan. "After all, the keys were in the safe and everything we've looked at has been locked up."

"Well, that's less to include in our stocktake," said Alex, "but we'll still need to check quite a lot of outdoor equipment."

"And see what sort of stock take Brad and his gang have done."

"Boom, boom!" said Alex, groaning. "That was a really pathetic pun, Dan."

"Sorry," said Dan, smiling.

"Puns aside, what shall we do about those pumps?" asked Nathan. "And how many *are* missing?"

He walked to the next tank and removed the pump cover. The pipe layout looked identical except that this time, a pump sat where it belonged.

"This one's okay. I wonder about those smaller tanks," he said, pointing to three tanks each sitting between a pair of cabins.

The three walked across to the closest tank and Nathan tried to lift the pump cover. It wouldn't move.

Looking at the back of the cover, he said, "A-hah! Good! This one has a padlock holding it down."

A check of the other two tanks showed that their pump covers were likewise padlocked in place.

"Well, that's good news," said Nathan, "but we'll still have to check the rest of the outside equipment to see if anything else is missing." He sighed again and went away to tell Tanya.

In the end, the extra inspection didn't cause a huge delay. One more pump was missing and the tank it was attached to was completely empty. Apparently the thieves had not closed the valve at the pump inlet properly, and there were signs of water leakage. Although the tank would not be required for the first camp, the lack of water might be important later in the summer.

Nathan asked Alex and Dan to keep their eyes peeled for any other places where equipment might be missing, and they all got back to work.

Once they'd finished inspecting the sports equipment, Alex took a walk around the site. He soon came looking for Nathan.

"I'm afraid the old toolbox is missing. Steve had to replace the generator a while ago and the new one was a bit bigger, so the toolbox wouldn't fit in the shed any more. It was padlocked closed, but it wasn't fixed down. I suppose the thieves just took it with them. It had Steve's name painted on it, though – perhaps the police could find it in Halls Gap."

"Maybe. Anyway, let us know if anything else is missing. Later, we'll need to replace those pumps."

Chapter 12

Reporting

"Of course there's no *proof* that it was Brad Jessop and his men, but they're the most likely culprits," explained Nathan.

"I'm sure you're right," agreed Terry. "I'll report this to the police. They may visit you at the campsite, but they're unlikely to be able to do anything about it."

"True. We also need to replace the pumps. I can jury-rig the piping to use two of the other pumps for now, but we'll need all the pumps before we host the larger groups in the new year."

It was Saturday morning and Nathan and Dan had made their way to Terry and Linda's house to report the thefts, leaving Tanya, Belinda and Alex to look after the campsite.

"The pump supplier is just over the railway line," said Terry, "but pumps are hard to come by nowadays. You saw what the convoys are like – oh, that reminds me! The convoy you came with was robbed on the way home, just a few kilometres beyond Beaufort. No-one was hurt, thankfully, but the gold shipment bound for Melbourne was stolen."

"What, all of it?"

"Yes."

"Is that unusual?"

"As far as I know, it's the first time ever," answered Terry.

"What will happen? What police would it be reported to?"

"I'm just hoping it won't cause too much trouble. The convoy brought a consignment of newly-minted gold coins and exchanged them for gold ingots from the mine. So now the Victorian government has neither the coins nor the ingots! They might decide to take some serious action beyond the margin."

"An invasion?" laughed Nathan.

"Times have changed, haven't they? Different governments, different currencies, and now perhaps an invasion."

"Do you know how much gold was stolen?"

"Not exactly, but rumours suggest about 40 million dollars' worth."

"Phew," breathed Nathan. "That's a lot of gold!"

"Yes, and stolen in the bushrangers' corridor."

"I wonder whether the armed men we saw in the back of that truck were involved," murmured Dan.

Shortly afterwards, Nathan and Dan visited the pump agents, but when Nathan provided the model number, the agent shook his head. They had none in stock and no expectation of getting any.

"You know the Victorian government's attitude to the margins and the towns beyond. As far as they're concerned, we're too much trouble to be bothered with. We can't place orders with the Melbourne manufacturers and importers as we used to, and trucks can't cross the margin anyway unless they're part of an 'approved' convoy. At the moment, we're investigating getting supplies from Adelaide instead."

Dan's ears pricked up. He hadn't completely abandoned the idea of travelling to Adelaide to meet Dave and his other relatives. "Can you communicate with Adelaide?" he asked.

"It's patchy, but, surprisingly, it's often better than with Melbourne. Telephone connections often work for a while, but we haven't been able to arrange any deliveries from there yet. Naturally, the suppliers want to get paid, and they're worried about the safety of transporting goods outside the margins. South Australia has drawn margins too, but at least the old border is open now."

"So it's just the same as Victoria."

"Not quite. South Australia doesn't charge taxes, or demand that people have formal permission before crossing their borders."

"So people can travel freely either way if they want to?" asked Dan, pleased.

"Yes. But it's a long way out here and no-one maintains the roads. Local councils only spend money on the bits they care about."

Nathan and Dan left with little hope of getting replacement pumps. As they were walking out to their car, Nathan's phone rang. Through force of habit he still carried it with him, but he hadn't used it since they left Ballarat.

It was Terry, advising that the arborists had said they would be beside the log at eight o'clock on Monday morning.

Dan groaned. "Another early start? We used to come to the Grampians to relax, but now we're having early starts all the time."

"We told you it would be hard work!" laughed Nathan as he hung up. "Would you prefer to be locked down in Melbourne?"

"No, but can't I have all the advantages of both?"

Nathan laughed again. "Sorry, son, it doesn't work that way."

"Rats. But that reminds me. You said we'd have this afternoon off. Did you have anything planned?"

"No. We should ask Alex to take us to a place we'll be taking campers."

"That sounds great. Could we go rock climbing?"

"Perhaps, or maybe just hiking. You know Belinda isn't keen on heights or rock climbing."

"True, but she loves clambering around on rocks – it's just the long drops she doesn't like. If we go rock climbing, there are always places for scrambling."

"We'll see," said Nathan.

Chapter 13

An Afternoon Off

"We'll be taking the campers to a few different places during this first camp, and we should visit them all before it starts," said Nathan as they ate a late lunch. "Can we mix work with pleasure and visit one this afternoon?"

"We've been to a couple of them before," said Tanya, "but I think it'd be good to see somewhere new this afternoon."

Everyone agreed.

"Did you want to go somewhere with rock-climbing?" asked Alex.

"That would be great!" said Dan.

"I think it'd be best to go somewhere with other options as well," said Nathan, looking at Belinda.

"I don't like rock climbing," said Belinda, "but I love rock scrambling."

"Alright," said Alex. "If we head north along the Mount Zero Road, that'll take us to Hollow Mountain or Mount

Stapylton. They've both got lots of scrambling, but the best climbing is in the amphitheatre on the way up Stapylton. Have you been there before?"

"No. We visited Mount Zero once on the way to Horsham, but we've never been to the others."

"I've seen Hollow Mountain on the map," said Belinda. "Is it really hollow?"

"There are lots of caves and hollows in the sandstone. One section has so many caves that it really does look like a hollow mountain. And if you climb up through it, you reach a path that works its way up a sloping plateau to Mount Stapylton. It's a really nice place to visit. I'm sure you'd love it."

"Are there any long drops?" asked Belinda, concern in her voice.

"I really can't answer that, Belinda," said Alex. "If you enjoy rock scrambling, it's hard to say whether any particular situation will scare you or not. The scrambling around there is good, but you need to work your way around tall cliffs at times. It might be best if we take the popular route up Stapylton, and then go across to Hollow Mountain on the way down. To climb the last section of Stapylton, you follow a ledge around the side of the mountain. It's not difficult as long as the wind isn't too strong, and if you can cope with that, I think you'd be able to climb down through Hollow Mountain too. None of it requires ropes or anything like that."

"That sounds like fun. How far is it?"

"Oh... I'm not sure. I've done it several times, so I should know, but I don't. A few kilometres. You'll have to look at the maps in the games room or read one of TT's books."[1]

---

[1] Tyrone Thomas wrote many books on bushwalking, including a couple on hikes in the Grampians.

Belinda immediately went looking for the maps and books. While they waited, Alex explained to Dan and Nathan that the rock walls of the amphitheatre were popular climbing walls. "One is the Taipan Wall, a sheer cliff of orange sandstone that towers over the amphitheatre. It's a wonderful photo opportunity, too, if you're there around sunset. But there are many climbing areas there; some easier, some harder."

It wasn't long before Belinda returned with a book of walks and a map. After studying them, she concluded that the walk to Mount Stapylton via Flat Rock and the amphitheatre was about two or three kilometres, while the track from the summit back to the parking area via Hollow Mountain would be about four kilometres. The complete walk would take about three-and-a-half to four hours. "And if it's going to take that long, we should go now," she said.

"You're right," said Tanya.

"We'll only have time to *look* at the climbing areas this time," said Nathan. "Sorry, Dan and Alex."

"That's okay," said Alex. "It gets pretty hot on the wall at this time of day anyway."

"I'll bring my binoculars to see what I can see," said Dan. "What's the road there like?"

"Good question," said Alex. "It wasn't much good when I last drove along it – lots of corrugations. It's probably even worse now with no-one looking after it."

"Don't worry, I'm sure Brad and his merry men will have used the money they're collecting to send a grader along," said Dan, sarcastically.

"Yeah, right," smiled Alex.

"We really need to know how long the campers will take to get there, so take note of the time," said Nathan. "We'll go in the four-wheel drive."

They carefully locked all the doors, sheds, padlocks and buildings before leaving. Nobody expected Brad Jessop's men to return while they were away, but it was best to be careful.

After piling into the four-wheel drive, they made their way to the Mount Zero road. It was a dirt road, and they immediately met the corrugations Alex had warned them about.

"This is terrible," said Nathan after unsuccessfully trying to find a part of the road on which the corrugations were not so bad. "We're only doing 20 kilometres an hour."

"How far is it, Sis?" asked Dan.

"About 13 kilometres."

Tanya groaned. "By then I'll be bruised all over!"

Fortunately, that first section proved to be the worst of the entire trip. After two or three kilometres, the road began to improve, and soon they were able to speed up significantly, despite the broken branches and fallen boughs that almost blocked the road in places.

Signage along the route was still intact, and they found the Mount Zero car park easily enough, despite the road's deterioration over the last few kilometres. However, as they turned off toward the car park, Nathan suddenly stopped. A fallen tree completely blocked the road, and there was no way around it. They left the car where it was and found their way to the bottom of Flat Rock.

"I can see why they call it Flat Rock," said Belinda.

"It may be flat, but it's sure not level!" said Dan.

A wide expanse of sandstone rose up on a steep incline in front of them, mostly uniform except for where water had worn paths down it.

"There are fluorescent arrows marking the path in rocky areas," said Alex, "but it's easy to miss them. Always keep your eyes open for the next arrow."

They started climbing and gained height quickly. Soon they were all puffing, and whenever they paused to catch their breath, they turned around to enjoy the delightful expanse of open country that was unfolding behind them.

"Do people use these walks anymore?" asked Belinda as they approached the top of Flat Rock. "Are we likely to meet anyone?"

"I have friends who still climb the Taipan Wall, but they come in on another path to avoid climbing Flat Rock," said Alex.

"I can see why! We're sure climbing quickly," puffed Tanya.

"Don't worry," said Alex, "we'll be going down again soon enough."

"Oh, no," groaned Dan. "It's not one of those up, down, up, down walks, is it?"

"Not really, but there are some downs, and one of them takes us into what's called the amphitheatre. After that we go up most of the way."

They reached the top of Flat Rock and followed the path down into a wide, fan-shaped area that sloped gently away from huge orange cliffs that rose to their left.

As they crossed the amphitheatre, following a sandy path between stunted trees, they passed many rough paths leading off toward the enormous walls.

"Rock-climbers follow those paths to the walls, but they don't look as if they've been used much lately. We'll follow this track across the amphitheatre and then climb up towards the bird."

"The bird?" asked Dan.

"It's a rock formation. You'll know it when you see it."

They reached a sloping rock pad that rose steeply in front of them and began to climb. After a while, Tanya stopped, puffing, and looked upwards. "Do we have to go all the way up here?"

"Yes," said Alex, smiling. "And... do you want the good news or the bad news first?"

"The good news, please," panted Tanya.

"Once we get to the top of this long sloping section of rock, the track levels out for a while – it even goes down a bit."

"And the bad news?" asked Belinda.

"See the top of the cliff on your left? That's where we're going." He pointed up to where the cliffs towered high above them, the huge sandstone crags dwarfing them. "All the way up there," he said.

"This walk sounded a good idea at the start," groaned Belinda. "But now I think I'll melt before we get there!"

"Let's keep going anyway," laughed Nathan.

"Hey!" exclaimed Dan, looking up the slope in front of them. "Is *that* the bird?"

He pointed to a large rock formation that looked remarkably like a bird. Perhaps it didn't accurately represent any particular type of bird, but it was undeniably bird-shaped.

"Yep," said Alex, "that's the one."

"I like it," said Belinda. "It looks like a chook. I'm going to call it Chook Rock."

"Last one to get to the bird is a rotten egg!" said Dan, striding off up the steep slope towards the bird-shaped rock.

"That's not fair!" said Belinda. "You got a head start."

"Hurry up, then," Dan called back. "Stop acting like a bird-brain."

"I'm flying."

"I don't think I am," muttered Tanya to Nathan.

"Nor I. They can have their hen. I like to breathe."

"Are those two always so competitive?" asked Alex, laughing.

"Yes – but they get on well together. Belinda would do anything for her big brother, and Dan would do anything for her," said Tanya.

"As long as he could do it without people thinking he was helping a girl!" added Nathan.

"Is Belinda really scared of heights? There are a few places along this walk that some people find difficult."

"Sometimes. If she has to walk along a rocky incline with sand on it, she does freeze at times."

"Okay. There are a couple of places that might be a problem for her: near the cave; and the ledge I spoke of. But I don't think there'll be much wind today. We'll see what she thinks of them when we get there."

As Alex spoke, Dan's voice floated down the hill to them. "Come on, Sis. I've been perched up here for ages." He had climbed up onto the top of the bird's head and was looking very pleased with himself.

"I'll get up there when I can breathe again," came Belinda's voice from behind the rock formation.

The others made their way up to the striking natural sculpture and Nathan and Tanya sat down in its shadow.

"It's good to be in the shade," said Tanya, breathing quickly.

"True, but I'll climb up to the head, anyway," said Nathan, "...once I get my breath back."

Alex had already swung himself up onto the body of the bird, where Belinda was sitting.

"Does this sort of climbing scare you?" he asked her.

"No, although I won't go over to that side where the rock drops away so quickly. I'm happy here."

"Look over there," said Alex, pointing towards Flat Rock and Mount Zero. "Do you think we're higher than the top of Flat Rock?"

"Yes," answered Belinda, promptly.

"What makes you so sure?" asked Dan. "Don't forget the earth is round."

"If I can see the horizon over the top of something, then I must be higher than it is."

"I guess that's true," said Dan. "I hadn't thought of that."

"You're right, Belinda," agreed Alex, "but I'm not so sure that we're higher than Mount Zero yet."

"We'll have to keep checking," said Belinda, "but I think we're almost equal with the top of Mount Zero now. How much further is it to the top?"

"Still a long way," laughed Alex, "but I think this is the hardest section." He turned towards the cliff and pointed upwards. "We want to get to the top of those cliffs, so we have to walk around behind the peak – unless you want to climb a vertical cliff!"

After enjoying the view for a few minutes, the younger climbers went on ahead, leaving Nathan and Tanya sitting comfortably in the shade. After a long climb, the three reached a flatter area and followed the path around a shoulder of the mountain before climbing gradually through shrubbery that was trying to reclaim the path. Chatting as they walked, they discovered many shared interests, including a great appreciation of nature, so they were all pleased when they saw a dark-furred wallaby. It spotted them at the same moment and hopped away into the bush.

Alex proved to have a good knowledge not only of sport, but also of botany, and he pointed out many different plants as they walked.

Surrounded by the sounds of the bush, and with the sun hot on their heads, they followed the path down into a quiet dell. They disturbed three more wallabies before reaching a narrow gully that led up to the gnarled and weathered sandstone that formed the crown of the mountain. There, Alex suggested they should wait for Nathan and Tanya, since it was easy to miss the path where it started up the gully. Sitting in the cool shade, they chatted and watched many tiny birds flit through the bushes and trees nearby.

After a while, Nathan and Tanya rounded the corner into the narrow gully.

"We saw four wallabies!" Belinda greeted them.

"That's good," said Nathan, "but guess what we saw?"

"A snake?"

Tanya shuddered, "No, thank goodness! It was a blue-tongue lizard. Quite a big one, too, as they go. It was just off the path and wasn't interested in us at all."

All together again, they climbed the steep gully and climbed onto a wide, steeply-sloping rock ledge. Despite the significant drop beside them, Belinda enjoyed the scrambling and was in the lead when they passed the entrance to a broad cave that sloped up into the mountain's rocky interior.

"Oh, look at that lovely white sand on the floor," exclaimed Belinda.

"And what are those footprints?" asked Dan, going in to explore.

"I don't know," said Alex. "There are always small footprints, but I've never seen anything actually walking in the sand."

"And look up at the roof," breathed Belinda. "It looks like a big sandstone carving with amazing swirls of colour and small hollows everywhere."

A swallow swooped in through the entrance, circled the large cave and sped out again.

"Swallows nest in here," said Alex, "and they don't seem very happy having us near their homes!"

"It's so co-o-ol in here," said Tanya, "and the sand on the floor is delightfully fine and smooth."

"I wonder what it would be like to spend the night here?" mused Nathan. "Some parts of the floor aren't too steep – you might be able to sleep in the sand."

"That's all very well," said Tanya, "but we need to get back to eat the chicken I left in the slow cooker."

"Mmm, that sounds good," said Dan, smacking his lips. "You know, we should have brought some snacks to eat in this cool cave."

"It really is an ideal spot," agreed Belinda.

"But we do want to get to the top, too," said Dan.

"So that we can get back for dinner?" teased Belinda.

"It's not very far to the top," said Alex, "and it's all rock scrambling."

"That sounds great," said Belinda. "Let's go."

They left the cave and made their way around to the front of the peak until they came to a rock chimney that led to the sloping ledge Alex had referred to. On their left, a cliff rose to the summit, while to the right, it fell away more and more steeply until it became a precipice, dropping to a rock platform far below.

Belinda leaned towards the rock wall and didn't look down as the track curved around the top of the mountain. It wasn't too bad.

After scrambling up one last slope of weathered rock, they reached the top of the mountain at last. A stunning view unfolded before them in all directions. Mount Zero, the northern-most peak of the Grampians, seemed small beneath them to the northwest, and beyond it were the open plains of the Wimmera. To the south, rank upon rank of purple mountains could be seen, dark green forests climbing their sides, but falling short of the rocky summits. None of these mountains were tall by international standards, but together they formed a vast expanse of rough, wild country stretching to the horizon. In places, the scars of old fires could be seen, and several roads and fire tracks picked their way through the bush. Below them to the north, the road they had arrived on curved around Mount Stapylton and Hollow Mountain, then past a large communications tower, before straightening out and heading south. The upper reaches of the tower were festooned with microwave dishes, incongruous and ugly amid the rugged beauty of its surroundings.

Dan stood on the highest point of the mountain and basked in the feeling of success which rewards a strenuous climb. After a few seconds, he took a few careful steps towards the edge of the cliff they had skirted on the way up. "Wow! It's a long way down," he breathed.

"Would I like to see it?" asked Belinda.

"I'm not sure," said Dan. "If you want to try, don't go too close to the edge. It really is a long way down."

"Maybe you should leave it this time, dear," called Tanya, concern in her voice.

"Hey, that looks like Bird Rock," called Dan. "Would it be, Alex?"

"Yes, you can see Bird Rock from where you are," said Alex. "It looks a bit different from on top, doesn't it?"

"I want to see it," said Belinda.

"Are you sure, dear?" asked her mother anxiously.

"Sure I'm sure," said Belinda, starting to scramble towards the edge. "Oooh!" she said as she got closer. "Maybe I'm not so sure that I'm sure. It's a long way down. And no soft mattresses at the bottom."

She stopped for a while, enjoying what she could see but trying to work up the courage to go closer to the edge where she would be able to see better.

"Can you see Flat Rock over there?" asked Alex, pointing.

"How far away?"

"Beyond the amphitheatre with the orange cliffs rising above it. If you look carefully, you can see the track going up beside the cliff to the top of Flat Rock."

"I see it," said Dan.

"So do I," said Belinda.

"Flat Rock seemed so high – even when we got to the top of it – but it looks so far down from here," commented Dan.

"Where is the camp site from here?" asked Belinda.

Alex pointed to the road below. "That's the road we came on. If you follow it southeast, it keeps going pretty much straight until you get to the Roses Gap Road."

Chapter 14

What Dan Saw

Relaxing on the summit and cooled by capricious breezes, their eyes drank in the vastness of the view that stretched away to a distant horizon in all directions. Birds darted to and fro and many insects buzzed in the afternoon sun.

Dan looked down on Flat Rock and traced the path they had followed. Then, finding out from Alex which crag was Hollow Mountain, he tried to imagine where a track to Hollow Mountain might go, but it wasn't easy to see. Remembering his binoculars, he took them out of their case and looked again, focussing carefully. With their help, he was able to see some small cairns that could mark the track.

Turning to face the ranges to the south, he scanned the communications tower where it sat in the middle of an open area, enclosed by a chainwire fence. With his binoculars still glued to his eyes, he suddenly noticed a smudge of dust nearby, approaching from the southeast along the Mount Zero road.

Studying the front of the smudge, he made out a large four-wheel drive – the first car they had seen since leaving the camp. As he watched, it slowed and stopped at the driveway of the communications tower.

Dan watched as the front doors opened and two men walked up to the gate. He was too far away to see clearly what they were doing, but they seemed to be yanking and shaking it. The driver returned to the car and re-emerged carrying something.

Dan wondered what they were doing.

After a while, they walked around the corner of the enclosure, stopping a short way along. A few minutes later, Dan saw that one of them was inside the enclosure.

"Hey, they must have cut the fence!" said Dan.

"What are you talking about?" asked Belinda lazily, leaning against a rock, watching a raptor cruise effortlessly high in the sky.

"Some men drove to that communications tower down there, and now they've cut the fence and gone inside."

"Maybe they forgot to take the keys with them."

"Or maybe they're breaking in. After all, it sounds like all the equipment is turned off, so no-one would be doing any maintenance on it anyway. Perhaps it's Brad and his men!"

"I can't imagine them finding anything useful in a complicated communications setup," said Alex.

"Maybe not," said Dan, "but a place like that might have emergency generators, solar panels – the type of stuff they were looking for at the camp."

"You could be right."

Dan turned back in time to see the men standing at a shed some distance from the main building. Once again, they seemed to be trying to open a door, and it wasn't long before they vanished inside. *I'll bet they broke the lock*, thought Dan, *or maybe even the door.*

He kept watching, and after a few minutes, the men left the shed and went to the main building. Eventually they opened a door and went inside.

"We should go," said Nathan, interrupting his vigil. "Mum and I have been discussing more work that needs doing, and it would be good to do some of it tonight."

"Let's start heading down then," said Alex.

"But I'm still watching that raptor," said Belinda. "It keeps gliding around and I'm waiting for it to find something to swoop on."

"You'll have to watch it another time," said Tanya.

"Oh, okay," said Belinda, disappointed. "But aren't they amazing to watch?"

"Beautiful," agreed Tanya.

"Which way shall we go down?" asked Alex. "We can go via Hollow Mountain if you think there's time, or just head back the way we came."

"It would be good to see Hollow Mountain," said Nathan, hesitating. "Look, I'll leave it up to you, Tanya. We can skip Hollow Mountain if you want."

"It should be okay," answered Tanya. "I'd like to see Hollow Mountain too."

"If we're going to Hollow Mountain," said Alex, "then we head along this ridge for a short distance, then scramble down towards two distinctive rocky outcrops on the lower edge."

Dan took one last look at the communications building, but there was no sign of the men. They were probably still inside. He wasn't sure what to do, but decided to keep quiet about whatever was going on down there. Perhaps he was imagining problems!

When they reached the cliff edge between the two outcrops, Alex pointed to a sloping tongue of rock that descended into a small canyon. "We climb down there, then turn around and go up the canyon for a bit."

Tanya was concerned about Belinda, but said nothing as the girl climbed slowly down.

"That wasn't too bad," Belinda crowed when she reached the bottom safely.

"It was bad to watch!" murmured Tanya.

Alex led them a short distance along the canyon before stopping at a stunted tree which grew beside the sloping rock wall. "We go up there," he said, climbing the rock easily. Soon they were all up on another rocky plateau that fell away gently in front of them.

"Stay close to this upper edge and follow the cairns."

As they walked, Dan had occasional views of the communications tower. The car was still there, but there was no sign of the men.

After a while, a deep cleft cut across their path.

"You can jump across it if you want," said Alex nonchalantly. "It's only a couple of metres wide, but the landing's rough and you'll fall quite a distance if you don't make it. Any takers for jumping?"

"Is there any other way?" asked Belinda, eyes open wide.

Alex laughed. "Yes, there is another way. I've never jumped it myself. We follow the cleft to the right, and in a while we can climb down past the end of it. Then we climb up the other side and keep going."

Reaching another place where he could see the compound, Dan was excited to see two tiny figures opening the gates. As he watched, one drove the car into the compound. Perhaps they were genuine workers after all.

"Come on, Danny Boy," called Belinda.

He hurried to catch up to the others and they worked their way around the end of the cleft.

As they approached Hollow Mountain, it was like following a secret trail. They edged their way along a log that spanned another deep but narrow fissure, then scrambled around the corner of a cliff and followed wind-carved tunnels down to the track that led to the top of Hollow Mountain.

This last stage pushed Belinda to the limit, but she overcame her fear and walked triumphantly out of the caves onto the track.

Dan revelled in the scrambling, but was disappointed to have had no further opportunity to observe the men at the communications tower.

"To get to the top of Hollow Mountain, you walk along to the end of this cliff here," Alex pointed, "then go around the end and walk up the other side towards the top. It's a bit like a staircase – the top is almost directly above us here. It's quite easy and there's a nice view from the top. Do we have time to go there, Mrs Turner?"

"Just call me Tanya," she answered, then added, "I think it would be best if we went straight back to the carpark."

They followed the track down to the sandy plain, then took a little-used path leading to the Mount Zero carpark. It wasn't long before they were back at their car.

By then, the sun was touching the horizon, and Nathan was eager to get back to the camp as quickly as possible.

"I don't think the place is in danger now that Brad knows we're there, but I don't want to be away too long."

As they drove past the communications tower, Dan scanned it carefully. The gate was closed and the steep driveway was empty.

Chapter 15

Tidying the
Games Room

After another late meal, all five gathered in the games room to see what was required to prepare it for the upcoming camp.

During inclement weather and the long dark evenings of winter, campers liked indoor entertainment, so games and puzzles filled the cupboards that lined two walls of the room. All of the games had to be unpacked and checked – the jigsaw puzzles would have to wait until they had more time.

"You don't need to join us, Alex," said Tanya. "You've already worked a long day, even if the afternoon was relaxation for us."

"No, I'll come and help, if that's okay. I reckon we'll all be busy right up until the camp starts. Anyway, I know how previous camps have been run, which might be useful."

"Thanks, Alex," said Nathan. "We really appreciate it."

"Well, I know my parents appreciate your help with the camp," said Alex, "so it looks like we're all helping each other."

"We do want to help Steve and Sylvia even though we've never met them," said Tanya, "but this is also a great opportunity for us."

"And an amazing series of coincidences," said Nathan. "If we hadn't met your grandfather in Ararat, we wouldn't have met your parents, and if we hadn't met them, we wouldn't be doing this."

"And if Sid hadn't been so friendly, we wouldn't have paid any attention to what he said about his daughter," said Tanya. "Nor would we have accepted this job if Linda and Terry hadn't shown themselves trustworthy. And you're just like your parents."

"Let's all praise each other," laughed Alex. "After all, my parents would never have asked you to do this if you hadn't convinced them *you* were trustworthy!"

"You wouldn't believe how many times Dad's told me, 'Honesty is what matters, son'!" Dan said the words in a good imitation of his father's voice and they all laughed.

"He's right," said Alex, "and he sounds just like my Dad. I can't copy Dad's voice, but he always says, 'Alex, if you don't have integrity, you don't have anything.' And that makes sense to me."

"If you don't mind me asking, Alex," said Nathan, "what does your family normally do on Sundays? It sounded like your parents are Christians. Is that right?"

"Yes, they go to a church in Stawell every week. Steve and Sylvia used to go to the same church whenever they could get away from the camp."

"Is that how your parents got to know them?"

"Partly, but also through the bank. Dad gets to know a lot of people through the bank, including some like Brad Jessop and his cronies."

Belinda looked questioningly at him, but said nothing.

"I suppose crooks put their money in banks, too," said Nathan, then laughed. "Perhaps they make bigger deposits!"

Dan had been scanning the noticeboards and bookcases that lined the other two walls of the room and had made a discovery. "Look! Bibles! I wonder if anyone reads them? They're in pretty good condition."

"Surely if anyone wanted to read the Bible they'd read it on their phone," said Belinda.

"Personally, I prefer to read a paper copy," said Dan. "That way I can see what's around the part I'm reading."

"That's true, but a phone is better if you're searching for things," said Alex.

"Do you read the Bible often, Alex?" asked Nathan.

"Oh, yes, I read it every day – almost."

"See, Dad!" said Dan, delighted. "I'm not the only one who thinks that's a good idea."

"I never said it was a bad idea," protested Nathan.

"No, but you don't do it, and you don't exactly encourage me to."

"You know that Mum and I have never got into Bible reading. We're not against it, we're just busy. We've found that being loosely attached to a church is better than joining. If you join, they think they own you."

"My parents had a really bad experience with a church in Adelaide," Tanya explained to Alex, "so I don't like getting too close to churches. I like the morality and the goodness that I find in many church-goers, but I'm a bit scared to get too involved."

"But I can't see why you include the Bible in that attitude, Mum," said Dan.

"I agree with Mum and Dad," said Belinda. "Christianity is good, but you don't want to become an extremist."

Dan looked at Alex helplessly. "We have this discussion every so often," he said, shrugging his shoulders and spreading out his hands, palms upward, "and I don't know how to get any further with it. I read the Bible because it answers my questions. I don't think that makes me an extremist."

"Don't worry, you're not an extremist, son," said Tanya, patting his arm, "and the friends you had at that last youth group in Melbourne were all good kids too. We just want you to be careful."

The conversation continued, but Dan tuned out briefly to muse over the exciting news that Alex read his Bible every day. He had already admired him for his sporting prowess, but this was an even better reason for admiration.

After they'd all been working for a while, Belinda commented, "It's amazing how much there is to check!"

"True, but it's been worth it," said Tanya. "That pack of playing cards you checked was missing the five of hearts, and one game of Ludo had three missing pieces – which I found in with the chess pieces."

"Do we throw away the games with missing pieces?" asked Belinda.

"At the moment, we'll just put them aside with notes about what's missing. We may find the pieces as we keep checking, or they may turn up over the next few months. If they don't and we can't get replacement pieces, we'll get rid of them then. To give people a really good camp, everything has to be complete."

The evening wore on and still the work was not finished.

Finally Nathan sighed and said, "I reckon it's time for bed. It's been a long day."

"What are we doing tomorrow?" asked Dan.

"We could go to church," suggested Tanya.

Nathan looked at her in surprise. "Well, I suppose we could," he said, "but I don't like leaving the place completely unattended for too long. We can't trust those trouble-makers from Halls Gap."

"I agree," said Belinda.

"You just don't want to go to church," scoffed Dan.

"You're right: I don't want to go to a church where we don't know anyone. But the other is true too."

"You might meet some new friends," said Dan.

"Maybe next week," said Nathan. "What do you think, Alex?"

"I don't mind staying here if that's what you want, but how would you feel about having a sort of service of our own?"

"What do you mean?"

"We could read the Bible and discuss what we read. I plan to have some bread and wine, but you don't have to do that."

Nathan and Tanya looked at him blankly, surprised by his suggestion that they could have church without a church!

Dan, however, answered enthusiastically, "That'd be great. I've never done anything like that before. What time?"

"How about after breakfast?"

"Breakfast will be at eight," said Tanya.

"So how about nine o'clock?" suggested Alex.

"Great," agreed Dan.

Chapter 16

The First Sunday

Despite the thick curtains in his bedroom, Dan woke early next morning. A magpie was singing outside his window and he wondered sleepily if it had woken him. Suddenly, he remembered what Alex had suggested for the morning and didn't feel sleepy any more.

Quickly he got out of bed, dressed, and went out into the cool morning air. Above him, the sun was already lighting the crags. To the south, its rocks glowing orange in the early morning sun, stood Briggs Bluff. His desire to climb that steep, angular peak was growing stronger each day. Was there a track to the top, he wondered. Perhaps there would be signs at the Beehive Falls parking area.

Suddenly it occurred to him that he had time before breakfast. It was only seven o'clock – he could easily walk to the parking area and be back in time to cook the toast.

No-one else was up, so he walked out of the camp alone and reached the empty parking area within minutes. Approaching the locked gate, he saw a sign which told him that this track could take him to Beehive Falls, Briggs Bluff and Mount Difficult. He passed through the pedestrian opening beside the gate, intending to walk a little way along the trail. Just inside the fence, however, he saw another sign, this one lying face-down on the ground. Though Dan didn't know it, this was the sign Alex had pulled up in annoyance. Seeing the hole left behind, Dan assumed that the sign had been pulled up by vandals. Perhaps he should put it up again – it might be important.

He turned the sign over and read, in large red letters, "Walking Fee."

Who would charge walking fees? He scanned the bottom of the sign, and read: "By order of Brad Jessop, Chairman of the National Park Management Committee."

"Hey!" he said out loud. "That's the bloke who came to steal things from the camp – the one Dad sent away."

The sign advised that, starting from Monday, 15 November, walkers would be required to deposit fees in a new "honesty box". "Why, that's tomorrow," he muttered to himself. "Sounds like those crooks'll be back soon to set up their box."

Brad Jessop was up to no good, he was certain of that. They had assumed Brad only intended to steal things that weren't fixed down, but perhaps they'd been wrong – particularly if the men Dan had seen up north were Brad's men! Perhaps Brad had had bolt-cutters with him at their first meeting – how would they know?

Maybe he'd planned to remove padlocks all over the campsite: from the pumps, the equipment sheds. Perhaps he'd come equipped to break into the cabins... or the administrative buildings.

He tried to slow down and marshal his facts.

One: Brad Jessop *had* come to steal things from the camp.

Two: Someone had *already* stolen some pumps and the toolbox.

Three: Someone had broken into the communications building near Hollow Mountain.

Four: Brad was trying to charge fees for walking on free tracks – tracks he had no control over.

Five: A complaint had been made to the police, but nothing seemed to have changed.

What did it all add up to? And what could he do about it? He was sure Brad Jessop was bad. He was also sure Brad had been involved in all those things, even the break-in he'd seen from the top of Mount Stapylton – but since the others had shown no interest, he wasn't going to mention it again until he could prove something.

Slowly he walked back to the campsite, wondering what they could do. Perhaps Alex would have some ideas. The thought of Alex abruptly redirected his musings by reminding him of their plans for the morning. Though Dan's parents went to church from time to time, they had never joined one, and he couldn't understand why. They never provided a clear explanation, just hinted vaguely that churches meant trouble.

Dan and Belinda had always been sent to Sunday School, and had belonged to three different church youth groups in the last four years – when the pandemic allowed. They both liked the people they met, but Dan also enjoyed the message of Christianity. After one particularly moving talk from a missionary, he had been inspired to read his Bible consistently. What he found there fascinated him, but also filled him with questions, most of which his parents couldn't answer. For a while, they had even seemed unhappy with his decision to read the Bible. He had persevered anyway, and was gradually becoming more familiar with it. The opportunity to talk to someone who read it every day was exciting, and he was looking forward to the get-together at nine o'clock.

He hurried along the camp driveway and made his way into the kitchen. Belinda was already there, setting the table for breakfast.

"Are you going to join Alex and me at nine o'clock?" asked Dan.

"Oh, I think I'll wait and see," said Belinda. "A sunny Sunday is too nice to waste sitting indoors. Which reminds me: where have you been? I was looking for you – it's time to start cooking the toast."

"I was wandering around outside," said Dan evasively, going to the pantry to fetch the bread.

Soon afterward, Nathan and Tanya arrived, pleased to see Dan and Belinda preparing breakfast together.

Alex followed them into the kitchen announcing, "If you want me to, I can fry some eggs in a special way my Dad taught me."

"I sure do," said Nathan.

"Nathan's always pretty eager for fried eggs," said Tanya. "If there's a new way to cook them, he'll want to try it."

"You make it sound like I'm addicted," laughed Nathan. "But perhaps you're right. My basic requirements are that the yolk is a lit-tle bit runny while the white is properly cooked."

"Well, as it happens, the way my Dad taught me to cook them will give you just what you want – with a bit of pepper thrown in as well. As far as I'm concerned, they're the nicest fried eggs I've ever tasted. Have we got any meat to go with them?"

"Yes, there are some sausages I cooked up a few minutes ago when nobody was in the kitchen," said Tanya.

"That sounds ideal. Some people like fancier meat, but sausages are good enough for me, particularly with fried eggs."

"Do we have sauce?" asked Belinda.

"Of course," said Tanya. "I wouldn't dare to suggest sausages without tomato sauce!"

Alex fetched the eggs from the fridge and took the pan Tanya offered him.

"There's nothing like a frypan that has already been used to cook meat when you want to fry some eggs," he said.

Soon it was ready, and the family pronounced the eggs delicious.

"A culinary masterpiece," said Belinda.

"Unsurpassed in the annals of history," added Dan with a serious look.

"A meal not to be trifled with," said Nathan.

"And definitely a cut above the average fried egg," finished Tanya.

"I must say that the sausages were pretty good too," replied Alex, gravely, "and the toast was exquisite. The table was laid to perfection and... er, did you do anything, Nathan?"

Nathan laughed. "No, I fear I contributed nothing to the feast except an appreciative spirit. As far as I'm concerned, this has been a delicious breakfast and I'm quite happy for the culinary competition to continue unabated."

"I can cook a pretty good fish finger feast," said Dan, "but I'm not sure that we have any fish fingers."

"I know you like them, so I made sure we got some," replied Tanya. "But I hadn't planned to have them for breakfast!"

"I can turn out some juicy porridge," said Belinda.

"Juicy?" grimaced Dan. "I wouldn't call porridge juicy!"

"Nor would I," admitted Belinda, "but I couldn't think of a better word on the instant, so juicy it had to be."

"Perhaps I need to develop some culinary delight of my own," said Nathan. "I can't be outdone by an upstart 15-year-old cooking juicy porridge."

"What about French toast?" asked Tanya. "That's about your skill level."

"Are you sure?" asked Nathan in mock concern. "It sounds too complex for me. Perfectly browned and generally superior toast might be within, as they say, my purview."

"They do? Perhaps they're exaggerating," said Tanya.

The food was enjoyed and so was the banter. Alex fitted in well with their sense of humour – and their sense of the ridiculous.

"What else are we doing today?" asked Nathan when everyone had finished.

"Alex and I are going to be reading our Bibles and talking about what we read," said Dan. "I'm looking forward to it."

"Oh yes, I'd forgotten about that. Can we join you?"

Dan was pleased with the request but looked to Alex for confirmation.

"That would be fine," smiled Alex. "It won't be like an ordinary church service – I don't have any religious qualifications, so if that's important to you, I can't help. Then again, Jesus didn't have any such qualifications either, and nor did his disciples."

"I suppose they didn't," said Nathan. "I'd never thought about that. They were mostly fishermen, weren't they?"

"We know that four of them were fishermen, but we don't know about most of the rest."

"Matthew was a tax collector, wasn't he?" asked Dan.

"Yes. Did you get that from reading the Bible?"

"I did. It was in the Gospel According to St. Matthew. Is that the same Matthew?"

"Yes, it's the same person."

"I guessed it was. Why is he called 'St. Matthew' in the book title in some Bibles, but just 'Matthew' in the text?"

" 'St.' is short for Saint. Later Christians gave that title to people they thought were particularly good. As you read the Bible more, you'll see that lots of people are called 'saints' – which just means 'holy ones'. In the Bible, 'saint' is more a description than a title intended to be used for certain special people."

"That's interesting, but what does 'holy' mean? I've seen it a lot, but..."

"Oh, sorry. 'Holy' means separated or set apart for God. So holy people – saints – are people who choose to be on God's side rather than siding with the rest of the world against God."

"I'm afraid that sort of separation is one of the things I don't like about churches," said Tanya. "Each church says they're right and everyone else is wrong."

"Okay," said Alex, nodding. "What about you, Nathan? Do you feel the same?"

"Up to a point. I can understand that there could be situations where churches are either right or wrong. After all, for any question, surely there can only be one truly right answer. In a maths exam, students can give lots of different wrong answers, but there can only be one that's right – and sometimes, nobody gives that answer!"

"That's true for a maths exam," said Tanya, "but religion isn't a maths exam. It's meant to be about spreading God's love, not trying to tell people they're wrong."

"But we don't give students exams so that we can fail them," Nathan pointed out. "It's quite the opposite – we're trying to find the students who *do* know what they're studying. We want everyone to pass, not fail!"

"I think that's a really good analogy, Nathan," said Alex. "The Bible tells us that God *wants* to save everyone, but it also says that for them to be saved, they have to come to a knowledge of *the truth*. It's not like a two-hour maths exam because God looks at how we live every day, but it does still depend on us knowing the truth from God and living it. That's what the Bible is there for – for us to read."

"I've never read the Bible," announced Tanya. "I think it gets used as a weapon, not a book of love."

"Why do you think it's a book of love?"

"That's what Christians say."

"I'm not trying to be rude, Tanya, but you're convinced that Christians misuse the textbook and yet you haven't read it. It's a bit like having a maths exam marked by somebody who never studied maths!"

"That's a good point, Mum," said Dan.

"Perhaps you're right. I've steered away from the Bible because of the problems religion caused in my family, so I've probably also stopped Nathan and my children from getting too close to it."

"I haven't fought very hard," admitted Nathan. "You know that. I've always liked goodness and morality, but I don't want to be tied down by a particular church's ideas."

"Please don't misunderstand me, because I already like all of your family a lot," said Alex, carefully, "but it seems to me that your answers are much more about *churches* than about *the Bible*. I believe the Bible is God's word, and it doesn't tell us to believe everything that other people tell us. In fact, the New Testament often warns about people who are misinformed or even deliberately trying to teach lies. We can't blame the Bible for that!"

"My father used to lump them all together after... after he had those problems with his church," said Tanya.

"I can understand why people might feel like that, but really, I think churches vary as much as people do. But there's only one Bible, and it doesn't change!"

"Well, if we're going to sit down and talk about this in fifteen minutes, why don't we wash the breakfast dishes quickly?" suggested Tanya. "Alex, you'll probably want to get ready to lead us, even if you aren't a pastor or whatever."

"That would be a help. But I can wash the dishes after lunch, if that's okay. I'll be over in the games room, every-one."

He walked out, but was still within earshot when Belinda asked her parents, "Do I have to come?"

Alex smiled to himself and kept going.

Reaching the games room, he sat down and pulled out the sheet of paper on which he had already made some notes. What with Dan's question about saints, and Dan's parents joining them too, Alex decided to change his plans a little. He skimmed the first chapter of Paul's letter to the Ephesians, and concluded that it was just what he was looking for: an encouraging letter that talked about saints from the very start. They could read it together.

By the time Dan arrived, followed closely by his parents, Alex was satisfied that the time they were about to spend to-gether would be helpful for Dan and his family – if they wanted it to be.

"Are we singing anything?" asked Nathan. "I should warn you that I'm hopeless at singing and don't know many religious songs."

"I can sing okay," said Tanya, "but I know even fewer religious songs than Nathan does."

"It looks like we won't be able to sing then," grinned Alex. "I'm not singing a solo!"

"What about you, though, Dan?" asked Tanya. "You sing very nicely. Belinda does too, but she decided not to come."

"What about 'Amazing Grace'?" suggested Dan. "You know that one, Mum, and I could play it on the piano."

"Oh, can you play the piano?" asked Alex eagerly. "I always wanted to learn, but we didn't have one and I never had any lessons."

"Dan plays very nicely..." began Nathan, then laughed. "At least, *I* think he does, but as I said, music isn't my forte."

Dan sat down at the piano and opened the lid. After trying a few notes, he began to play the well-known chords of Amazing Grace. He really did play nicely, although the piano didn't flatter him, having the unprepossessing quality of most camp pianos.

"Does everybody know the words?" asked Alex.

"I know the first verse," said Tanya.

"There are some books of music over there on the shelf," said Dan, "and I think there's a hymn book too. You might be able to find Amazing Grace in it."

Nathan took down the book and looked in the index. Sure enough, Amazing Grace was listed there, with the music as well.

"You don't seem to need the music," said Alex, "but let's agree on the number of verses to sing. There are three verses in this book. Shall we start?"

Dan began to play and they sang together, "Amazing grace! How sweet the sound, that saved a wretch like me."

They were finishing the first verse when Belinda walked in, asking, "Can I join in?"

"Of course," they all said.

"Would you like us to start again?" asked Alex.

"Ooh... yes, please," said Belinda.

So Dan started again and they all sang the three verses together. Nathan had been a little hard on his singing skills and the music sounded quite nice. It was clear that everyone enjoyed it.

"When I was originally thinking about what to do this morning, I was just planning to pray and read the Bible for a while, but all of you joining me has made it much grander and more enjoyable," began Alex. "Thank you. Nevertheless, when we are thinking about God, prayer and reading the Bible are both good things to do, so let's start by talking to God in prayer. I'll say a prayer and you can listen to it. If you agree with what I say, then at the end, you can say 'Amen' to show that you agree and want to be part of it."

Accordingly, Alex prayed, thanking God for the morning and the opportunity to read the Bible and worship. It was a simple prayer, praising God also for his work of creation. When he concluded with "Amen", the others chorused "Amen" also.

"That was a nice prayer," said Tanya. "Who taught you to pray like that? It sounded as if you were just talking to God."

"My grandfather, Dad's Dad, loved the Bible and always used to pray before meals when I went to visit him and Grandma. I loved his prayers."

"Are your Dad's parents still alive?" asked Tanya.

"No," said Alex, and it was obvious that he missed them. "They both died of the virus last year when the worst of the outbreaks happened in the country. They were vaccinated, of course, but that didn't help much with some of the later variants. I went to visit them one Thursday afternoon, and by Sunday they were both dead."

"How tragic," said Tanya. "I know many people lost loved ones like that in that outbreak. We were glad our relatives were in South Australia, which was spared the worst of it."

"My other grandma, Sid's wife, died of the virus two years ago. Grandpa Sid caught it too, but thankfully he recovered."

"You've had some trouble, haven't you?" said Nathan, sympathetically.

"But you still believe in God," marvelled Tanya. "Not like my Dad and Mum."

"What else could I do?" answered Alex simply. "Creation convinced me that God was real long before those sad things happened, and nothing can change that."

"I suppose not, but things like that often seem to make people start questioning."

"I used an example from maths at breakfast, and now I'll use another," said Alex. "Two plus two didn't stop being four just because my grandparents died, and nobody would suggest that I should think it might, so why should I doubt that God is in control just because things happen that I don't like?"

"You seem to have a different approach to life from what most young people have," observed Nathan.

"And old people, too," added Tanya.

"Shall we read some of the Bible now?" asked Alex. "I chose Paul's letter that he wrote to the believers at Ephesus, or St. Paul as it might say in Dan's Bible. Does it, Dan?"

"No," answered Dan, when he found the place. "It says 'The letter of Paul to the Ephesians'."

"Ah, you must have a newer version."

"I don't know, but who were 'the Ephesians'?"

"Ephesus was the name of a town in the area of modern-day Turkey, and people who lived there were called Ephesians," said Alex, "just like people who live in Melbourne are called Melburnians."

"They should be called Lockedownians," said Belinda.

They all laughed, glad to be free of such constraints themselves.

"I wanted to read the first chapter of Ephesians," said Alex. "Dan has a Bible and he's found chapter one, but what about the rest of you? You can just listen if you want to, or Dan can help you find it in one of those Bibles on the shelf."

They all chose to listen, and just before Alex started he said, "I want you to notice how the word 'saint' is used in the chapter, because that will help to show what Paul meant by a saint."

As Alex read the chapter, Belinda put up her hand each time she heard the word 'saint'.

When Alex finished, he asked Dan, "So, what do you think Paul means when he talks about 'saints'?"

"I think he just means any believer, but I suppose he might mean some special believers."

"Try reading the whole letter later and then let me know if you still think it might mean special believers. For now, can you please read Ephesians chapter 5 verse 3?"

Dan found the verse and read: "But sexual immorality and all impurity or covetousness must not even be named among you, as is proper among saints."

"Do you think Paul is saying that goodness only matters for some special believers?"

"No. The Bible says everyone has to be good."

"You're right. Saints are holy people, and God wants everyone to be holy, his people... saints."

"That's interesting," said Dan. "And challenging too, I guess. We can't just leave all the hard work of being good to some special people – we *all* have to be holy."

"I prefer grace," announced Belinda. "Grace like we sang about in that song. That's when God forgives us even though we don't deserve it, isn't it?"

"Yes, it is," agreed Alex, "although I don't know how we could ever *deserve* to be forgiven – without avoiding sinning in the first place! And then, of course, you wouldn't need forgiveness."

"So you're saying that all forgiveness is showing grace?"

"Yes. And when God shows us grace, he wants us to be thankful. You know, there's a passage in Ephesians that's very closely connected with that song. Ephesians chapter 2 verses 8 to 10."

"Can I look that up?" asked Belinda.

"Sure," said Alex.

"Do you know how to?" asked Dan.

"Not really, but I'm sure you'll help me, Danny-boy," said Belinda, sweetly. She took down a Bible from the shelf and opened it to the table of contents.

"Ephesians is in the New Testament," said Dan.

"Okay. I suppose I should have known that from Sunday School. Anyway, this gives me the page number and... here it is."

"So you should be able to find chapter 2 verses 8 to 10," said Alex.

"Yep, there it is. It says: 'For by grace you have been saved through faith. And this is not your own doing; it is the gift of God, not a result of works, so that no one may boast. For we are his workmanship, created in Christ Jesus for good works, which God prepared beforehand, that we should walk in them.' "

" 'Amazing Grace... that saved a wretch like me.' It does fit, doesn't it?" said Tanya.

"And it's not because of what we do," said Dan. "That's what we were taught at Sunday School."

"Good, and did you notice the next sentence too?"

"The next sentence? You mean, 'For we are his workmanship, created in Christ Jesus for good works, which God prepared beforehand, that we should walk in them'? Hmm. Just wait while I think about that.... Not of *our works*, but created by God in Jesus *to do good works*. I think I see. As Christians, we have to do good works, but that's not what saves us. Is that what it means?"

"It sounds a bit confusing," frowned Belinda.

"I think it's mostly about motives, really," said Alex. "If we're doing good deeds to show everyone how good we are, that won't save us. God expects us to do them because of Jesus' sacrifice."

"You mean it's working for God, not for yourself?" said Nathan. "Is that right?"

"Yes, I think so. So, if you're doing something good, who do you hope will get glory through that work? Yourself or God?"

"I like that," said Nathan. "That makes sense."

"Well, I think that's enough for the time being," said Alex. "And I've thought of another song you'll probably all know which has a really good message: Great is Thy Faithfulness."

"Yes, I know it," said Tanya eagerly, and the others agreed they also knew it.

"And I can play it, too," said Dan; "...I think."

Nathan looked in the index of the hymn book and found the song. "Three verses here, with the chorus after each. Is that what you're used to, Dan?"

"Yes," said Dan, and started playing an introduction.

They all joined in, singing with enthusiasm and enjoyment.

As they finished, Nathan asked, "Can we have another prayer like that first one, Alex?"

"If you want to, but I was thinking that this time we could all say the Lord's Prayer together. Do you all know it?"

"Yes, we do," said Tanya. "I may not have done a good job of teaching Christianity to our children, but I did at least make sure they knew the Lord's Prayer!"

They said the Lord's Prayer together, and although the words they used differed in places, there was pleasure in praying to God together.

Chapter 17

Clearing the Road

Monday morning didn't start according to plan. Having decided to drive the camp's small tractor to the fallen tree, Nathan got up a little early to allow for the slower travel, but when he turned the key, there was no response, not even a click.

As he was climbing down to check the battery, Belinda came over to report that the shower wasn't working. It took a few minutes to find a loose connection on the pump and tighten it, and by then, there was no time to look at the tractor – they would have to do without it for the time being.

Right on eight o'clock, Nathan, Dan and Alex met the arborists at the fallen tree on the Roses Gap Road. Stopping on opposite sides of the great trunk, they shook hands over the top.

"We're Nathan and Dan, and I guess you already know Alex."

"G'day to you both, and yes, we know Alex. I'm Trevor and this is Ewen. Big tree."

"Massive," agreed Nathan. "We're looking forward to getting rid of it. I reckon the trunk must weigh about a tonne per metre near the base."

"That sounds about right," said Trevor.

"I tried to bring the little tractor from the camp," said Nathan, "but it wouldn't start. I'll see if I can get it working later, but for now it might be best to cut the trunk into pieces small enough to move by hand."

"Well, 10-centimetre slices would probably only weigh a hundred kilograms or so," said Trevor. "We should be able to manage those together – just roll them off the road."

"We brought the big trailer so we can take some of it back to the campsite," said Alex. "If any of it looks particularly nice, we might be able to use it for outside furniture."

"And we'd keep the rest for firewood," added Nathan.

"Okay," said Trevor. "We'll see what we can do. Let's start in the middle of the road and cut it into fairly thin slices. In the past, we'd have just made a few cuts, then used a crane to dump the bits beside the road, but it's not easy to get cranes now, so we spend more time sharpening the chains! The thin sections will be heavy, but I reckon we should be able to roll them away."

"Wouldn't it be good to remove just enough for a car to fit through?" asked Dan. "That'd be an interesting tourist novelty."

"Until someone misjudged the gap," laughed Nathan.

"I suppose so," said Dan, disappointed.

"We could paint it with reflective paint," said Ewen, quite keen on the idea of a tourist attraction. "People couldn't miss it then."

"But we want them to miss it, Ewen!" laughed Trevor.

It wasn't a great joke, but Nathan's was no better when he added, "We really don't want it to be a great hit with tourists!"

They all groaned, then Trevor and Ewen put on their hard hats, overalls and safety glasses before starting their large chainsaws. It took less time than Dan expected to cut through the massive trunk, but it looked like hard work! With their long guide bars and powerful motors, the chainsaws seemed heavy and unwieldy, but in the hands of experts they cut quickly, sending out showers of sawdust. On one side of the road, the branches held the trunk up off the road, so Trevor expertly cut through the log from underneath, allowing it to settle onto the asphalt. Then he began to slice up the log in the middle of the road while Ewen worked on the separated upper section, cutting off branches that fell into the paddocks beyond.

Having tidied up the branches, he crossed to the base of the tree and examined it. The roots and lower part of the trunk had been badly damaged by insects until finally there wasn't enough timber to keep the tree standing. Ewen began to wield his chainsaw again, throwing out a shower of sawdust and chunks of badly decayed timber. It wasn't long before the cut was complete and the stump with its roots slumped back into its original hole.

Now only the trunk blocked the road, and Trevor had already cut it into several pieces.

"Some of the timber in the roots and the bottom of the tree is really rotten," said Ewen. "It's no wonder the tree fell down!"

"Let's have a look," said Trevor, walking towards the stump. It didn't take long to find living insects in the timber, so Trevor advised them to keep that section away from the campsite where the insects might spread and damage other timber.

Back in the middle of the road, Trevor kept cutting the log into pieces. After a while, they decided to load some of the thinner sections, starting with the round ones that would roll best. They rolled away the first one until it stood, a little wobbly, beside the trailer.

"How do we get it on?" asked Dan.

"Four of us should be able to lift it, while one moves things for us," said Nathan.

It was awkward, but eventually they got it onto a piece of carpet in the trailer. Nathan and Dan then used the carpet to slide the wood towards the front of the trailer.

"That timber looks really nice," said Trevor.

"I wonder how old the tree is," mused Dan. "You can see the growth rings pretty clearly."

"If you want to count them, try smoothing it off with a sander first," suggested Trevor.

After manhandling another three sections of trunk into the trailer, the large floor area was well filled.

"They look pretty good, don't they?" said Ewen. "You could use them for really solid benches and tables."

"Do you want any of the timber yourselves?" asked Nathan.

"I'll take some of the smaller branches," said Trevor.

"None for me, thanks," said Ewen. "I'm about to move house!"

"Can we put any more on the trailer?" asked Dan.

"If we're up to lifting more, the trailer could carry it," said Nathan. "What do you all think?"

"Let's try another layer," said Trevor.

They found that loading the second layer was much harder, but finally they managed it.

"Now there's plenty of room for people who are walking or riding a bike," said Ewen.

"But I wouldn't want to try driving through, even with a small car like mine," laughed Alex.

"Imagine going through that gap at full speed," said Dan.

"Scary," said Alex.

"Don't forget that in two weeks the campers will have to drive through," said Nathan.

"Let's keep going until we have one lane properly clear," said Trevor. "We can roll the pieces to the side of the road, but we'll have to hurry. We need to get to our next job soon."

They continued cutting the trunk and piling up the pieces at the edge of the road. Once one lane was completely clear, Trevor and Ewen hurriedly cut the rest of the trunk into larger pieces about three-quarters of a metre long. Nathan planned to return later with the tractor to clear them from the road.

"We'll leave a folding warning sign on each side of the road in both directions," said Trevor.

"Okay. We'll bring them to Stawell for you once we've cleared the road," said Nathan.

Trevor and Ewen packed up their equipment, shook hands, called "Cheerio" and hurried off to their next job, while Nathan, Alex and Dan slowly towed the loaded trailer back to the camp.

Chapter 18

Driving the Tractor

Nathan and Dan examined the tractor as soon as they arrived back at the campsite.

"The battery is where it should be," said Dan.

"And it's properly connected," added Nathan. "Can you turn on the headlights, Dan? Then we'll know if there's any charge in the battery."

Dan studied the control panel and found the switch. "Hey! It's already turned on! Someone must have left the lights on when they finished using the tractor."

"Or turned them on deliberately," said Nathan, grimly. "Let's try charging the battery."

Finding a battery charger in the machinery shed, they connected it to the battery and left it charging.

When Nathan tried starting the tractor after lunch, it started easily and ran smoothly.

Taking some slings from the shed, Nathan used the tractor to unload the pieces of trunk from the trailer. Soon they were ready to return to where the log still blocked part of the Roses Gap Road.

"We have a problem," said Nathan. "I want to put two larger chunks of trunk across the track where they cut the padlock off the gate, to make it harder to get through. And that means we need two drivers: one for the four-wheel drive towing the trailer, and one for the tractor. I'll go and see if Alex can spare the time."

"But I can drive the tractor, Dad," said Dan, eagerly.

"You've never driven anything like that, have you?" frowned Nathan.

"No, but it should be pretty easy."

"How about I show you how to drive it first."

"Now?"

"I suppose so. Get up and I'll show you how the controls work."

Nathan showed Dan how the gears and brakes worked, but ignored the specialised tractor controls. Dan had got his learner's permit on his sixteenth birthday and had some experience driving the family four-wheel drive. Once Nathan was satisfied that Dan knew what he was doing, he let him drive the tractor around the campsite for a few minutes.

"You can set off when you're ready," called Nathan when Dan drove near him again. "Remember to keep left and keep well out of the way if anyone drives by. It's only a few kilometres, but it'll take a long time. I'll follow with the big trailer once I've finished a few things around here. How does that sound?"

"Great," said Dan.

"Well, be careful!" said his father.

Dan set off, carefully negotiating the track out to the main road. He was surprised how much he bounced on the tractor with its short wheelbase and tall tyres. About a kilometre from the camp, he met a white four-wheel drive, speeding by in the opposite direction. He saw two men inside, but the car had no identifying markings, not even registration plates. Normally this would have intrigued him, but he was too busy concentrating on his driving to give it much thought.

Not far from the log, Nathan passed him with the trailer, and when Dan arrived he greeted him with a smiling, "How was the journey, son?"

"Phew!" answered Dan. "It was rough. The tractor vibrates a lot and bounces you all over the place, but it was still fun."

"At least we've got it here to move the log, so let's get on with it."

Nathan had already backed the trailer close to the log, and the pair discussed how to use slings to load the heavy pieces onto the trailer. The trailer could safely carry two of the log sections; the challenge was to get them safely onto the trailer, fastened securely for the journey.

Eventually, they managed to tie two slings snugly around a section of trunk and attach them to the bucket arms of the tractor.

"Can the arms lift far enough to get the log into the trailer?" asked Dan.

"I think so," said Nathan. He climbed onto the driver's seat and waved Dan some distance away just in case the log slipped and rolled. The slings tightened and the front of the tractor sank lower, then the heavy log rose into the air, but Nathan soon lowered it safely onto the trailer. Carefully, they fastened the log in place with tie-down ropes, then loaded a second log section. The gap in the middle of the road was now wider, but still not wide enough for two vehicles.

"Let's move a few of these pieces off the road," said Nathan.

They were getting used to attaching the slings, so moving the next few sections was much quicker.

"Will that do?" asked Dan. Very little of the log still intruded onto the asphalt of the road – with care, two cars could easily pass in opposite directions at the same time.

"Yes, that'll do. I think we should still leave the warning signs...." Nathan stopped and looked around, just as Dan did the same.

"Hey! Where are those signs?" asked Dan.

"Trevor and Ewen set up four of them, didn't they?"

"Yes, but they're not there now."

"Someone must have stolen them," said Nathan.

Dan remembered the four-wheel drive that had passed him: were those two men the culprits?

Nathan was obviously remembering something too. "You know, as I was driving here, I noticed two men near the gate at the Beehive Falls parking area. If I hadn't been coming to meet you, I'd have stopped and checked what was going on."

"Did they have a white four-wheel drive?" asked Dan.

"Yes."

"A white four-wheel drive was going the other way as I came here. It's probably the same one. Perhaps they pinched the signs on the way past. But what would they want them for?"

"Maybe it's just a habit," said Nathan, sardonically.

"I forgot to mention: I saw a sign there yesterday saying walking fees must be paid from Monday, 18th November. That's today!"

Privately, Dan also wondered if this was the same four-wheel drive as he had seen at the communications tower near Mount Stapylton. It was the same colour – but then, white cars were very common. Were these the same men?

❧

Dan was thoroughly sick of bouncing around on the tractor by the time he approached the Beehive Falls parking area, so he was pleased to see the family four-wheel drive parked there. Relieved, he stopped, then climbed down and stretched his back. He could still feel the vibration in his hands and arms.

There was no trace of the men, but what they had left behind had made Nathan just as angry as Alex had been.

The sign Alex had pulled up had not only been hammered back into the ground but also welded to the gatepost. Welded next to it was a padlocked steel box with a slot in the top, while a second sign demanding an outrageous fee for walking in the park was tied onto the gate with wire. Fees were to be placed in the "honesty box". A crude picture of a video camera accompanied a statement that the site was under surveillance and that fee avoiders would be prosecuted.

"Under surveillance!" said Dan in disgust. "Crooks watching honest people to extort money from them."

"You know, Dan, I've been looking around, and I don't believe there are any cameras here. There's no sign of a power supply or mountings, or any trimming of trees to give a clear view around the gate. I reckon they hope their threats will scare people into paying their fake fees."

For a moment Dan couldn't believe it, but after looking around carefully, he nodded. "I think you're right, Dad. They're just con men."

"But it might be a different matter if you met them here when they were checking their 'honesty box'. From what Alex said, they were very threatening."

"Did Alex meet them?"

"Yes, on Friday. I didn't mention it because I didn't want to scare your mother."

"Did he chuck the sign behind the fence?"

"Yes, but not until after they left. They threatened him and only left when he warned them they'd get caught if they did anything to him."

"It didn't stop them for long. I wonder if the police have gone there yet."

"Is there anything we can do about these signs? They're mounted better this time."

"First, let's take the sign off the gate. I've got some pliers in my toolbox, so I can cut the wire they've tied it up with."

"Should we really do that, Dad?"

"Yes. We know these people aren't genuine. They're bullies and thieves with no right to collect money or put up their blackmailing signs."

Nathan got out the pliers, then paused. "I think I'll take photos of these signs as they are first. It could be useful." He took the photos, then cut the ties while Dan held the sign.

"Imagine if there really are cameras somewhere after all," laughed Dan. "Think how they'd feel watching us pull down their signs just after they put them up."

"It would serve them right."

"Yes," agreed Dan, "but didn't you say they threatened Alex? What'll they do when they find this?"

"I have no idea, but I think they'll be too busy putting up signs on other trails to come back for a while. I must go to Stawell soon and tell the police."

"What about the money box?" asked Dan. "Can we make sure people can't put any money in?"

"Good idea. There's lots of gravel around here: will it fit through the slot?"

Dan found that he could fit fine gravel through the slot, so he filled up the box, leaving no room for money. "That's better," he said.

"Good job," agreed Nathan.

Chapter 19

Getting Ready

The work of preparing the campsite for their first camp kept the family and Alex very busy for the rest of the week. Despite this, Nathan took time off on Wednesday to drive into Stawell and speak to Terry about the missing signs and the signs demanding fees from hikers. Terry was furious and immediately took Nathan with him to the police station.

The constable recognised them and said, "We visited Brad Jessop on Monday morning, and he agreed they wouldn't claim to be authorised representatives of a council or the National Park. At the moment, I think that's all we can do."

"Well, on Monday afternoon, signs with his name on were put up at the Beehive Falls parking area," said Nathan. "I can show you photos."

"That would be useful new evidence and would give us reason to act more forcefully. Did you leave the signs there?"

"We left the main sign – they'd welded their post to a gatepost so we couldn't easily remove it. The other sign was only attached with wire, so we cut it off and threw it into the bushes."

"Welding anything to the gatepost is criminal damage," observed the constable, "and making fraudulent claims about being an official with authority to levy charges is an even more serious offence. We'll go back and see him again. We might lay charges this time."

"We also filled up their so-called 'honesty box' with gravel to stop anyone putting in money. I didn't want anyone helping Brad Jessop."

"Good," said the constable, smiling. "That was an excellent idea."

Before leaving Stawell, Nathan also visited Trevor and told him about the missing signs – missing presumed stolen.

Trevor reassured him. "We lose them from time to time, but they often turn up again. All of our signs have our initials on them, 'STLS' for Stawell Tree Lopping Services, so we know they're ours if anyone finds them out on a road somewhere. It's amazing where those signs turn up."

∞

Dan and Alex spent a lot of time together that week making sure the sporting equipment was properly inspected and tested as necessary, from balls to boats, from ropes to rubber mats. In particular, the climbing ropes, harnesses, carabiners and clips were all examined carefully – somebody's life might depend on this inspection.

Dan was amazed at just how much equipment was needed to offer adventure holidays for more than a hundred people. Their first camp would only have 30 attending, but later camps would require all the available equipment. Since

Alex knew it had not been checked for some time, they inspected it all.

As they worked, they took the opportunity to talk about the Bible. Dan had started reading the book of Genesis just before the family left Melbourne, and had now reached the history of Jacob and his children, particularly Joseph who had been roughly Dan's age when his brothers sold him as a slave! What impressed Dan most was that Joseph remained determined to obey God even when he was alone in Egypt with no-one to check up on him – he even refused an Egyptian woman who tried to seduce him.

When Dan said this to Alex, the young man agreed. "Yes, if anyone worships God when nobody's watching, that's genuine worship."

"Exactly," said Dan. "That was the real Joseph. I want to be like him."

Since both of them wanted to read the Bible every day, they decided to read it together and discuss what they read. Dan had no real plan to his reading, but had mostly been going through one book at a time as his fancy took him. Alex suggested that they keep going with Genesis, but also read through the book of Galatians, which he had been about to start reading. Dan agreed, and each day they met in the games room before breakfast to read the Bible out loud together. They took turns reading a few verses each, pausing whenever either of them had a question or comment. Dan had so many questions about Galatians that they didn't always get very far, but Alex patiently answered any questions he could, taking others on notice and thinking about them during the day. He normally came up with good answers, and Dan was getting more and more impressed with Alex's knowledge of the Bible.

"I've been reading the Bible since I was about 15, just like you, Dan," Alex explained, "although now I wish I'd started earlier. I'm not complaining, but my family didn't read the Bible much at home, so I only learned things at Sunday School and church until Grandpa started talking to me when I visited. When I was 15, Grandpa hurt his leg quite badly in a tractor accident, so I started mowing their lawns for him. Grandpa loved the Bible and would talk about it to anyone who'd listen – and he always made it interesting. So I got a Bible of my own and began reading it myself. Grandpa answered all of my questions, always using the Bible, which impressed me. He didn't have any religious qualifications, but he'd read the Bible many times. He told me once that he'd only really begun to understand it in the last few years. That discouraged me for a while, because he'd been reading it for about forty years by then."

"Forty years! And he was only just starting to understand it? Whew! If it takes that long, I'm..."

"It wasn't that he didn't understand it at all, he just felt he'd missed some really important details for many years. Once he saw them, he was amazed how well everything in the Bible fitted together. He used to say, 'Never forget that one God wrote the whole Bible, Alex. If you remember that, you won't get lost like I did.' "

"What did he mean?"

"He meant that since God wrote both the Old Testament and the New Testament, we should expect to meet the *same* God in both parts of the Bible."

"O-kay," said Dan, thoughtfully. "But... we do read different things in the Old and New Testaments, don't we? The Old Testament tells us about heroes like Joseph and David, while the New Testament has the gospels about Jesus and letters telling churches how they should behave. Isn't that different?"

"Yes, but the same God wrote them both and his *character* is the same in both. What's the best-known verse in the Bible, Dan?"

"I guess it must be John chapter 3 verse 16, about how God loved the world."

"Exactly. And if you look in Exodus chapter 34 where God talks about what he is like, he says that he is 'merciful and gracious, slow to anger, and abounding in steadfast love and faithfulness.' Doesn't that sound just the same as that famous verse in the New Testament?"

"I suppose so."

"Once I expected to find the same God throughout the Bible, that's just what I found. And when I come across things in the Old Testament that I don't understand, I can't just ignore them – I need to work hard to understand them."

"Hmm. I'll have to think about that."

Time flew by whenever they discussed the Bible, and Dan found that he was enjoying thinking about the Bible more than ever before.

Alex worked equally hard on camp work, never skipping important tasks even if they were tedious – such as one morning when the pair visually inspected the carabiners. After studying a hundred or so, Dan said, "These are all fine, can't we just skip it? After all, the campers will see anything that's wrong with them when they start using them."

"Campers often haven't used this sort of equipment before, so they'll just assume it's normal even if there's something wrong. We're the ones who know how it should work, so *we* do the checking."

Dan couldn't argue with that logic, so he continued examining the carabiners carefully one by one. He was rewarded a few minutes later by discovering one that didn't work properly and could have been dangerous.

He showed it to Alex and the young man smiled. "Now you won't want to cut corners, will you?"

"No!"

In the afternoons, Alex and Dan checked whether Nathan needed help with other work around the camp. If he didn't need them, they went on with their own work, but sometimes he needed a hand with testing equipment or carrying heavy parts. He was careful to take the opportunity to show them how each of the systems in the camp worked, and Dan and Alex were glad to broaden their knowledge. Alex had always concentrated on sporting activities, but was eager to learn about the power, water, drainage and wastewater systems that kept the campsite going.

"I've been looking at the electrical system," said Nathan one afternoon. "I'm not quite happy with the solar panels. Based on their ratings, we should be getting more power, so I'm going to try a few tricks. Otherwise, I'm concerned we'll have to run the generator whenever we get a few clouds – and we'll run out of fuel pretty quickly doing that."

"What do we do, then?" asked Alex.

Nathan led them to the solar "farm", where many racks held a host of panels, all facing the sky.

"For a start, each panel has clear protective glass on the front. If the glass is dirty, less light gets through and the panels generate less electricity."

"These look pretty dirty."

"Yes, which can make a few percent difference to the output – which becomes important when there are clouds and a full quota of campers."

Together, they cleaned the panels. It was a big job, but checking the gauges afterwards showed that Nathan was right: the power output had improved.

"Anything else?" asked Dan.

Nathan pointed upward and traced a path across the sky as he said, "Obviously the sun moves across the sky from east to west each day, but these frames hold the panels in a fixed position. Ideally, each panel would adjust itself through the day so it's always at right angles to the sun, but that requires motors and expensive equipment – and the extra power gained won't justify the cost. However, we can manually adjust the angle of the frames to point the panels towards the sun as much as possible. Does that make sense?"

"Yes, but how can we do that when the sun moves so much?" asked Dan.

"Well, it only goes in one line each day," Nathan pointed out.

"So we're aiming for some sort of best guess?" asked Alex.

"More 'optimisation' than 'guess'," laughed Nathan. "You know, you can even adjust the angle as the seasons change, say between summer and winter. However, that's a lot of work with so many panels. For the time being, we'll use the best angle for a setup that stays the same all year. Later, I'll do some more research and work out a schedule of adjustments to wring a bit more power out of the panels, particularly to get the most we can from them during winter."

"I've heard that solar panels aren't much use during the winter," said Alex.

"Winter days are shorter and more likely to be cloudy, so the panels can only generate about half as much power. However, you can recover about half of those losses by changing the angle of the panels for winter. Since the sun is always lower in the sky during winter – much closer to the horizon – the panels should be tilted up much closer to vertical during winter."

"And that must save money on generator fuel," observed Alex.

"Yes. For the moment, however, we'll just use a 'set and forget' angle which will work quite well over the whole year.

The angle we'll use is a few degrees less than our current latitude. So now a general knowledge question: what's our latitude here?"

"I've seen signs for the 37th degree of latitude on the roads somewhere around here, haven't I?" asked Dan.

"You're right," mused Alex. "There's one on the road to Navarre."

"Yes: we're very close to 37 degrees south here. You can check it with the GPS on your phone if you want – GPS doesn't need a mobile phone signal! These panels are all facing a few degrees east of north, which is really good, and we'll set the angle of the panels to 30 or 31 degrees from the ground. I've checked a few and they vary. They don't seem to have been set either as part of a regime of frequent adjustments or for the single 'set and forget' approach."

"How do we measure the angle?" asked Dan.

"For today, I've made this simple jig. We hold the straight piece of wood against the vertical legs of each panel and line up the panel with the other piece, which is mounted across the first at 59 degrees, or as near as I can make it."

"And that gives us a 31 degree angle to the ground," said Alex. "Sounds pretty simple."

Each frame was attached to two vertical legs mounted in the ground, and the angle of the panel could be adjusted by undoing two nuts and setting it to the preferred angle. Nathan's jig made it quick to adjust each frame, but it was still quite a big job with so many panels.

Once they had finished, Nathan said, "Let's see if we're getting more power from the panels." Again, the gauges showed that they were getting a little more, despite the sun having gone down somewhat while they made the adjustments.

"So how much difference does it make if we get the angle right?" asked Dan.

"Just a few percent – but it's important. Otherwise, we'll have to run the generator more, and that's noisy and expensive."

❧

Tanya and Belinda were equally busy preparing for the camp, cleaning all the required cabins inside and out and equipping them with comfortable bedding. They also checked the doors, lights, curtains, toilet facilities and other features, calling in Dan, Alex or Nathan to help as necessary. Steve and Sylvia had done the best they could, but Sylvia's failing health had left plenty of maintenance and tidying to do. By the end of the week, Tanya and Belinda were very pleased with the results of their hard work.

The camp was looking spick and span, ready for campers to arrive in just over a week.

Chapter 20

Another Afternoon Walk

After the events at the Beehive Falls carpark on Monday afternoon, Nathan made sure the camp site was never unattended. However, when they had seen no more of Brad and his men by Friday, he began to feel less concerned. He also hoped that the police had visited Halls Gap again and put an end to Brad's grand schemes.

Saturday rolled around again, and after working hard all morning, they were ready to take the afternoon off.

Alex announced that he would visit his parents in Stawell for an hour or so and then return, while the family decided to take another hike.

Dan suggested visiting Beehive Falls and then climbing Briggs Bluff. A study of the maps had convinced him that they could easily get back before the sun set.

Alex had already left when they set off on foot after lunch. Despite their appreciation of the country habit of leaving things unlocked, Nathan locked everything that could be locked, just in case.

On reaching the carpark, they found it refreshingly empty. The signs were just as they had left them and the 'honesty box' was still full of Dan's gravel. Clearly, Brad's men hadn't returned.

They set off along the track towards Beehive Falls. It was a hot afternoon and they were all wearing hats, with sunscreen daubed on their arms and legs. Alex had warned them that the upper parts of the walk had very little cover.

The track to Beehive Falls passed through alternating shade and sunshine, and Dan was feeling very hot by the time they reached the falls. There wasn't much water flowing over the falls, but the pool at the bottom was cool and clear.

He enjoyed the coolness until Belinda and his parents caught up, then left the pool, climbing the steep zig-zagging path to the top of the cliff. Alex had told them that an older, unmaintained path went off to the left not far beyond the top of the cliff. Apparently it crossed the creek, then climbed steeply towards the bluff until it reached a plateau, which it traversed before rejoining the new trail. Although Dan had never travelled either path, he preferred the sound of the old path and soon found where the unmarked path left the main track. He was quite a distance in front of Belinda at the time and decided to investigate.

Following the curved path down, he was almost at the bottom of the valley when he saw it lying on a sunny rock only about two metres away: a thin rounded body in the shape of a letter 'S'. His heart leapt with shock, but in an instant, he was relieved to observe that the snake's slightly flattened head was facing away from him. The browny-green body bore some indistinct diamond markings along it.

He took a few cautious steps backwards, but stumbled over a rock and almost fell. The snake turned in an instant and lifted its head.

Dan regained his balance and ran away a step or two, then saw that the snake had stopped and was lying still once more.

His heart was thudding painfully as he reminded himself that most snakes in the Grampians were not aggressive unless you got too close or trod on them – but he also knew that they were all venomous. Taking a deep breath, he tried to look at the snake objectively, doing his best to appreciate its attractive markings and smooth, slightly shiny scales, but he couldn't. Snakes were terrifying. Dan always liked to be first when the family walked together, so this was not the first time he had met a snake, but whenever he did, he felt a leaden, scared feeling in his stomach which lasted until the end of the walk. It didn't stop him wanting to be in front, though!

"Belinda," he called tentatively, ashamed to hear a quaver in his voice. "Belinda!" he called again. That was better.

"Where are you?" she answered, her voice coming from where Dan judged he had left the main path.

"I'm down here in the valley. Follow the path off to the left," he called, keeping his eyes glued on the snake.

☙

Dan arrived at the top of the bluff first, quite a way in front of Belinda, who was walking with their parents by then.

It had been a longish walk, and steep in parts. He was very hot, but the view from the rocky ridge made it all worthwhile. It didn't take Dan long to get his bearings. Across the Roses Gap Road he could see a valley, surprisingly green among the dark grey rocks and grey-green shrubbery of the surrounding hills. He knew that the campsite was in that valley, but it was hard to make out much because of the campsite's many trees. Looking carefully, he recognised parts of the track they had followed past Beehive Falls and up to the bluff where he now sat, and was pleased to see that they were all empty. His childhood memories of the Grampians were of a place that was always quiet and lonely, but he was sure that in the past they used to meet *some* other hikers. Yet they had met nobody walking up Mount Stapylton, and now none climbing Briggs Bluff either. Times had certainly changed! To be honest, he liked it, but part of him couldn't help wondering what would have happened if he had trodden on that snake before he saw it. He knew about applying compression bandages and staying still in the event of a snake bite, but that assumed people would find you and care for you! Not even his family had known where he was in that valley, and if he had been bitten or fallen and hit his head, would anyone have found him?

He shook his head to dismiss the unwelcome thought. The solitude was delightful and he was thoroughly enjoying their Grampians escape, even though it wasn't at all what he'd expected. It was genuine adventure! And he was learning a heap and enjoying his work.

Had the police charged Brad Jessop, or "taken him into custody" as they used to say on the news? He and his men were causing more than enough trouble! Were the two men in the four-wheel drive near the log the same ones as he had seen from Mount Stapylton? And why would they have visited a communications tower? How could they make money from that?

Dan didn't have any answers, so he turned his thoughts to the future instead. Dad and Mum had agreed to manage the camp for three months, but what would they do after that? The cost of getting back inside the margin would be prohibitive. They might *never* go back to their old home. All the goods they had left behind might be permanently out of reach.

Did he care?

As he mulled over that question, he looked back along the track he had climbed. His parents were approaching the final steep ascent, with Belinda a hundred metres or so behind. He still had a few minutes before they arrived.

Belinda seemed to be enjoying this unexpected adventure, but how would she feel when school started next year?

And how would he feel himself? University seemed like a distant possibility now, but that didn't really upset him. He was enjoying his work and learning a lot. Although Alex was quite a bit older, he was quickly becoming a good friend. He knew a lot about the Bible, and Dan was glad for the chance to learn more about it too. Perhaps he could stay here and find a job like Alex's. He didn't know what qualifications he'd need to lead climbing groups or supervise people on high ropes courses, though.

If only Dave was with them, he mused. It was so long since they had been able to spend time together.

The sun was hot on the treeless sandstone summit, but a cool breeze kept Dan comfortable as he sat and thought.

Suddenly, mingling with the sound of his parents' approaching voices, Dan noticed the distant sound of a car. Excitement rose within him and he turned quickly to scan the road which passed below him on the edge of the plain. There it was – a dust cloud coming from the direction of Halls Gap. He watched with fascination as it drove past his vantage point, making out the roof of a white four-wheel drive. "Not again!" he groaned to himself. "Is it those goons again?"

The car slowed and turned left onto the Roses Gap Road. With so many trees around, he couldn't see clearly, but the car seemed to stop at the Beehive Falls carpark.

Quickly Dan stood up and called out, "Dad, I think Brad Jessop's men have just stopped at the carpark."

"Oh, no!" gasped Nathan, and ran the last 30 metres up the steep rocks to where Dan sat. "Where are they?" he panted as he arrived.

Dan pointed towards the carpark, but there was nothing to be seen through the trees.

"Are you sure?"

"As sure as I can be without actually seeing the car," said Dan. Pointing at the road towards Halls Gap, he explained, "A white four-wheel drive came from there, then turned left and disappeared behind the trees near the carpark. You can't hear much from here, but the noise stopped about when they would have reached the carpark, and I haven't seen it go anywhere else."

"And that carpark's only two hundred metres from the camp driveway. Oh, if only we could get down there straight away!"

"I don't think they went to the camp, Dad. The sound stopped too soon. And they won't walk there – they only ever seem to drive places."

"I wonder if Alex has got back from Stawell yet."

"I hadn't thought of that."

Just then, Tanya reached the summit and Nathan quickly explained the situation.

"Should we hurry down now?" asked Tanya.

"I don't think so," said Nathan. "It'll take us more than an hour to get down, so they'll probably finish whatever they're doing before we get there anyway."

"What's going on?" asked Belinda when she also joined them.

"Some men have stopped in the carpark," said Dan.

"Wow!" said Belinda, opening her eyes wide. "Really?"

Dan dropped his head into his hands and sighed. "Girls!"

"Yes, Danny-boy, girls – or at least, one girl. A breath of fresh air and sweet reason."

"I suppose you don't know anything about the trouble with the men from Halls Gap?"

"What trouble?"

"Oh, nothing much – just stealing things and trying to extort money from people with signs and 'honesty' boxes. You know, the signs we saw at the carpark."

"I didn't read any signs. Most signs aren't worth reading."

" 'Sweet reason', did you say?"

"Are you going to tell me this news or not?"

⚬⚬

Sitting helplessly at the top of the bluff trying vainly to see what was going on in the Beehive Falls carpark quickly became unbearable. Before long, the family was hurrying down.

Once more, they followed the old path, since Alex had said it was shorter, and this time Belinda did her best to keep up with Dan. The two of them walked swiftly along the sloping rocky plateau. On their left, the rocky plateau rose gently then fell away steeply, forming an almost vertical cliff in places. On their right it sloped down into a valley that grew steadily deeper as they followed the plateau.

"Look at those caves," said Dan, pointing across the deepening valley as they approached the place where the path left the plateau, crossing its upper edge and following a steep valley down to the dry creek bed where Dan had seen the snake.

"Yes, I saw them on the way up," said Belinda.

"I wonder if they're like the big cave on Mount Stapylton?"

"Probably, but we can't look now."

"I didn't say we could," said Dan irritably. "But I love caves. Maybe we can look another time."

Soon they were descending the steep zig-zag track that led to the bottom of Beehive Falls. Belinda almost ran into Dan as he stopped suddenly.

"Listen," he said.

Belinda heard a faint sound of a hammer striking steel – unexpected in the quiet of the bush. They looked at each other, then hurried quietly on.

"Ssshhh," said Dan as they got closer, putting his finger to his lips.

"Der," breathed Belinda, rolling her eyes.

Dan stopped and whispered earnestly to his little sister, "Look, smarty pants, there are some troublemakers around who might be dangerous. You haven't met any of them, so you can't know how important it is to make sure they don't see us."

"I'm not stupid, Danny-boy! How about we keep going until we can see this hammerer."

They continued carefully, hurrying as much as possible. Suddenly, Dan rounded a slight corner in the path and came in clear sight of the pool below. He ducked hastily behind some large rocks beside the path, and Belinda followed suit. Together they crouched and watched.

A man was standing near the pool, trying to hammer a star picket into the ground. He was obviously having diffi-culty finding anywhere with enough soil, and they heard him swearing as the picket struck rock in each new place he tried. At last, however, he found a location where he could drive the picket well into the ground.

"You finally got it right, Darren," commented a harsh, sarcastic voice.

Dan and Belinda took a moment to work out where this new voice was coming from, but then they saw a man lounging on a large rock holding some wire and a pair of pliers.

"Then I'm doing better than you, Craig! We're still waiting for *you* to get something right. See if you can get the sign facing the right way this time."

"Yeah, yeah, yeah," growled the man. "We all make mistakes sometimes."

"Come on, get the sign up and let's get out of here. I'm scared the police will turn up. Those fools at the camp keep dobbing us in."

"Yeah. Maybe we should go to the camp and see if they're around. If they're not, we can burn down a few buildings. I've got some petrol in the car."

"If you use petrol, it's pretty obvious someone started the fire – and we'd be the first suspects, since we've been here a few times recently."

"I s'pose so. Anyway, come and hold this sign while I tie it up."

"So *I* have to carry the star picket up here and *I* have to find somewhere to hammer it in while you laze around sneering, but when *you've* got the simple job of tying up a sign with wire, you need my help? No way!" Darren lay down on another rock with his hands behind his head. "Make sure you get it level."

"You get over here and hold it level," growled Craig, his rasping voice threatening.

"Hold it yourself," whined Darren.

"Come here and hold it. Now!"

Darren reluctantly stood up and walked across to where Craig was holding out the sign, grumbling, "You can't even do simple things. We wouldn't get far if I was as hopeless as you!"

"Shut up and hold the sign."

Darren shut up and held the sign.

Standing silently behind their rocks, Dan and Belinda exchanged glances. This man Craig was a bully!

With the sign wired in place, Craig said, "Done. Let's go."

"Should we climb up to the top of the falls and see what's there? Doesn't the Grampians Peaks Trail go somewhere along there? We'd catch more suckers on it than coming to see this so-called waterfall."

Dan and Belinda looked at each other. Their rocks sheltered them from below, but wouldn't hide them from anyone climbing the path! Dan was just reaching for Belinda's hand to lead her silently out of hiding, hoping that Craig and Darren wouldn't see them hurrying back up the path, when they heard Craig's harsh voice again.

"Nah, too much effort going up there. You go and have a look around. I'll wait down here."

"If you don't think it's worth going up there then I'm not going either," whined Darren. "You can't make me!"

"I could," said Craig coolly, "but this time I won't. Let's go back to the car."

Dan heaved a sigh of relief and watched as the pair left.

"Whew!" said Belinda after a moment. "They're a nasty pair!"

"I'll say."

"I saw the one called..." began Belinda.

"They were the two men Alex met at the carpark," interrupted a voice behind them.

Dan and Belinda spun around in surprise and saw their parents emerging from behind another rock that had obviously given them a clear view of the events below.

"When did you get here?" asked Dan.

"While they were tying up the sign," said Tanya. "We heard the hammering some distance away, so we climbed down carefully. We were glad to see you were safe."

"What do we do now, Dad?" asked Belinda.

"Follow them back to the carpark. I don't think they'll go to the camp, but I'd prefer to be close behind them, just in case."

"I'm going to try to catch up with them," said Dan, "but don't worry, I'll stay out of sight!"

"Be careful," warned Nathan.

Dan quickly caught up with the men and followed them back to the carpark, keeping carefully out of sight. Spotting the gate around a bend, he stopped and waited behind some trees. When he heard a car drive away, he ran to the gate and found the parking area empty.

Looking around, he saw that the sign he and his father had removed was attached to the gate again – this time with more wire than ever.

Somehow, both signs looked a little different, so he read them carefully to see what had changed. That was it: all reference to Brad Jessop had been removed. Instead of the signs claiming to be 'by order of Brad Jessop, chairman of the National Park Management Committee', now they were just 'by order of the National Park Management Committee'.

"Hey, look, Dad!" he called, seeing the others approaching. "They've taken Brad Jessop's name off the signs – painted over it."

"I wonder why?"

"Maybe the police told him he had to."

"That was quick."

"Dad," said Belinda, "You know that Darr...."

"Sorry, dear," interrupted Nathan. "We need to get back to the camp straight away, just in case those two decided to drop in for a visit!"

Chapter 21

Learning

The day was already heating up when Dan awoke next morning. A northerly wind stirred the trees outside with the dry rustling sound so typical of hot days in the bush of western Victoria.

He checked his phone. Seven o'clock. Quietly, he got up and went outside to look around. The morning felt as if it were going to be the first really hot day of the season.

Fallen leaves swirled in eddies among the gum trees, and more dry leaves were fluttering down to join them.

The sky was a deep blue and the sun already felt burningly hot. Since Sunday was a day off, he decided to ride his bike to the Troopers Creek Campground before it got too hot and check whether any of Brad Jessop's signs were there. He'd been so busy working that he hadn't done any riding yet, and he missed it. He hadn't flown his drone either.

An early morning ride sounded great, and if he left now he could be back in time for breakfast. According to the map, it was only about seven kilometres to the campground – hopefully none of it too steep.

Dan got the key from the office and collected his bike from the sports equipment shed. After a perfunctory check of the tyres, he put on his helmet.

Soon he was riding uphill in a squally wind, dodging the worst of the twigs and branches strewn over the road.

There was a quiet freedom in riding along a lonely country road, the wind in his face. He met no-one on the road, and when he turned, puffing, into the Troopers Creek Campground, he found it almost empty too. If Brad's men had put up a sign here, it would probably be beyond the camping area at the start of the walking track.

There was only one tent in the entire campground: a compact one such as a lone hiker might carry. In front of it sat a man, frying an egg in a very small frying pan over a very small fire.

As Dan cruised by, the heady smell of cooking reminding him that he needed to hurry back soon to prepare breakfast, the lone camper called out, "Hey, lad! What are you doing here? Not many people in the Grampians nowadays. I've hardly seen anyone since I left the Gap."

Dan stopped and leaned his bike against the fence that bordered the parking area. Here was an opportunity to find out more about Halls Gap and possibly Brad Jessop.

"I'm working at the Roses Gap Camp at the moment and came out for a morning ride. My name's Dan."

"Morning, Dan. I'm Fergus – Fergus Norton. I've been walking the Grampians Peaks Trail and I'm disgruntled."

"Disgruntled?" laughed Dan. "Why's that?"

"The trail is good, but what got my gruntle was the thugs who've taken over the campsites along the way."

Dan's interest quickened. "Thugs? What do you mean?"

"Have you ever heard of the 'National Park Committee'?"

"Have I ever! They keep making trouble around here," said Dan.

"Well, these blokes all claim to be from the NPC. As far as I can tell from the enquiries I made in the Gap, the committee is a lucrative fabrication."

"A what?"

"A rip-off, a scam, a rort, a confidence trick. Daylight robbery if you like."

"Ah. Yeah, that's what we decided."

"I worked my way up from Geelong to Dunkeld, keeping out of the way of the unfriendlies, and made my way across the margin. Don't ask me how because it wasn't strictly official, and, no, I didn't pay the 'requisite taxes and charges'. I thought that'd be the worst of it, but following the GPT was a real eye-opener."

"I've heard it's expensive."

"I'd heard the same – that's why I saved my money on the requisites."

"Was it worse than you expected?" prompted Dan.

"Much! They'd have taken my breakfast eggs from their shells if they could have. Folks in Dunkeld did warn me, though. They said the old 'Approved Operators' who sold hiking packages and ran the trail camping areas had been driven away by some blokes they called the 'NK2-ers'."

"Does that mean what I think it means?"

"Yep – a new version of the Ned Kelly Gang."

"Is NK2 connected with this National Park Committee?"

"Without question," said Fergus, nodding his head until his chin quivered. "It's not the Grampians like I used to know them."

"No, that's for sure. Who's this new Ned Kelly then?"

"I'm not sure. Some people suggest it's a bloke called Brad Jessop, but I met him in the Gap and he's far too... too gentle for anyone to connect him with Ned Kelly!"

"But he's a thief and a cheat!" blurted out Dan.

"He's all that and worse, but he's not the sort of man who'd bump someone off just because they got in his way, like Ned Kelly did."

"Well, if Brad Jessop isn't NK2, then who is?"

"That's a go-o-o-ood question, Dan. Perhaps Brad's just a second rate con-man trying to look like a brutal bushranger, but he does seem to have a lot of men working for him."

"I guess so. You say he's got men collecting money at the GPT camping areas, and there are others at toll booths and putting up signs all over the place."

"Yet Brad Jessop doesn't seem like the sort of bloke who could control such a large group of crooks," observed Fergus. "Maybe he's just very good at hiding how brutal he is."

Dan checked the time on his phone. It was later than he thought. "Look, I've gotta get back to the camp for breakfast," he said. "Are you heading north today?"

"Not today, it's too hot – would've been a total fire ban in the past. I'll eat my eggs, put out my little fire and try to stay cool in the creek, a little way up the track."

"Have you got any transport from Stapylton?"

"No, nothing," laughed Fergus. "Maybe I'll have to walk back to Dunkeld again."

"If you come back this way, why not come and see us at Roses Gap? I know Mum and Dad would welcome you. We could probably even arrange to take you somewhere if we didn't have other campers at the time."

"That might get you into trouble with Brad and his cash collectors! I saw what one of them did when a victim was a bit slow to fork out his dough. That was why I had to move on from the Gap in a hurry. Not that anyone saw me except the victim, and I encouraged him to move on quickly himself. I didn't have this beard then."

"Did you attack Brad's goon?"

"Not exactly, but I stopped him from carrying out his threats."

"Are you a policeman?" Dan didn't know why, but he suddenly had a feeling about this man.

Fergus glanced hastily around, then asked quietly, "Why do you ask?"

"I don't know. It just seemed the most likely thing."

"You've taken me down a peg or two, Dan," said the man who called himself Fergus. "I thought I was acting like a genuine hiker, if a little eccentric."

"So you *are* a policeman?"

"Yes – sort of. Put it this way: I'm trying to track down NK2 and his merry men with a view to making them feel less merry."

"None of Brad's men look merry anyway! Are they really NK2-ers?"

"I'm not sure. NK2 has carried out some vicious crimes. He's very quick to use violence, and so are his men, yet most of Brad's men are not so bad – except that one I dealt with in the Gap."

"Maybe they're two different groups then," suggested Dan.

"Mmm, perhaps. But some of the men in the Gap were speaking as if they were NK2-ers, so I'm not sure."

"I'd better get back for breakfast before it gets any hotter. The wind is getting stronger, too."

"A seriously hot day with a blustery north wind," said Fergus. "I hope no-one is careless with fire today!"

Dan was halfway back to the campsite when it struck him – he hadn't looked properly for that sign!

☙

Dan hurried into the kitchen, only to find Belinda waiting for him again. She peppered him with questions, but when he tried to answer her, she just shushed him and told him to hurry, not talk, or breakfast would be late.

Despite everything, breakfast was ready on time. Dan pointed this out triumphantly, but Belinda retorted, "That's because I hurried you up. Otherwise we would've been late."

Dan was speechless with frustration, but Nathan and Tanya laughed at Belinda's clever answer. Breakfast was filled with the usual light-hearted banter, but Dan stayed aloof. He was annoyed and decided to get his own back by keeping the news about Fergus Norton to himself. As he ate, he gradually calmed down – even deigning to taste some of Belinda's "juicy porridge" – but remained quiet. Suddenly, he remembered that they were having another session of Bible readings with Alex that morning and felt a little embarrassed at his sulkiness.

Once everyone had finished, Alex said, "I'll go to the games room and get ready for our worship time. Are you all coming?"

"We'll come, won't we, Tanya?" said Nathan, looking for confirmation.

"Yes, I enjoyed it last week."

"I think I need to wash the dishes," said Belinda.

"Belinda!" said Tanya sternly. "You don't have to come if you don't want to, but don't use the dishes as an excuse!"

"Sorry." She looked at Alex apologetically. "I don't think I'll come today, Alex."

Dan and Alex walked to the games room, discussing what songs they could sing.

"I like 'How great thou art'," said Dan.

"I do too," agreed Alex. "It's so true that creation shows God's amazing power. Shall we sing that first?"

"I'd like that," said Dan, holding open the games room door for Alex. "Would you like to sing another song at the end like last week? You choose one and I'll see if I know it."

"How about, 'The Lord's my Shepherd'?"

"Yes, I like that," answered Dan, "and I can play it."

"Good," said Alex. "I also want us to read chapters 14 and 15 from Mark's gospel."

"What are they about?" asked Dan, doubtfully.

"Judas' plan to betray Jesus, the last supper, and Jesus' trial, crucifixion and death."

"That doesn't sound very nice."

"No, but it was necessary – and it's good to think about what Jesus did for us."

"I suppose so."

Just then, Dan's parents walked into the games room. "I hope we're not late, Alex," said Nathan.

"No – we've only just finished choosing the songs and readings."

"What are we singing?" asked Tanya. "I really enjoyed those songs last week."

" 'How great thou art' and 'The Lord's my shepherd'," answered Dan.

"I like those. I think Belinda would enjoy them, too."

"It's her choice not to come," said Dan, shortly. Her smart-aleck comments still rankled.

"True," said Nathan, "but maybe she'll get more interested if she sees you setting a good example."

Dan didn't answer. He hadn't thought of that.

Alex explained his plans for the morning to Nathan and Tanya, and then they were ready to start. Dan sat at the piano and they all began singing "How great thou art". They hadn't got far before Belinda came in, just as eager to join in as she had been the previous week. Dan was irritated, but restarted the song without verbal complaint.

They weren't a large choir and their singing wouldn't have won any awards, but they enjoyed it, singing together in the wilderness they all loved.

"Let's pray to God," said Alex when they finished, "but before we do, would anyone like me to include anything particular in the prayer?"

"Can we ask that there are no dangerous fires today?" asked Tanya.

"And how about some help in dealing with Brad and his men?" added Nathan.

"I'd like God to look after our relatives in Adelaide," said Dan. "It's ages since I saw my cousin Dave."

Alex began to pray, repeating some of the words of praise from the song, then simply expressing the others' requests and adding some of his own. He asked God to care for all those suffering because of pandemics and ongoing wars. When he finished, they all said "Amen" together.

"I wish I'd heard more clear and simple prayers like that when I was young," said Tanya. "I might have paid more attention."

"You can always say your own prayers," suggested Alex.

"Perhaps I will," said Tanya, looking at Nathan to gauge his reaction.

"Good idea," he nodded. "Living closer to nature makes God seem more real – even with people like Brad Jessop around."

Dan was tempted to cheer, but managed to keep his mouth shut.

Belinda was neither pleased nor tactful. "Are we becoming a *religious* family?" Her tone made it clear what her opinion of that was!

"Let's wait and see, dear," answered Tanya. "For now we're just giving it the fair go we never gave it in the past."

"And why does that song use 'thou' and 'art' and 'thy'?" asked Belinda, getting onto one of her pet peeves.

"There are two reasons," answered Alex. "Firstly, many Christian songs and hymns were written a long time ago when those words were in common use. Secondly, some people still feel that those old-fashioned words show more respect to God than using everyday language."

"Why not just use *new* songs?" asked Belinda, never one to let an argument go without a struggle.

"We've been through this before," said Dan. "You could ask the same about works of art, or classical music, or old buildings."

"Come to think of it, even old *people*," teased Tanya.

"I suppose so," admitted Belinda, "but I get so frustrated with those old thees and thousts."

"Did you like that song?" asked Nathan.

"Yes," said Belinda, "but..."

"Then just enjoy it. Don't look for problems."

Belinda subsided and Alex picked up his Bible and told them what he wanted to read.

"*Two full chapters?*" asked Belinda. "The Sunday schools and youth groups we went to only ever read a few verses. Why two whole chapters?"

"I'm glad you asked that," said Alex earnestly, "because it gives me a chance to explain just how important I think reading the Bible is. I believe that only the Bible can teach us how to get eternal life. Jesus lived all his life in obedience to God and then *died* for us when he was not much older than I am, which shows how important he thought it all was. If you only ever read just a few verses, it's like drinking one drop of water and thinking that's all you need for the day, or learning the symbol for one element and thinking you understand the periodic table!"

"I suppose so," acknowledged Belinda grudgingly.

Alex read the first chapter and asked Dan to read the other. When Dan finished, Alex spoke simply and sincerely about Jesus' life and death. Dan learned a lot and even Belinda seemed interested.

After that, they sang "The Lord's my shepherd", filling the room with joy. They were beginning to learn to sing together – even Nathan! Alex offered a prayer of thankfulness for Jesus' death and resurrection and everyone said "Amen" when he finished.

"Wow, look at the wind outside," said Belinda, looking out of the window for the first time since they had started.

"Phew," breathed Nathan. "No-one could stop a fire in that gale."

"How hot is it?" asked Alex.

Belinda ran to the door and opened it. The wind snatched the door from her hand and slammed it against the stopper. The glass rattled.

"Careful," said Tanya. "The camp's not ours!"

After a few seconds, Belinda hung her head down and panted like a dog. "It's hot," she said. "Really hot."

"Then shut the door, you dill," laughed Dan. "You'll let all the cool out."

ℭℜ

It was too hot to do anything outside that afternoon, and lunch stretched on as they nibbled and chatted, enjoying the air-conditioned comfort while outside the trees lurched and twisted in the searing gale.

At about three o'clock, Dan suggested they return to the games room and while away the rest of the afternoon there.

"Why don't you go and turn on the AC," suggested Belinda, "and we'll come once it's cooled the place down a bit."

"Wimp," said Dan, scornfully, but he got up and went anyway.

As he walked out of the house, it really was like walking into an oven. The heat almost took his breath away. He sniffed the air with its hot, dry smells, thankful that there was no smell of smoke or fire. Abruptly, he wondered what they should do if a fire approached – particularly if it happened once there were campers depending on them! He made a mental note to check with his father and Alex.

As expected, it was hot in the games room, so he turned on the AC and got out some of the games the family liked to play. The room was already beginning to feel cooler when he went out onto the porch again. He looked up towards the mountains and suddenly saw a frightening sight: a thin wisp of white rising from the trees before being quickly dispersed by the strong north wind.

Smoke!

He ran back to the house, tugged open the door and shouted, "Fire!"

Nathan and Alex sprang to their feet.

Tanya squealed. "In the games room?"

"No, somewhere up north," Dan answered urgently. "It doesn't seem very far away, maybe near that camp on the peaks trail."

"North?" said Alex. "That's bad. Is the wind still northerly?"

"Yes," answered Dan. "It's strong, too."

"If there's a fire, the north wind will bring it straight towards us," said Nathan. "Let's go outside and have a look."

Standing on the porch, they all saw the thin column of smoke.

"How far away is it?" asked Belinda.

"It's hard to tell," said Alex, "but I'd guess about one to three kilometres away."

"Then we've got a hard decision to make," announced Nathan. "If the fire is near a track, we could get there in, say, ten to thirty minutes. It's a small fire now, but it could grow while we're on the way, leaving us facing a quickly growing fire that could easily outpace us. On the other hand, if we get there quickly enough, we may be able to easily contain the fire before it takes off and burns thousands of hectares and threatens many lives."

"That sounds dangerous," said Belinda, eyes widening.

"It is," agreed her father, "and if we do nothing, the first option is much more likely. In fact, if we don't go and look for the fire *right now*, we should get into our cars instead and look for a place of refuge."

"I've got an idea, Dad," said Dan.

"If we're going to look for this fire, we've got to get moving, Dan. Is it important?"

"Yes. My drone has a range of about five kilometres. We could use it to guide us to the smoke or warn us if things get out of control."

"Good idea," smiled Nathan.

"Well done, Danny boy," said Belinda.

Dan ran to his room and fetched the drone, glad he'd been keeping it well charged despite being too busy to use it!

Within a couple of minutes, the drone soared aloft, its droning buzz fading as Dan directed it northward towards the column of smoke.

"Let's go," he said.

"I think I'll stay," said Belinda, looking cautious for once.

Dan, Alex and Nathan hurried along the track that led along the valley towards the Grampians Peaks Trail and Barigar Camp.

Before they reached the creek crossing, the drone camera showed Dan that the spiralling smoke wisps rose from Barigar Camp itself. There was actually quite a lot of smoke, but the gusty wind dispersed most of it close to the ground.

"I think it's a fire in a metal rubbish bin," said Dan, bringing the drone down low from the north.

"But there are no rubbish bins along the trail," objected Alex.

"It looks like a portable bin, but quite large."

They hurried on, Dan controlling the drone carefully and keeping his eyes on the view through its camera. They could all see the rising smoke more clearly as they approached the camp site.

Guided by the drone, they quickly found the old steel bin just outside the camp. Alex hurried across to it, worried by the flames rising above the sides of the bin. For some reason, the fire was only now beginning to take hold. Something must have been holding it back.

"We need to put this out," said Alex, urgently.

"Yes, but how?" asked Nathan. "It looks like it's just getting going, and there's all this bush around, and a strong, hot wind."

Dan landed the drone and collected it.

"There's quite a bit of sizzling in the fire," puzzled Alex. "I'm wondering if there's a lot of water in that bin. If so, maybe we could tip it over and the water would help us put out the fire."

"The bin will be too hot to touch," said Nathan. "I'll find a branch to hook over the edge of it. That might give us a hint as to how much water there is. Wait here."

Alex stayed near the rapidly growing fire while the other two hunted for sticks long and sturdy enough to tip over the bin. When they returned with two or three sticks each, Dan took the thickest and began pushing at the bin. "It sure feels heavy," he announced.

Nathan had found a stick with a short side branch that he could hook onto the bin and pull it towards him. He stood opposite Dan and pulled. Together they slowly tipped the bin, causing more loud sizzling.

"I think you're right about the water, Alex," shouted Nathan. "Grab a stick and push with Dan. We'll tip it over slowly so that it falls towards the area where the flames are growing the quickest."

As the bin fell over, the growing flames sputtered and seemed to pause. The bin hit the ground and dirty water flooded out, carrying with it many white cylinders which they instantly recognised as rolls of toilet paper. Some were burning, some smouldering and some completely soaked. As some of the burning cylinders started rolling downhill towards the main camp, Alex and Dan used their sticks to stop them. With the spilled water and the many waterlogged rolls, the smouldering and flaming rolls were surprisingly easy to put out.

Within two minutes, the crisis was over. The three stood and looked at each other.

Nathan asked the question that was foremost in all their minds: "Why would there be a bin of soggy toilet rolls at a camping ground on the Grampians Peaks Trail?"

"And who would have lit the fire?" asked Alex.

"And when?" finished Dan.

The tension and fear were released and they laughed at each other.

"I have no evidence, but I reckon it was probably Brad Jessop's gang," said Dan, remembering Fergus' comments that morning about them having commandeered the GPT.

"I can easily imagine them *doing* something stupid like this," snorted his father, "but I'd like to know *why*!"

"What do we do with all these toilet rolls?" asked Alex.

"Put them back in the bin and tip it upside down?" suggested Dan. "Once they dry out, we can carry them back to the camp and get rid of them – if no-one comes and collects them first."

"Not many people are likely to collect soggy toilet rolls," said Alex.

"Well, at least we stopped the fire, even if we don't know what caused it in the first place," said Nathan.

Chapter 22

Countdown

Less than a week remained before their first camp would begin and the campsite was almost ready. True, they had never run a camp there before, but Nathan and Tanya felt that everything was under control.

Alex was satisfied that the adventure equipment was ready for the camp and pleased with Dan's progress in learning what was required.

On Wednesday morning, Nathan and Tanya decided to visit Terry and Linda in Stawell that afternoon to discuss the upcoming camp and make sure they hadn't missed anything obvious.

However, as they were enjoying some morning tea, they heard a car on the gravel outside. Thinking of Brad Jessop and his men, Dan hurried out to investigate.

A minute later, with a loud "Ta-da!", he presented Terry and Linda as if he were a magician performing a magic trick.

"Mum and Dad!" said Alex, jumping up to give them each a hug. "It's good to see you."

"We thought you might all like one last chat before the camp starts on Monday," said Terry. "There are sure to be some questions that only come up when there are just a few days to go."

"And we've brought some news, too," added Linda.

"It's not all good news," warned Terry, "but there is really good news about Steve and Sylvia."

"They're on their way back!" said Linda, happily. "Sylvia has responded very well to treatment. They just want her to have one more week of recovery in Ballarat before returning to 'the rigours of life beyond the western margin'."

"Apparently that's literally what they told her," Terry laughed.

"What does 'rigours' mean?" asked Belinda.

"Difficulties," said Dan.

"But we've had a lovely time here!" said Belinda, brows furrowed.

"Even without Derek?" teased Dan.

Belinda stuck out her tongue at him. "I'll never see Derek again," she said, "and I won't miss him. At least, not much."

"I'm glad Sylvia wasn't here on Sunday afternoon," said Tanya. "There was a scary fire at Barigar Camp."

"It was only a small fire in a big rubbish bin," said Nathan.

"But you said yourself that if you three hadn't got to it quickly, it would've spread and got out of control. If Dan hadn't gone to the games room when he did..."

"And the games room was where we asked God to make sure there wouldn't be any bad fires that day," said Dan. "I guess God answered our prayer."

He was still ashamed that he hadn't noticed the answer to prayer when it happened. Not until he was praying that Sunday evening had he suddenly remembered it and thanked God. This was the first time he had mentioned his conviction to the others.

Nathan and Tanya looked thoughtful, Belinda sceptical. Alex said, "You're right. I hadn't noticed that."

"It's too easy to ask God for things and not even notice when he gives us what we ask," said Linda.

"True, and I've got to agree with you about Sylvia, Tanya," said Terry. "It's good she wasn't here. Fire danger is one real difficulty of living around here. Also, some people skate much closer to the edge of criminal behaviour when they think there aren't many police to catch them."

"We've only seen problems with Brad Jessop and his men, and maybe NK2," said Nathan.

"There's a bit more than that in Stawell," said Terry. "You're having a camp with people from the mine – well, we've heard reports that some of the workers at the mine have been helping themselves to some high grade ore."

"Is that unusual?"

"It's always been a problem with gold mines, so they do their best to make sure valuable ore doesn't leave in people's pockets! They've found a new quartz vein with some extremely rich pockets – rumours suggest *kilograms of gold per tonne of ore*. That's about a thousand times richer than most of the ore they've been mining."

"Do they ever find gold nuggets?"

"I don't believe so, but with such high yields, there'd be plenty of visible gold in the ore. But returns have been below expectations and the amount of ore brought out doesn't match the volumes calculated for the work done."

"Terry means that some of the ore seems to be going missing," explained Linda.

"But a miner can't just put a tonne of ore in his back pocket and walk out!" said Tanya.

"And how many people would have any opportunity to help themselves anyway?" asked Nathan.

"Tongues have been wagging about this all over Stawell, so when the boss of the mine visited the bank, I asked him about it. He said they've given up trying to track down the thieves for the moment because they can't tell where in the process the ore is disappearing."

"That must be frustrating!" said Nathan.

"Yes. Of course, it's all been reported to the police, but here's the thing: they're not *completely* certain it isn't just an accumulation of rounding errors! They process thousands of tonnes of ore and less than 0.1% is believed to be missing – just a few tonnes of special ore that was expected to yield a thousand times more gold than average. But it's possible that the ore just wasn't as good as the core samples suggested and it's not missing at all."

"I suppose they'll be going over all their records, checking and double-checking," said Nathan.

"Yes, I believe so."

"Gold attracts thieves, doesn't it?" observed Belinda.

"Well, God says don't steal," said Dan, "and didn't Jesus say, 'You can't serve both God and money'?"

"Talking about money," said Terry, "Darren came into the bank yesterday."

"The guy who works for Brad Jessop?"

"Yes. He looked a bit edgy and wanted to talk to me about the bank's attitude toward this self-proclaimed 'National Park Committee'. He was concerned his money might be impounded if the police decided Brad's business was fraudulent."

"I saw him in the bank the day we first met you," said Belinda.

Terry paused and looked concerned. "Really?"

"Yes – you were at the door of your office talking quietly to someone, while Darren was standing in line nearby, waiting to see the teller."

Terry took a deep breath. "Well, well, well!" he said. "That may answer a few questions about the mine." He stopped and shook his head. "The man I was talking to was John, the boss of the mine. I know him well and he was excited because they'd just finished some development work that would allow them to get to that new quartz vein I mentioned. I was trying to quiet him down a bit, but he has quite a powerful voice. I guess Darren would have heard everything he said. I wonder...."

"Darren wouldn't be able to cause any trouble on his own," said Alex.

"No," agreed his father, "but he might have told someone else."

"So there could be a connection between Brad and thefts from the mine?"

Chapter 23

Heatherlie Quarry

Another Saturday came around. The morning was full of urgent, last-minute checks as they all made the most of this last morning of work before the camp began on Monday morning – the real test of their preparation.

After breakfast, one of the wastewater pumps suddenly began to squeal, and when Nathan went into the shed to check it, the light fizzled and died! After replacing the light, Nathan and Dan swapped over the entire pump, thankful that Steve and Sylvia kept spares of various important items.

Shortly afterwards, a slicing machine in the kitchen failed and none of their efforts could restore it to working order. Thankfully, only thirty people were to attend this first camp.

The failures shook Nathan's confidence as he hurried through the work he had planned for the morning.

After a late lunch, Nathan threw up his hands and abandoned the rest of the work he had hoped to do. They still had to inspect the historic Heatherlie Quarry, since the camp programme included a visit there. The family had visited briefly about five years earlier, but none of them remembered much about it. Alex had never seen it and planned to join them.

Accordingly, they all piled into the four-wheel drive and drove south to where a track led off to the old quarry. As they turned into the parking area, they were surprised to find it almost full of cars. It was the biggest collection of cars they had seen in the national park area since their arrival!

What was going on? There was no-one in the carpark, so Nathan parked the car in the one available space and they climbed out. As they began to make their way up the track towards the quarry area, they saw two men walking down the track towards them. Fluorescent jackets over the top of camouflage clothes seemed a strangely contradictory mix, but the really disconcerting feature of their attire was the pistol that each carried in a holster on his hip.

"I don't like the look of those pistols," said Nathan quietly as they walked on.

"And I don't like the fact that there are more men further up the track," murmured Alex. "What's up?"

"Is this more of Brad Jessop's work?" whispered Dan.

"Let's see how being nice goes," said Tanya under her breath, then said brightly as the men approached, "We've been looking forward to seeing the relics at Heatherlie Quarry. This is where they quarried the stone for Victoria's Parliament House, isn't it?"

"Dunno, lady," said the first man, "but the National Park Conference..."

"Committee," corrected the other.

"Ah, yeah," acknowledged the first. "The National Park Committee is doing important maintenance work on the paths and buildings right now."

"We're rangers in the National Park. We're here to make sure everyone stays safe," added the other.

"Yeah," nodded the first. "So the old quarry is closed."

"Closed?" asked Tanya, the artificial smile fading from her face. "But we came to see the boilers and the old houses where the workers lived."

"Sorry. We're using tractors and other equipment, so we can't have tourists in the way," answered the first.

"It wouldn't be safe," added the other.

"Can't we just walk around carefully? We'll make sure we keep away from your equipment. We'd really like to see the stone houses."

"No," said the first man, obviously annoyed by her persistence. "We're working on the houses to..."

"...to make sure that the roofs won't fall in," finished the other.

"And they're doing all this work now, are they?" asked Dan.

"Yes," snapped the first. "Now we've answered your questions and explained why you can't come in, that's it. Go away."

"I think we'll go for a walk along the road first," said Nathan. "Isn't there a camping ground over the other side of the road, a bit closer to Halls Gap?"

"How should we know? Why don't you drive along and find out?"

"Well, since we can't see the quarry," said Nathan, "we'll at least get some exercise if we walk."

"I s'pose so," said the first guard, grudgingly.

"But don't forget, if you go for walks in the National Park area, you have to pay the new fees," said the other. "Those fees pay for the maintenance work."

"And when we open up the quarry again, there'll be a visitor's fee here too," said the first.

"And armed guards to make sure people pay, I suppose!" said Alex, bitterly.

"No, no, no," said the first guard. "We're only here to make sure the maintenance work can be done safely. After that's finished there'll be signs here and an honesty box, same as other places."

"We've seen the signs around," said Nathan, "and we've got no intention of paying any bogus fees like that!"

"What do you mean, bogans?" said the man angrily, putting his hand on his pistol. "We're not bogans, but we don't carry these guns for fun. If you're looking for trouble, we can give it to you!"

The other guard laughed and put his hand on his companion's arm.

"Hey, Jonno, calm down. He said 'bogus', not 'bogans'. It means fake." He turned to Nathan. "All these arrangements are made by the National Park Management Committee. Brad Jessop is the chairman and everything he does is for the good of the National Park. After all, that's what we need the money for."

"Okay, you can think that if you want," replied Nathan. "We'll go for a walk along the road now and come back to get our car in a while."

"Don't take too long."

They turned away from the two guards and walked down to the road. Once out of earshot, they began to discuss what had happened.

"Dodgy as!" said Dan, and Belinda nodded.

"Why, what's wrong with them?" asked Nathan.

"Are you serious, Dad?" asked Dan. "Couldn't you see that everything they said was lies?"

"Of course, but tell me what *you* see."

"For a start, it's Saturday afternoon. Rangers wouldn't be around in a place like this on a Saturday afternoon. They said there was equipment working, but we can't hear any – and what would it be doing on a Saturday afternoon anyway?"

"True."

"They claimed to be rangers, too, but didn't know about Plantation Campground."

"They aren't rangers," scoffed Alex.

"Except maybe *bush*rangers," said Belinda.

They walked along the gravel road until they came to another track leading up towards the sandstone range.

"Where does that track go?" asked Dan.

"No idea. Have you got maps on your phone?" asked Nathan.

Dan took out his phone and looked at a map. He began to look excited. "I think it must go up to another track that leads back to the quarry area," he said. "That could take us up past those guards."

"Or it could take us right to them," said Tanya.

"Can you imagine what they'd do if they found us coming in from another direction?" asked Belinda, wide-eyed.

"Not very happy," said Alex, frowning, "but I'm suspicious of what's going on."

"I am too," said Nathan, "but those men are armed and there must be quite a few of them, given the number of cars in the carpark. Let's go back to the camp and finish off the work we couldn't do this morning."

"But Dad..." said Dan.

"Your father is right, Dan," interrupted Tanya. "Let's go."

Dan argued, but not even Alex supported him, so they were soon walking back to the carpark. The two guards they had met were standing there, chatting.

"Leaving?" asked one.

Nathan nodded as he unlocked the car.

"Good," said the other guard.

They got into their car and drove off.

☙

Back at the camp, Nathan said to Dan, "I'm going to do those final checks I didn't finish this morning, but you were meant to have the afternoon off, so you don't have to come and help."

"Okay. I'll go for a ride instead," said Dan.

Nathan's concentration had already switched to his work, so he agreed absent-mindedly and walked away.

Dan fetched his bike, thinking this was a good opportunity to see if there was one of Brad Jessop's signs at Trooper's Creek camping area.

Before he reached the road, however, a more radical idea occurred to him: he could return to that track beyond the Heatherlie car park and see if he could get into the quarry area behind the guards. He was sure there was something suspicious going on! It must be roughly ten kilometres to the quarry, so riding there and back would take about an hour altogether. If he also spent an hour at Heatherlie, then... he had to hurry or he would be late for dinner! He hurried off, but soon began to understand how the lack of road maintenance slowed his riding! Occasional larger branches and fallen trees covered parts of the road, while smaller branches and twigs were scattered everywhere. Following the tracks of earlier vehicles proved to be the quickest way to travel, even when they left the road to avoid a couple of larger fallen trees.

Eventually, he reached the track that led off to Heatherlie Quarry and raced past without turning his head. He didn't want to meet those guards, and if they saw him, he didn't want them to think he was interested in their precious site. Another minute's riding and he came to the track they had seen earlier. It was rough – probably only intended as a walking track – but led up towards the range of mountains that marched south beside the road. After a while, he met a 4WD track running parallel to the main road. This must lead towards the old quarry! Dan turned to follow it cautiously.

Darkness was still hours away, but already the shadows of the looming mountains stretched across the bush. Dan was confident that he knew where he was going from the tracks shown on the map. Walking tracks marked the streets of the never-completed township of Heatherlie – reclaimed now by bush, and popular among wildflower lovers. He was more interested in the quarry itself and the historic buildings those guards claimed to be repairing. He couldn't imagine Brad's men doing any useful work, so what were they really doing?

The map showed this section as a bicycle track following the path of the former railway line from Stawell towards the quarry, but it was far too overgrown to ride a bike along. He climbed off and hid his bike in the bush near the track, making sure he could find it again later.

Back on the track, he listened for sounds of people, but all he could hear were buzzing insects, bird calls and the multitude of other noises that echo through the bush whenever you stop and listen.

This quarry had an interrupted history, starting in the 1860s soon after the gold rush, but abandoned several times when the demand for stone dipped.

The most recent re-opening had provided stone to refurbish the Victorian houses of parliament in Melbourne. After closing for the last time, hard-working volunteers had refurbished the empty stone houses and tidied up some of the heavy equipment on the site. Paths and boardwalks led interested tourists around the site, past coloured placards describing the quarry's history to patient readers. Dan, however, knew nothing of this except for what the maps on his phone presented so confidently.

After fighting his way through the undergrowth for some time, he reached a place where the track had been cleared and a narrow track led off to the right, down, he guessed, to the former township area.

Ahead, Dan saw a folding aluminium frame with a bright orange sign bearing the words "Tree lopping work ahead". For an instant, he thought maybe genuine maintenance work *was* going on, but as he approached, he noticed four letters painted at the bottom-right of the sign: 'STLS'. Suddenly Dan recognised it as one of Trevor's signs, stolen from near the fallen tree on the Roses Gap Road. Brad's men again! He seemed to have his fingers everywhere, and one of his signature tactics was stealing.

Dan checked his location again. He was approaching the track they had tried to walk up earlier, and listening carefully, he could hear distant voices.

Hurrying towards the quarry area, Dan stifled a cry of surprise as he almost fell over a man seated on a fallen log with his back against a gum tree.

The man's eyes were closed, his mouth open. Asleep. Unlike the other guards they had met, this man wore no hi-vis jacket, but he did have a holstered pistol on his hip. Dan's heart thrilled with shock and surprise, but he forced himself to keep walking until the path turned a corner and he could breathe again.

Moments later, he wondered if he had blundered out of the frying pan into the fire!

No more than twenty metres away, six or eight men sat around a table leaning towards a box that sat in the middle of the table. A crackly voice came from the box, its lack of clarity saving Dan from immediate discovery – the men were concentrating so hard on listening that no-one noticed him. Yet it was inevitable that he would be seen eventually if he didn't find somewhere to hide. Once again, he kept walking. A bright yellow front end loader with backhoe was parked beside the track, and soon he was behind it, hidden from the men.

Dan crouched down. Now he had one man behind him and several more in front. He tried to position himself beside the backhoe so that he could not be seen by the men at the table, but would also be invisible to anyone following him along the path.

"...the police are causing trouble," said the crackly voice, "but I kept them happy. They'll leave us alone for a week or so, and that's all the time we need. After that, we'll be able to take over the areas we want."

The voice sounded familiar, but Dan couldn't quite place it.

"So when will we get the consignment we're burying?" asked one of the men at the table.

"Probably Thursday evening. Make sure the hole is ready by then, and fill it up as soon as you can after that."

"We've already started digging. It's not easy: lots of rocks, but at least it's not solid rock."

"Good. And when you fill it in, don't forget to put enough extra soil on top to allow for settling."

"Yes, boss," answered the man, and Dan could imagine him rolling his eyes at the obvious instructions. "We know that."

"And spread the extra gravel on top and around the buildings so it looks as if you were upgrading the gravel path for tourists."

"Yes, boss. They'll never know what they're walking on top of!"

All the men at the table laughed.

"We hope not. Just don't bury it too deep," said the voice over the radio. "We might be in a hurry when we dig it up."

"Sure, boss. And, boss, we had a family of snoopers come this afternoon, but we got rid of them."

"Snoopers?"

"They came to see the quarry and didn't want to take no for an answer."

"Was it the family from the Roses Gap Camp?"

"No idea. They came in a four-wheel drive."

"Doesn't everyone?"

Dan recognised one of the guards they had met as he leaned forward and said, "An older man and woman." Mum wouldn't like that, thought Dan.

"A young man who looked a bit familiar," added the other guard they had met.

"And two stupid teenage brats," finished the first.

It was Dan's turn not to like what he heard.

"That sounds right. They're harmless enough, but keep an eye out for them. If they cause trouble, don't be afraid to grab them and bring them here to the lockup."

"Okay. They looked a bit too stupid to cause us trouble."

"I'm sure you're right, but be careful. We're on the verge of something big and we don't want to lose it, not for all the gold in Timbuktu."

There, Dan had it! The voice was Brad Jessop's. He'd used that expression the first time Dan and his father had met him.

Brad and his men kept talking, but Dan remembered that he needed to get back to the campsite. How could he get away without the men seeing him? Off to the right, between him and the men at the table, the track led down to the parking area, but he couldn't go that way without being seen. Since he couldn't stay until dark, he'd have to go back the way he'd come. His decision made, he was about to stand and walk smoothly and steadily away from the front-end loader when he heard Brad Jessop say, "Okay, that's all, fellas. I've got another meeting to go to. Over and out."

Dan froze.

One of the men at the table reached over and turned off the radio. "Sounds like the boss has everything under control."

Two of the men stood, as if to walk away, and Dan hurriedly checked that he really was hidden from view.

"Well, yes and no," replied another, remaining seated. "I didn't like that bit about calling ourselves 'NK2-ers'." Dan's ears pricked up at the mention of NK2! "NK2 has a bad reputation, bad enough that the police won't have any difficulty enlisting support from the farmers against us – perhaps even from the Victorian government. Seems a bit risky to me."

"But NK2 is pretty famous," said one of the men who had stood up. "Aren't people more likely to listen to us if we say we're part of his gang?"

"That's what Craig was saying last week," said another. "He reckons all publicity is good publicity."

The two who had stood sat down again. Dan relaxed a little.

"Well, I don't agree," said the first complainer. "Some publicity is too much publicity. If we keep a low profile and work locally in the National Park, they'll leave us alone, but taking over the entire Wimmera or the Mallee or controlling some corridor between here and the margins will attract the attention of much bigger players. Possibly even the Victorian army. We don't want that."

"Have you said this to Craig?"

"Oh, no!" answered the man, smiling as he shook his head. "We don't get along. But Craig never listens to anyone anyway. He has grandiose ideas, but he's lazy. He'll never get anywhere."

"You better be careful what you say," warned another. "Remember Rick?"

"Mmm, yes. Maybe you're right."

"Where is Craig anyway?" asked yet another, and the rest joined in to answer.

"He went away early yesterday. Said he had other things to do."

"Did Darren go with him?" asked someone else.

"I don't believe so. In fact, I haven't seen Darren for a few days."

"Strange. Craig works with Darren most of the time."

"...using him as his personal servant," sneered the complainer. "Maybe we'll soon be using Darren as a cautionary tale instead of Rick."

At that moment, Dan made his move. Keeping the front-end loader between him and the men for as long as possible, he walked away as quietly and calmly as he could, not looking back.

Each step seemed age-long, yet no shouts announced his discovery. After what seemed like an eternity, he reached a slight bend in the path and rounded it with a few more thankful, tottering steps.

He stopped and took a deep, incredulous breath. Surely it was a miracle. How else could they possibly have missed seeing him? He pulled out his phone and checked the time.

It was almost 5:30, and he needed to be home by 6:30 for dinner! He broke into a jog, then just as suddenly slowed to a walk as he remembered the sleeping guard. "Oh, no," he said, involuntarily.

"Dan," hissed a voice from nearby. It was Alex's voice, but where was he?

"I'm here," said Alex, stepping out from behind a gum tree beside the track. "I was heading back towards my bike when I heard you coming and hid behind this tree. What are you doing here?"

"No time to talk now," said Dan. "There was a sleeping guard along this track. We've got to get past him."

"While I was fighting my way along that overgrown so-called bike track, just before it opened out, I saw a guard walking towards me. He didn't see me and followed the track towards the township, so I sneaked along here while he was away. Perhaps we could do the same again if he has a regular beat."

Dan nodded, "Let's wait here until he comes, then follow him when he goes back the other way."

They hid in the shrubbery and waited.

Suddenly they heard footsteps coming along the track from the direction of the quarry. Fortunately, they were well hidden from view from both directions, but who was this?

"Max!" called a voice which Dan recognised as belonging to the man who had complained about Craig. "Max! Where are you? There's news from Brad."

The man hurried past and Dan and Alex watched him disappear along the track.

"What do we do now?" whispered Dan, urgently.

"Let's wait for a few minutes and see what happens."

After a while, they heard voices and saw two men returning.

"I was just having a cigarette," whined the man called Max. "There's no point in walking backwards and forwards all the time. No-one's going to come here. Seriously, who'd go to a disused quarry in the back of beyond?"

"You agreed to be the guard today, and all you've been doing is sitting around smoking. If I hadn't come, that butt you tossed away would have started a fire. You did the same at Barigar Camp last Sunday, and there would've been a huge fire if I hadn't dumped it in that waterlogged bin. You're just too careless, Max."

So that was the cause of the fire at Barigar, thought Dan.

"Aw, cigarette butts never hurt anybody," scoffed Max. "Anyway, what was the news from Brad?"

The other man began to repeat Brad's instructions as the pair walked on, and soon their voices faded away.

Dan and Alex moved carefully out of the bush and hurried along the track together. But curiosity was eating at Dan, and it wasn't long before he turned to Alex.

"How did you get here?" he asked, just as Alex asked him the same question.

"By bike," they answered together, and laughed.

"Where's your bike?" asked Alex.

"A little further along here. Where's yours?"

"I hid it in the bush where this track meets the one that goes down to the road."

They retrieved their bikes without difficulty, then hurried down to the road and sped back to the campsite with no chance to compare notes.

After taking a few moments to catch their breath, they were able to sit down to dinner with no questions asked.

Chapter 24

Sharing the News

Tanya and Belinda had prepared a special dinner to celebrate the family's success in getting the campsite ready – and not merely on time, but more than a day early! Alex joined in, practically part of the family although they had not known him for long.

Nathan wasn't one for speeches, but he began the meal with a short expression of thanks for the excellent, tireless work they had all done since arriving at Roses Gap.

A mouth-watering dessert followed the delicious first course, but Dan was so eager to learn what Alex had discovered at Heatherlie that afternoon that he paid little attention to either. He even refused the chocolates that followed, prompting his mother to raise her eyebrows and ask if he was unwell!

Dan protested that he was fine and thanked Tanya and Belinda for the meal, then left the table, looking meaningfully at Alex. He was also eager to tell Alex of his own discoveries.

As he headed for his bedroom, he was pleased to see Alex rising to leave. Soon, the two of them were standing in the corridor outside Dan's room.

"Can we go to the Games Room and talk?" Dan asked.

"Good idea," said Alex.

Excitedly, Dan led the way, shutting the door of the Games Room as soon as Alex was inside. Then he blurted out, "How long were you at Heatherlie? And what did you find out?"

"About an hour," smiled Alex.

"Longer than me!" said Dan with chagrin.

"Quite a lot of it was just listening to chit-chat," said Alex, "but I did hear some interesting things in the end."

"What did you do when you arrived?"

"Hid my bike and followed that pretend bike path. When I spotted that guard ahead of me, I watched him until he sneaked down into the township area, then I hurried along the track to the quarry. From what we heard, I guess he went to have a smoke."

"Then he must have come back and fallen sleep before I arrived," said Dan.

"Yes. I didn't know where to go, so I made my way up into the quarry area and looked around, but there was no-one there. Away from the workings, I noticed some buildings and followed a track towards them. Then I heard people talking, but fortunately there was quite a bit of undergrowth, so I was able to hide and listen. I worked my way closer to them and found a group of people in army fatigues sitting at a table, including those guards we met earlier. They were just chatting, but if the police had been there to hear them, they'd all have been arrested. They talked as if stealing was fun!"

"I wonder if they'd feel the same if people were stealing *their* stuff."

"Probably not," laughed Alex. "That's why Jesus warned us, 'Do to others what you want them to do to you,' didn't he?"

"Yes. And I reckon that makes sense."

"Incidentally, they mentioned a visit to the Roses Gap Camp one night to steal a pump – apparently they needed it in a hurry. They shone the tractor's headlights on the water tank so they could see."

"Why didn't they turn off the lights when they finished?"

"Maybe it was easier for them to see the way back to their car, but they did seem to find it funny that they'd left the lights on so the battery would go flat. We obviously don't have the right mindset to be crooks, Dan!"

"Did you hear anything else?"

"They talked about various things, but no details. They're obviously hiding something there."

"Was everyone armed?"

"Yes. Mostly with pistols, but a few had rifles too."

"Yet the men we've seen before haven't been dressed like that or armed. What's the difference?"

"Maybe they're two different groups in Brad's organisation – or perhaps the job at Heatherlie is more serious."

"What else did you see or hear?" asked Dan.

"The men sitting at the table were obviously waiting for something, and after a while I heard a crackly voice that must have been coming through a radio."

"Was it Brad?" asked Dan, excitedly.

"Apparently, although I didn't work it out until that bloke who kicked up a fuss said there was news from Brad," answered Alex.

"So we both heard Brad's call," said Dan. "Though I didn't hear it all. I came in somewhere in the middle."

"Where were you?" asked Alex.

"Hiding behind the digger."

"Well, I was on the other side of the table, up near one of those stone buildings – but not the one with the guards at the door."

"What did they talk about at the start?"

"Brad told them to use the tag 'NK2-ers' for themselves and to make sure they carried their guns all the time to look the part, but said they shouldn't be in too much of a hurry to use them unless…"

Just then, Belinda opened the door and walked in. "Sorry to interrupt your discussions, gentlemen. I wanted to borrow a hymn book to see if I can find some good songs for tomorrow morning." Her words were casual, but her eyes were open wide.

Dan looked at her suspiciously. Why would wide-eyed Belinda be interested in a hymn book?

"By all means," said Alex, graciously. "Help yourself."

Belinda fetched a hymn book from the bookshelf, then said goodnight and left.

"Hmm," mused Dan as the door closed and they heard Belinda's footsteps descending the stairs outside. "How long was she listening?"

CR

The next morning, Belinda brought the hymn book to breakfast and announced the two songs she wanted to sing that morning, pointing out triumphantly, "They don't have any theeses or thouses."

"It doesn't sound a very good basis for choosing hymns," laughed Tanya.

"And why are you trying to take over a meeting you don't want to come along to anyway?" complained Dan irritably.

"I'm not taking over," said Belinda sweetly, "I'm just making my contribution to our continuous improvement."

"Maybe you could do that best by not coming along," grumbled Dan. He knew he shouldn't say it and his parents wouldn't like it, but Belinda was so bossy sometimes that it got annoying. When his father responded, however, his words surprised Dan.

"That's not a very gracious attitude, Dan," began Nathan. "Yes, Belinda is being pushy and trying to get her own way, but don't let her behaviour control yours. It's up to you and Alex what songs we sing – after all, you two took the lead in trying to get us all to think about God."

Belinda looked at Nathan for a few moments, then said, "I suppose Dad's right. Sorry. I'll come along and sing whatever you two choose."

It was the start of a delightful Sunday morning.

Once again, Alex and Dan discussed what their time of worship should include, and Dan even suggested that they sing one of the songs Belinda had chosen.

When the family gathered in the games room after breakfast, Belinda was there from the beginning and the atmosphere was happy and relaxed, mixed with an awareness of the God they had come to worship. Outside, it was a cool, pleasant morning, much cooler than the previous Sunday, and they left the door open, enjoying the sounds of the bush outside. Dan was very content in this unexpected sanctuary, away from the dangers of pandemics and city life.

They really were learning to sing better together, and the sound of their enthusiastic voices not only filled the room with praise but also spread across the campsite. Even the magpies stopped their songs for a moment to listen.

Having been thinking about Brad and his criminal helpers, Alex chose to contrast the beauties of trust and faith with the ugliness of theft and violence.

God's gift of his son showed his amazing generosity, while the NK2-ers seemed to know only greed.

When Alex finished their worship with a prayer, he asked that God would continue to give them peace, even when people like Brad Jessop were doing their best to bring trouble through theft and violence.

Chapter 25

The Camp Begins

The sun rose over the campsite the next morning in a glorious profusion of colours, while wispy tendrils of cloud traced tenuous pictures. Sadly, no-one in the camp took the time to enjoy the beauty. Since their contented celebration on Saturday evening, each of them had remembered extra tasks that simply *must* be done – and the deadline was so near that everyone ran around like chooks without heads.

Alex was familiar with the excitement and stress of getting ready for a camp. He also knew that, while it was best to be completely ready when the campers arrived, there were always opportunities during a camp to do any urgent work that was required to make the camp run smoothly.

Nathan and Tanya had experience with helping to run church youth group camps, but this time they were in charge. There was no-one else to ask for directions. Breakfast was a tense time.

At 8:30am, the mine's camp organiser arrived. Nathan strode out of the office and greeted him. "Good morning, Paul."

"Morning, Nathan. Glad the tree's gone from the road. Must've been a big job, that one!"

"I'll say. But it also gave us enough firewood to last for a good long time. We're even thinking of making some tables with it."

"If you have good strong tables, the council might want some to put in parks around the town. Might cover your cleanup costs."

"Good idea. It was a lot of work, and parts of the trunk are really fine timber."

"It's hard getting used to doing the road work that the roads department used to do, isn't it? We've found that with a lot of work around the mine – things the council used to do but can't afford to pay for now, so we have to decide how much we need them. If we need something enough, we pay for it ourselves. Fortunately, the mine's quite profitable at the moment. The new workings are just coming online and producing nicely."

"Does that mean you need more staff?"

"Yes, and most of them have precious little experience in mining."

"How many new workers are available now? And how do you advertise to a larger audience?"

"You're spot on. Those are exactly the problems we face. Anyway, I'm meant to set up a registration table with an information pack for each camper in the games room. But I can't remember where that is."

"Follow me," said Nathan.

"Thanks."

They left the office and Nathan led Paul to the games room where Dan had already set up two tables to lay out the welcome packs, ready for the campers when they arrived.

"You read my mind!" said Paul.

The campers were to arrive between nine and ten o'clock, and it wasn't long after nine when the first car drove into the carpark from the Roses Gap Road.

Within minutes, several more cars appeared, and Dan marvelled at the sudden change from hushed tranquillity into a busy ants' nest of people. Some strode around purposefully, while others looked slightly lost. Nathan took it as a good sign when the last camper collected his welcome pack before ten o'clock.

Tanya confirmed with Paul that the number of campers was as expected and went to the kitchen to make sure that the supplies were all correct.

Paul had already arranged morning activities for the mine staff, and Alex and Dan were free until they helped serve morning tea at eleven o'clock. Lunch would follow at half-past twelve and the afternoon activities an hour later.

This was when Alex and Dan would take over, presenting the pre-arranged activities that must satisfy the campers. Dan had been worrying about it all morning, and by lunchtime, he was positively shaking in his boots.

There were 30 campers and four different activities, so Paul had already divided them into groups of seven or eight.

When the campers gathered after lunch, Alex announced the groups and explained the goals of the different activities. Each group would be awarded points based on how well its members performed each activity.

Alex and Dan had already checked the written instructions and set up the equipment, and Nathan and Tanya were on hand to supervise the remaining two activities.

Dan was very impressed by the cool and relaxed way in which Alex went about his work and noticed how the campers responded to his friendly attitude.

The competition between the groups was stiff, but it was clear that everyone was enjoying themselves greatly. By the time Belinda arrived with the afternoon tea on a trolley, the shouts and laughs of the mine staff had convinced Dan that the camp had started well.

Chapter 26

A Quick Visit

By Wednesday, Dan was familiar with the daily rhythm of the camp. Morning activities were run by Paul and other mine staff who travelled to the camp as necessary to train the campers in technical and operational matters. Alex and he arranged and ran the afternoon activities, and it was obvious that the campers were enjoying them. The weather was not too hot, and the campers made many approving comments about the food and the camp facilities.

On Wednesday evening, Paul told Nathan that mine management had approved his proposal to run another training camp for staff who had joined since this camp was planned. It was wonderful news, and Alex and the Turners were particularly pleased for Steve and Sylvia, who were to arrive in just a few days.

Thursday, however, was the day Dan and Alex were waiting for. They were determined to disrupt Brad's plans for the expected shipment.

After morning tea, they went to the equipment shed to get what they needed for the afternoon. Since they couldn't visit Heatherlie Quarry, team sports would be held at the camp site instead.

No sooner did they reach the equipment shed, safely away from the others, than Dan burst out with the question that was uppermost in his mind: "How can we get to Heatherlie tonight without Mum and Dad knowing?"

"A secret delivery is sure to happen after dark," said Alex, "but if we ride there in the dark, someone might notice our headlamps."

"And we couldn't ride without lights – there's not much moon at the moment. Let's ride there after dinner before it gets dark."

"What about your parents?"

"And what about me?" said a voice behind them.

The boys turned quickly and found Belinda standing in the doorway of the equipment shed.

"What are you doing there?" asked Dan, irritated.

"Listening to your deep-laid plans, Danny-boy."

"Why don't you make some of your own?" grumbled Dan, quickly replaying what Alex and he had said. How much had Belinda heard? Heatherlie. Dark. Secret delivery. Or had she been eavesdropping on Sunday evening too, in which case she already knew it all?

"We're just going to watch a special delivery of... ah... gravel at Heatherlie," he said lamely.

Alex looked doubtful, but Belinda responded, "You sure are! That special delivery must be...."

"Shush!" hissed Dan, hurriedly. "Here come Mum and Dad!"

His warning was barely in time. Nathan and Tanya were almost upon them.

"Ah, you three," said Nathan, "just the people we wanted to talk to. Can you come to the office?"

Dan, Alex and Belinda exchanged glances and agreed.

Once they were in the office, Nathan began, "We've been thinking about what Brad Jessop might have to do with the thefts from the mine and what's going on at Heatherlie. We think Brad must be hiding the high grade ore there, so we wondered whether you could have a look around with your drone, Dan. What do you think?"

Dan's mouth fell open. How could his parents have grasped the situation so clearly? Their conjecture that Brad had hidden the ore at Heatherlie hadn't occurred to him at all. Yet now that the suggestion had been made, he suddenly knew that it was wrong.

"The delivery tonight," he blurted out, turning to Alex, "it must be the stolen high grade ore from the mine!"

"Well, of course," said Alex and Belinda together, looking at him as if he were stating the obvious.

Dan looked around at them all. Everyone else seemed to have solved the mystery of the missing ore already – yet he had only worked it out when they gave him a hint! So much for solving the mystery himself!

He must be stupid, he thought in disgust. The suggestion that he could use his drone let him push the thoughts aside, so he said eagerly, "I could go there with the drone now."

"Can't we leave it until after the camp finishes tomorrow?" asked Nathan, puzzled.

"I don't think so," said Dan. "They're expecting a delivery tonight, and it's probably the ore."

"Dan and I agree it probably won't arrive until after dark," added Alex.

"But if we fly the drone over now, we could see if they've done anything to the buildings or finished digging a hole for the ore," finished Dan.

"How do you know about this delivery and their plans to hide something?" asked Tanya, frowning.

"That's what I was about to ask," said Nathan.

"Alex and Dan went back to Heatherlie Quarry last Saturday afternoon and heard the bad guys chatting," said Belinda.

"So you *did* hear that!" said Dan angrily. "Is there nowhere you don't eavesdrop?"

"I went to the games room to get a hymn book but stubbed my toe on the step, so I sat down and gave it a good rub. Then I heard you and Alex talking. I wasn't trying to eavesdrop, but you weren't listening or you would've heard me kicking the step – and you didn't try to keep your voices down either. Really, you should be more careful. To be honest, Danny-boy, if you don't start taking more care, you're going to get yourself, and maybe us, in serious trouble!"

"You should stand taller as you lecture him," laughed Tanya, "and wag your finger at him like a know-all old maid teacher. I had one when I was young and you sound quite a lot like her."

"But it's true," protested Belinda.

"Perhaps," said her father, "but it's also true that listening to conversations that aren't intended for you won't make you popular."

"I suppose Belinda's sort of right, though," said Dan, grudgingly. "So I'll try to be more careful. If Alex drives us there in his car, we should be back in plenty of time for the afternoon activities."

"I'd prefer it if your mother and I did the investigating," said Nathan, "but we're not as good with the drone as you are."

"Can I come too?" asked Belinda.

"Yes," said Alex, "but who will you listen to afterwards if you already know what Dan and I have been doing?"

"Sorry, Alex," said Belinda.

They set off a few minutes later, after collecting Dan's drone, the controller and two spare batteries. Dan looked at the maps again as they travelled. As they passed the track to Heatherlie, he said, "Keep going another 300 metres or so and turn right onto a short track. It has a small turning area at the end where we can park."

Alex soon found the track and drove to the end where he turned around and parked, ready to leave in a hurry if necessary.

"I can fly the drone from here," said Dan as he climbed out of the car. "I think we're about a kilometre from the houses at the quarry, and the camera will show us what's going on."

Quickly Dan made sure everything was working properly, then the drone was away, flying almost silently towards the quarry. Many retrieved golf balls and disc golf discs had paid for the latest in super-quiet rotors and a good quality camera on the drone. Dan was confident he could record high quality video from above without anyone suspecting they were being watched. On the video screen of Dan's controller, the three of them could see the backhoe of the front-end loader digging a hole between two of the houses.

"How much ore will they have to bury?" asked Belinda.

"A few tonnes, I guess," said Alex.

"Would they just drop it in the hole?" asked Belinda.

"Not even they would be that stupid," snorted Dan. "There's not much point in getting high grade ore and mixing it with dirt!"

"I see five people standing near the hole," said Alex. "I wonder how many others there are? I didn't see any cars in the carpark as we drove past, so where *are* they parked?"

Dan steered the drone back along the track where the railway line had once been and they looked carefully at the place where it met the track that led down to the carpark, trying to see if there was any guard as there had been when Dan had almost tripped over him last time.

"There he is!" Dan pointed to the screen.

"Yes," said Alex. "That's six."

"And one using the digger," said Belinda. "Seven."

Dan flew the drone down towards the carpark and they saw another two guards down near the historical information sign where two cars were parked just off the track.

"So that makes nine," said Alex.

"Plus the men who make the delivery," said Dan.

"And probably a few others, just to see the show," said Belinda.

"Which means about 15 to 20 men altogether," said Alex.

"How can just a few of us stop them?" asked Dan.

"We could let them bury the ore and get the police to dig it up later," said Alex.

"Maybe we could get the police to catch them red-handed tonight!" said Belinda, excitedly.

"The police?" asked Dan, snorting again. "Can't we look after it ourselves?"

"What, like you managed to keep me from hearing your secrets?" asked Belinda.

Dan felt hurt. He turned back to his controller and flew the drone back to them, landing it gently on the sandy track. He picked it up.

"Sorry, Dan, I didn't mean to be nasty," said Belinda. "I'm just worried that if we try to deal with the crooks ourselves, someone will get hurt. Let's get the police."

"How?" asked Dan, sarcastically. "Ring them?"

"Yes, why not.... Oh. I still can't get used to not being able to use our phones!"

"But they do work sometimes," said Alex, pulling out his phone. "Look, I've got a signal now! I'll try ringing Dad." He called the number but got a recorded message saying: "No service."

"I'll try mine," said Dan, pulling it out of his pocket. "I've got a good signal too. What's your Dad's number?" Alex gave him the number, but Dan got the same response.

"Maybe it's a problem with Dad's number," said Alex. "Can I ring you, Dan?" Dan gave him the number, but the result was just the same.

They tried various numbers, but the same disembodied voice answered every call.

"And we're not getting missed call messages either," said Dan. "It's as if we're trying to connect through the wrong network."

"It looks like we'll have to go to Stawell if we want to tell the police," said Alex.

"I don't think we've got time," said Dan. "We need to get back to the camp now or we won't be ready for the afternoon activities."

"You're right," said Alex. "Let's put the drone in the boot and head back. Maybe we could show the video to the police. Digging in the old National Park should pique their interest."

Alex opened the boot and they packed the drone away. Belinda stood at the door of the car, obviously thinking. As Alex shut the boot, she said, "You know, I've been thinking about..."

"Yes, yes, yes," interrupted Dan, loudly, "you're always thinking about the different places we could visit in the Grampians, but you seem to have got this one wrong. This can't be Heatherlie Quarry. We've looked all around the place and there's no quarry, no stone houses, no signs, nothing!"

"You're right," said Alex. "Let's go."

For a moment, Belinda looked from one to the other in bewilderment, then suddenly she seemed to pick up a warning.

"I suppose so..." she said.

"What are you kids doing here?" asked a harsh voice behind her.

Belinda turned and saw two men dressed in camouflage outfits with fluorescent vests standing close enough to have heard every word she said.

"We came to look around Heatherlie Quarry," said Alex calmly.

"You can't," said one of the men, "it's closed."

"We didn't see any sign saying that," said Dan.

"Well, you won't see any signs here – this isn't the right track for Heatherlie Quarry! Say, have you kids seen anyone flying a drone around here?"

"We haven't met anyone flying a drone," said Dan truthfully.

"I did *hear* a drone a few minutes ago," said Alex, "but I can't hear it now."

"Okay. We'll keep looking. But Heatherlie Quarry is closed, so you kids might as well go home."

"When it will be open again?" asked Belinda.

"No set date, but we should be finished by next Tuesday."

"Finished what?" asked Dan. "You didn't say why it's closed."

"Maintenance – improving some paths and fixing up the area around the old stone houses."

"Then we can see the place if we come back in a week or so?" asked Dan.

"Yeah, sure," said the man, smirking at his mate.

"And we'll check the map again," said Alex.

Dan, Belinda and Alex got into the car and Alex drove thankfully away.

"Whew!" said Belinda. "That was close."

Dan agreed. He was tempted to remind Belinda of her lecture, but Alex caught his eye and shook his head slightly. Dan took the hint. "Did we learn anything new?" he asked instead.

"We learned that they're moving quickly," said Alex. "They plan to bury the ore and take away whatever they have in the houses in the next few days: five at the most."

"And I learned that even super-silent drones are still noisy enough to get you into trouble," said Dan. "I suppose there's less background noise in the country."

Back at the camp, they were about to get out of the car when Belinda said, "I'm sorry I almost got us into trouble back there, particularly after what I said about you two not being careful! Thanks for not rubbing it in."

❧

Dan couldn't concentrate on the sporting activities that afternoon. The first activity involved him giving some simple archery lessons and supervising a short competition. It was just the sort of thing he loved, but he was distracted by the question of what to do after the activities finished.

When the campers swapped activities, he checked his phone and saw that he had coverage. He rang Alex's phone, but received the now-familiar, "No service."

One of the men from the mine was standing nearby and noticed his frustration when the call failed.

"No coverage? It's not like the old days, is it?"

"Oh, there's coverage, but the call won't go through. It just says, 'No service.' "

"Okay. That sounds like a network access problem. Have you changed carrier recently?"

"No."

"Hmm. Perhaps you should contact your carrier."

"It's funny – when we first came here, there was never any coverage, so we got used to it. Now there's coverage, but it doesn't work!"

"Maybe they've restarted some of the towers but made configuration changes." The man paused, then said, "Look, Dan, I'm Glen. I do a lot of communications work for the mine, but I used to work for a telco, so I know a lot about mobile phone services." As he spoke, he took his own mobile phone out of his pocket and looked at it. "Signal strength looks fine. What's your number?" Dan gave him his number and he tried to ring. Dan could hear the voice from the phone, "No service."

Glen confirmed Dan's carrier, then started tinkering with the configuration of his own phone. It made no difference. "For some reason, the network thinks our SIMs are not authorised to use it – I'm sure it's a configuration problem. Strange."

"Is it a problem with the tower?"

"It could be. Really, I'm surprised there's *any* signal. The two remaining carriers switched off all the towers around here." He pursed his lips. "I think I'll talk to some friends in Stawell and Horsham after the camp finishes."

⌘

When the afternoon activities finally finished, Dan and Alex went to see Nathan. Belinda had already told him what had happened at Heatherlie, and he was only waiting for Alex to finish before going to Stawell and telling the police all they knew.

"I need you to stay here at the camp, Dan," said Nathan. "You can help Mum and Belinda prepare and serve dinner."

"But..." objected Dan.

"Alex and I will talk to the police and hurry back. Brad and his men will be at Heatherlie tonight while somebody makes a delivery, and there aren't enough of us to interfere. Maybe we don't need to, though. If they're just delivering the ore and burying it, I guess we can leave it to the police to dig it up whenever they're ready."

"But what if they're doing something else as well? Something we *do* need to know about?" asked Dan.

"Let's wait and see what the police say."

"Do you really think they'll tell us what they plan to do?"

"I hope so, but probably not."

"Then how does it help to wait for their answers?"

"There's a chance they will, and it can't hurt to wait. Anyway, you know we need their help to bring these thieves to justice! If they don't, this gang will only get more confident, and have more money to fund their operations."

Chapter 27

A Surprise

As Dan was helping to clean up the tables after dinner, Glen approached him.

"I've been thinking about that comms problem," he said. "And the more I think about it, the more I wonder if someone has hijacked the network. There's been no news of the telcos reinstating mobile coverage, so that seems unlikely. With fewer people travelling around, and the regions still trying to get re-organised after Spring Street[2] dumped us, it's much easier for people to act outside the law. The towers were physically turned off, so someone must've broken in and turned them on again. If they knew what they were doing and had some special equipment, they could easily make the necessary changes to the tower config. I reckon I could do it myself."

---

[2] Spring Street in Melbourne is the location of the Victorian Parliament buildings, built with stone from Heatherlie Quarry.

"What would be the point?" asked Dan.

"It's an easy way to get a private communications network by locking out everyone except a few select users. Their phones would just work, but nothing would work for anyone else."

"Do you really think someone's done that?"

"I don't know. Let's ask about everyone's coverage now and see if anyone else can get through."

Most people still carried their phones with them from force of habit even though there was rarely any coverage outside the towns. Since quite a few campers were still chatting in the meal hall, Glen called out and asked people to ring his number. Everyone tried ringing Glen. As Glen expected, those using the alternative carrier had no coverage at all. Those on the same network as Dan and Glen all reported the "No service" message – except for one woman. When she rang Glen's number, there was the normal delay of a few seconds and then his phone rang.

He picked up the call, and said, "Miranda, can you hear me through the phone?"

"Yes," she answered, giggling.

"I'll hang up and try to ring you back," he said. Swiftly he did so, only to be greeted by the usual message.

"It doesn't work," he announced, putting down his phone. "Well, thanks, Miranda."

Glen turned back to Dan. "Let's go outside and see how things work out there."

Deciding that cleaning up could wait a few minutes, Dan followed Glen.

Once they were out of earshot, Glen said quietly, "Miranda's our new receptionist. If her call got through, she must be on the approved list."

"Why? She doesn't look like a dangerous criminal."

"No, but she is one thing that might be important. Do you know Brad Jessop?"

"Yes. He's head of the fake National Park Committee."

"He's been a troublemaker for years. Miranda is his youngest sister."

"So you reckon Brad Jessop has taken over the network?"

"That seems logical. We're not far from the Hollow Mountain exchange and tower – let's go and check for evidence of a break-in. I've worked there before, so I know the place."

Dan was in a quandary. Dad was relying on him being on site to help Mum and Belinda. But this was an important clue and could show what the men he'd seen from Mount Stapylton had been doing. What should he do?

Chapter 28

Hollow Mountain Exchange

Greg pulled the door to so that it appeared locked – the same position as they had found it.

"Okay, what are you fellas doing here?" asked a voice from behind. Dan spun around, sure that he recognised the voice but unable to place the owner. Two figures stood behind them, but the first thing he registered was a gun, pointed at the ground but obviously ready for use.

"Dan!" – another voice he recognised. Yet surely that was impossible?

"Dave?" he said tentatively.

"Hey, it's Dan," said the man holding the gun, and Dan suddenly realised who he was.

"Everyone seems to know *you*, Dan, but who are they?" asked Glen.

"Dave is my cousin," said Dan, smiling at Dave and patting him on the shoulder, "and Fergus is... do you mind if I say what you are, Fergus?"

"I'm a special agent of the Victorian Police Force," said Fergus, pocketing the gun. "Brad and his men are implicated in a few crimes I'm trying to solve."

"And this is Glen," said Dan, completing the introductions. "He works for the Stawell Gold Mine, and we're investigating how Brad Jessop got himself a private communication network. Apparently his men have hacked the exchange here – and probably all the towers in the National Park."

"That's clever," said Fergus. "Surprisingly so."

"Hey, Fergus, did you know that Brad has a sister?" asked Dan.

"Yes, but we don't think she's involved in any of his shenanigans."

"She's linked in to their private network!"

"Is she?" frowned Fergus. "Interesting."

Dan turned to Dave. "It's great to see you, Dave."

"And you," replied Dave. "It's been years. You really have grown!"

"Why aren't you in Adelaide?"

"We left Adelaide in a hurry," answered Dave, "and we won't be going back in any time soon."

"*We?*"

"Yes. Mum and Dad brought me, and Grandpa and Grandma Turner came too. It's a long story."

"How did you meet Fergus?"

"He was camped in Mount Stapylton Campground when we stopped for lunch, and after we'd chatted for a while, he said that he knew you."

"I told them where you were staying," said Fergus, "and they offered me a lift to Roses Gap."

"When Fergus spotted a car parked at the exchange, he asked us to stop and we walked back here together. That's when I found out he was a policeman."

Dan wondered why Fergus cared about a parked car, but before he could ask, Fergus spoke up.

"Anything else to do here?"

"No," chorused Glen and Dan.

"Then why don't we head for Roses Gap? If we're welcome, that is?"

"Of course," said Dan. "You're all very welcome! There's a camp on at the moment – that's why Glen's with us – but I'm sure we can still fit everyone. I'll need to explain a few things once we see my Dad and Alex."

"Who's Alex?"

"Terry and Linda Holland's son, from Stawell."

"Ah. I've... heard of Terry. He's a bank manager in Stawell, isn't he?"

"Yes – and a close friend of the owners of the camp."

Fergus digested this information, but as he seemed about to respond, Glen said, "Let's head back to the camp before it gets dark."

"Good idea," said Fergus.

They gave Dave a lift back to his family's four-wheel drive, and Dan briefly greeted his uncle and aunt and his grandparents. Glen then drove Dan and Fergus carefully back to Roses Gap, watching out for kangaroos and wallabies in the gathering dusk. Dan caught up with Fergus' last eleven days, and Fergus pumped Dan for information.

Dan told what he could in Glen's presence. Fergus obviously understood and avoided asking difficult questions or giving away unnecessary information.

At the first opportunity, Glen brought up the subverted network. His examination of the equipment in the exchange had shown that the tower had indeed been hacked so that it was only available to a list of about a hundred numbers. Fergus said that this confirmed his estimate of how many people were involved in Brad Jessop's operation.

It was almost dark when the two vehicles drove into the Roses Gap campsite. They all climbed out and Glen quickly excused himself.

Fergus watched him go. "I should follow his polite example, but I won't, if you don't mind. I have a feeling this is urgent. Am I right?"

"Yes, I think so," Dan answered cautiously.

"Lead me to your parents, then. Actually, take your family. I'll follow in a few minutes."

Accordingly, Dan led the way into the residence attached to the office. "Dad! Mum!" he called.

"Dan," came his father's stern voice. "Where have you been?"

He walked into the kitchen and saw his parents sitting at the table with Alex, while Belinda was curled up in a chair nearby, reading.

"At the Hollow Mountain Exchange with Glen," said Dan, "and guess who I met?"

"Who... Mick!" Suddenly seeing his brother a few steps behind Dan, Nathan ran to greet him.

"And Robyn," said Tanya, greeting her sister-in-law warmly.

"And Dave," said Belinda as Dave followed his mother into the room. Before anyone else could move, two older people also entered the room, smiling.

"Mum and Dad!" said Nathan, excitedly. "What a lovely surprise!"

After several years of lockdowns and travel restrictions, it was a joyous reunion. Everyone soon found somewhere to sit, and conversation ran freely.

Dan was introducing Dave to Alex when Fergus walked in quietly and joined them.

No-one else seemed to notice.

As the main conversation turned to their life at the camp, Tanya suddenly stood up and invited Dave's family to see their living quarters. Almost everyone rose and trooped out of the kitchen.

Dan, Dave, Alex and Fergus remained.

"Let's go into the office," said Dan, motioning with his hand in the other direction.

CR

Dan led the way into the office and closed the door behind them.

"I'm Fergus Norton," said Fergus, holding out his hand to Alex.

"Fergus Norton? I'm sure I've heard that name before," said Alex, looking thoughtful. "Do I know you?"

Fergus smiled. "No. I'm what you might call the black sheep of the family. Your father is my cousin, but I haven't been part of the family for years."

"Ah, yes. Well, if you're the black sheep, sir, you're the black sheep they speak of admiringly in hushed whispers."

"Perhaps not a black sheep, then, but definitely one who chose a different path from the rest of the family."

"There certainly aren't any other police marksmen in the family."

"Well, I'm not a marksman any more, Alex. I'm a special agent working on assignments arising from governmental responses to COVID-19. The breakdown of the commonwealth, the separation of the states, and states excising margins from within their boundaries have left no consistent police cover across the country. Jurisdiction can sometimes be hard to define."

"I suppose so," said Alex.

"This may well be my last assignment, anyway, so I need to get on with it. Dan said you went to see the police in Stawell this afternoon. What happened?"

"Nathan and I went to see the police and told them about some sort of delivery Brad's men are making to Heatherlie Quarry tonight. They didn't really believe us, though – or wouldn't admit that they did. All they said was to 'stay home and leave it all to them'," he finished in disgust.

"You should always listen to police advice, young man," said Fergus with a twinkle.

"And let Brad get away with whatever it is he plans to do?"

"Don't forget, Alex, that while Brad doesn't seem a dangerous man, some of the things going on around him are very dangerous indeed. Some of his men love violence, and then there's the question of NK2."

"I think I've worked out..." said Dan.

"What's NK2?" interrupted Dave.

"A new version of Ned Kelly and his gang," answered Dan.

"A *dangerous* new version," insisted Fergus.

Dan explained to Dave, "A bloke called Brad Jessop leads a gang around here that's taking over the old Grampians National Park, charging fees for entry or using walking tracks, and for maintenance – which they never do."

"And they're also stealing ore from the Stawell Gold Mine," said Alex. "The police didn't seem to believe us on that one either."

"And some of us wonder about a connection between Brad Jessop and NK2," said Fergus.

"If Brad is NK2, then he's much more dangerous than he seems," said Alex. "NK2 has carried out several violent robberies."

"So we need to be careful tonight," said Fergus. "It'd be best if you kids stayed here."

"I'm no kid!" protested Alex. "And you wouldn't know about this delivery if we hadn't told you about it. We've gone to Heatherlie three times and found out lots. We want to solve the puzzle and stop the crooks."

"These men are armed and dangerous," argued Fergus.

"We know they're armed," objected Dan, "but if we don't come with you, you won't have any transport, and you won't know where to go or who's there."

"Okay," said Fergus, "you win, but only because I don't know anything about Heatherlie. I don't want you involved up close. What would your parents think, Alex?"

"They don't need to know about it," said Alex, "but let's get going. We may be missing the action!"

Chapter 29

That Night

The four moved quickly to the parking area and climbed into Alex's car, Fergus in the front and Dan and Dave behind. As Alex drove off, he asked, "Should we go back to the same parking area as this morning, Dan?"

"I wonder if it's safe," pondered Dan. "After all, we met those two guards there."

"Good point. Well, I noticed there was a 4WD track almost directly opposite the track to the quarry. I don't know what condition it's in, but we could probably park a short distance along it. That might be safer."

"Could be – let's go there."

By that time, they were out on the Roses Gap Road, heading towards the road to Halls Gap. As they neared the intersection, they saw lights approaching along the Roses Gap Road.

"Hello," said Fergus, "who's out driving this late?"

"It may be connected with the delivery to Heatherlie," said Dan, excitedly.

"In which case we don't want to be in front of them," said Fergus, as Alex slowed down to turn right towards Heatherlie. "Don't turn, Alex. Keep going along this road for a while instead."

Alex accelerated again and continued along the Roses Gap Road as the other vehicle passed them. They couldn't see much of it except that it was a four-wheel drive, probably white.

"I *think* the driver was the only person in it," said Dave.

"I agree," said Dan.

"And now it's turning off towards Heatherlie," said Fergus, looking back. "Okay, it's gone. Let's do a U-turn and follow them, Alex, but don't get too close. It may not be any of Brad's men, but if it is, we don't want them to know anyone's following them."

Finding a safe place, Alex turned the car around and drove back to the intersection. By the time they reached it, the 4WD must have been two or three kilometres ahead. Alex followed carefully, the gravel road showing no sign of any car in front except for the dust in the air.

Alex didn't hurry. If the other driver planned to stop at Heatherlie, they wanted him well and truly off the road and up at the quarry with his comrades before they arrived.

"We're nearly there," said Dan after a while, and Alex slowed down even more. A bush night is full of countless bird, animal and other noises, but man-made sounds carry a long way on a windless evening.

This evening was particularly still. Not a breath of wind moved the trees, and dust raised by previous cars hung lazily in the air over the road. Alex turned left onto the rough four-wheel drive track and cautiously picked his way along, looking for somewhere to hide the car. After about 50 metres, they saw a gap in the bush that looked good enough in the dark. Alex steered the car in and switched off the engine, leaving the car far enough into the bush to be invisible from the main road.

"Can you make sure the lights in the cabin don't turn on when we open the doors?" asked Fergus. "It might be important when we come back."

Alex fumbled around and did as Fergus requested.

They opened the doors and climbed quietly out into the still darkness of the night. Each held a torch, but they kept them pointing towards the ground. Flashes of light can be seen from a long way away and they didn't want to advertise their presence to Brad and his men.

"Listen," said Dave. "Engines running."

They stood still and listened to the low rumble of large diesel engines in the distance.

"Is that the delivery trucks or the front-end loader moving earth?" asked Alex.

"Probably both," drawled a voice. All four spun around and shone their torches on a tall, thickset man standing on the track a little beyond their parking spot. "Brad said the delivery arrived just before dark, so I hurried back from up north." The man gestured over his shoulder with his thumb. "I'm parked a bit further down."

With a sudden shock, Dan recognised Craig, the bullying thug he had seen with Darren at Beehive Falls and heard spoken of with fear by the gang members at Heatherlie. He wondered if Alex had recognised the man who had threatened him at the Beehive Falls carpark.

"Let's go up and join the rest," said Craig, obviously mistaking them for gang members.

"Sure," said Fergus, and they followed Craig.

They emerged from beneath the arch of trees onto the Mount Zero Road, and Dan noticed a delicate sliver of moon edging its way down behind the inky black silhouette of the mountain range in the west. Directly above, the Milky Way formed a vast river of stars across the sky, even the darkest areas scattered with swarms of pale blue-white dots. The warmth of the summer evening accentuated the stillness as branches and leaves hung silent and unmoving.

Had one been relaxing in the midst of a carefree camping holiday, the serene beauty of the night would have first triggered then satisfied the innate human yearning for beauty in its most delicate form. It was a flawless display of the creator's love of beauty, shared freely with any who might attend.

Yet for Dan and his friends, the night was filled with malevolent danger, and a very real part of that danger – Craig – was walking with them, sounding almost friendly as he reflected on the gang's success in snagging the most valuable ore the mine had ever produced. He even stopped in the middle of the road to laugh, deriding mine management's futile attempts to track down the thieves. "Do you blokes know any of our men at the mine who pulled it off?" he asked.

"No," they all answered together.

"They did a good job, I can tell you, and so did the lovely Miranda who made sure the work records were confused enough that no individuals could be held responsible. In fact, they couldn't even be sure a theft had taken place at all! It's pretty well the perfect crime, isn't it? You're part of a pretty good outfit, right?"

There was an awkward pause, but Craig didn't notice. Perhaps he didn't really expect an answer; perhaps he was thinking of the lovely Miranda. Whatever the reason, he changed the subject. "Look, Brad should be arriving in a few minutes. I'll wait for him here."

"Okay," said Fergus. "Can I ask a question?"

"Sure." To Dan's ear, Craig sounded rather pleased with himself.

"Who came up with the plan for stealing the ore?"

"NK2, I believe," answered Craig, a smirk in his voice.

"You mean Brad?"

Craig laughed. "Haven't you heard Brad deny it before?"

"I'm just getting mixed messages about NK2 in the gang," said Fergus. "Some proudly say they're NK2-ers, while others deny it. It's the same with Brad. Do you know the truth?"

"It's called deliberate obscurity. What happened to Ned Kelly?"

"He was hanged."

"That's not what I meant," said Craig, and for a moment his drawling voice held irritation. "No, he was so famous he couldn't stay hidden, and that's why he was doomed – everyone ganged up on him. NK2 is different. He's famous, alright: everyone's heard of him, right across Victoria, to the margins and beyond. But no-one can say what he looks like. Nobody's sure where he lives, who his gang is or anything much about him. All they know is that he steals what he wants and it's dangerous to resist him."

By the end of this speech, any hint of anger in Craig's voice had changed to admiration.

"But there seem to be a few groups claiming to be NK2-ers," said Fergus. "Some of Brad's men here, a group over beyond the eastern margin, one beyond the northern margin, and even one inside Victoria."

"Brilliant, isn't it?" said Craig. "Magicians call it 'misdirection'. The police don't know where to look, and robberies keep happening everywhere."

"So do *you* think Brad is NK2?" asked Fergus. "He's smart enough, isn't he?"

Dan wondered what game Fergus was playing. When he'd first met him at the Troopers Creek campground, Fergus had declared Brad not violent or brutal enough to be NK2, yet now he was suggesting he *was* NK2!

Craig snorted. "Brad? Look, Brad's a great guy – after all, you all follow him and do what he tells you. But Brad as NK2?" He snorted again.

"So who is?" asked Fergus, puzzlement in his voice.

"Hmm. Maybe we'll just have to wait and see."

No-one spoke for a few moments, and Dan heard the sound of an approaching car above the diesel engines up near the quarry.

Craig heard it too. "That must be Brad," he said. "I'll have a chat with him when he arrives. You lads head up to the houses and we'll see you there."

Remembering that Fergus didn't know the place at all, Dan led the way up the track, his torch pointing to the ground with his hand blocking most of its light. The others followed, and within a few steps the faint starlight was swallowed up by the blackness under the trees. As the sound of a car grew louder, Fergus asked in an urgent undertone, "Where will Brad stop? I want to hear what those two say, but Brad mustn't see me – he'd recognise me. Does he know any of you?"

"Yes," answered Dan and Alex together.

"And Craig mustn't see Alex either," said Dan, turning off his torch.

"No," agreed Alex. "He might recognise me too."

"Who's Craig?"

"The man we were just talking to," whispered Dan.

"Ah. I didn't know his name. Well, *he'd* better not see me properly either."

"They'll probably use the carpark. It's just here."

They hurried into the carpark as the car slowed down and stopped out on the road. The diffused light from the headlights showed Dan that eight cars already filled the small carpark, leaving no empty spaces.

"Hi Brad," they heard Craig say, but the driver's response was inaudible.

"Okay, just drive into the carpark," said Craig after a few moments.

Dan and the others hurriedly ducked behind various cars while Brad turned off the road and followed the track the short distance to the carpark. Seeing that there were no free spots, he stopped in the middle of the carpark. He turned off the car, but left the parking lights on as he climbed out. Dan couldn't see him from where he was hiding, but he recognised Brad's distressed voice as the man asked, "Why did you kill Darren, Craig? Hasn't there been enough violence without that?"

"He was going to rat on me," growled Craig. "He withdrew all his money from the bank and was going to the police when I met him. Thankfully, I worked it all out before he got there. I've been worried about him for a while."

"Darren wouldn't have ratted on us. He was too scared."

"Why else would he pull out all his money?"

"Probably because he was afraid the police would take it all away from him. Haven't you heard him saying that?"

"He was a fool and a coward. I've often told him what he deserved."

"You probably drove him to it."

"Why was he going to the police station, then?"

"How do you know he was?"

"He was walking down Patrick Street straight towards it. And he looked guilty when he saw me."

"He was probably just *scared* of you. Novel idea, hey?" asked Brad, sarcastically. "But remember the police talked to me recently? They wanted me to fill out a form, so I asked Darren to go to the Magistrates Court to collect it for me. Remember where the court is?"

It was too dark to see whether Craig looked guilty or not, but no hint of guilt found its way into his voice. "Next to the police station."

"Exactly. So you murdered him for doing just what I asked him to do."

"Oh, he deserved it. Anyway, at least we'll get some value out of his death. I left the body where the police will find it, with some hand-written notes that will bring them here – after we've booby-trapped the place."

"Still trying to kill policemen, too, Craig?"

"I've got scores to settle."

"I know, I know," said Brad, sarcastic again. "Sergeant Smith gave you a hard time when you were a trainee criminal, and Corporal Jones stole your first girlfriend."

"Shut up, you fool!" snarled Craig. There was a brief scuffle and Brad let out a cry of pain. "Don't forget you're only leader here because I want you to be. You could never run an outfit like this by yourself!"

He pushed Brad away contemptuously and Brad staggered back against the bonnet of the car Dan was hiding behind.

"I'm *so* close to my first major triumph," said Craig, "and half-wits like you and Darren start causing trouble." He stepped forward and grabbed Brad by the front of his shirt, pulling him forward as he said through clenched teeth, "Now, who told you I killed Darren?"

"Harry, of course. You knew I was going to get the toolbox from him. And you were... you were *stupid* enough to get him to help you with the body. Do you know..."

Craig swore and flung Brad backwards against the car so that he fell onto the bonnet. Brad lay there, gasping for breath. "You fool... Craig... do you... what do you know about Harry?"

"What do you mean?"

"*He's Darren's brother!*"

"You're kidding!"

"You got Harry to help you chuck a body in the dumpster last night. Then, just as you left, you told him who it was. And you didn't even know that he would care!"

Having recovered his breath, Brad slid off the bonnet and stood up, straightening his shirt. "You've always needed me, Craig. I treat the men like people, and you don't know how to."

Craig didn't answer for several seconds, then said slowly, "So what do you think he'll do?"

"I don't know," said Brad.

"Well, we'd better get going anyway," said Craig. "Did you bring the toolbox?"

"Yes. Harry gave it to me because we're friends, but he almost refused. He certainly didn't want to help you!"

"Ah well. It can't be helped now."

"And why did you put the body in the dumpster at the mine? That's madness. I don't want anyone associating my men with the mine!"

"Don't worry. I put a notebook in his pocket with notes about how he planned the ore robbery."

"But when will they find the body?"

"Since the theft, mine management have been inspecting the dumpsters before they're emptied, and they get emptied tomorrow morning. So they'll look tomorrow morning, and the police will be here a few hours later. They'll dig up the ore we've buried and Harry's masterpiece will blow them all sky-high. By then, we'll be long gone with the loot."

"That's what Darren was hanging out for."

"Don't mention Darren again," said Craig, a chilling menace in his voice. "Let's go and see how the boys are going with the ore."

"It's getting late," said Brad. "Let's drive up there."

The two men climbed into Brad's car and Dan and the others made sure they were well hidden from the anticipated light. Brad backed the car out of the carpark and drove off up the track towards the quarry.

"Well, we all heard a clear confession of murder there, and a few other crimes too," said Fergus grimly. "Let's follow them, but don't use your torches. Dan and Alex, can you lead without any light? I'll use my torch carefully if I have to. How far is it?"

"About 500 metres," said Dan, leading the way with Alex.

"How could he murder his friend like that?" he whispered.

"Do people like Craig have friends?"

As they picked their way carefully towards the quarry site, Dan wondered what Fergus was planning to do. The noise of the diesel engines increased as they approached, and finally Dan saw light ahead of them through the trees.

Dan and Alex expected to find guards watching the track, and so it proved – but conditions gave the friends an unexpected advantage. The irritating, insistent sound of the front end loader's warning beeper easily covered any small noises they made, and its garish flashing light threw quick-moving shadows across the bush, rendering the guards' job of keeping watch even more difficult.

Not only so, but Brad's four-wheel drive and a tray truck stacked with barrels were parked at the intersection, providing convenient cover. Dan and Alex crept past Brad's car, then made their way safely around the corner, hidden by the truck. Fergus and Dave followed, and they all edged their way along the curving track. After about ten metres, the track had curved enough that they would have been invisible from the intersection, even if the truck had not been there.

As they moved closer to the open area that surrounded the old stone cottages built by the quarrymen, voices occasionally became audible above the noise of equipment.

Dan reached the next corner and crouched down behind the bushes close to the table where Brad had spoken to his men by radio. Alex crouched beside him, and Fergus and Dave soon joined them. Not far from the bushes, a trailer with floodlights lit the open area in front of them.

It seemed that they were just in time. Two blue barrels stood near the hole between two of the cottages, and as they watched, the front end loader picked up one of them and lowered it into the hole.

"Those must be the last ones they're burying," whispered Dan.

"What's in them?" asked Dave.

"Ore stolen from the mine," answered Alex.

The front end loader picked up the final barrel and turned to place it in the hole.

"Look, there are Brad and Craig," said Dan.

Brad and Craig stood on the far side of the hole with a large toolbox between them. As soon as the last barrel was lowered into place, Craig signalled to the driver of the front end loader, who immediately moved the bucket near to one edge of the hole and about a metre below ground level, then turned off the engine. A sudden silence fell and the driver climbed down out of his cabin.

"Now for Harry's masterpiece," said Craig. "I'll put it on the barrels and then I'll set it." He picked up the toolbox, and the watchers could see the letters 'SJ' painted on the side.

"That's Steve Jones' stolen toolbox," whispered Alex urgently.

Using the bucket of the front end loader as a step, Craig disappeared into the hole. To Dan's surprise, Brad immediately hurried away from the edge of the hole and signalled urgently to his men to do the same. They began to follow his instruction, but in moving back from the hole, two of them walked straight towards the friends' hiding place! Dan turned to flee down the track, but Fergus was right behind him. There was nowhere to go.

Suddenly, everything happened at once. A loud explosion sent earth and stones flying from the hole. With a sound of breaking glass, the lights on the front end loader went out, and stones and dirt began to shower all around.

Amid the confusion, Fergus jumped up and Dan saw that he held a pistol as he ran towards Brad.

"You're all under arrest," he called, aiming his pistol at Brad. "Tell your men to stand still!"

At first Brad didn't react, so Fergus made sure that he could see the pistol and commanded, "Quickly!"

"Okay, men," shouted Brad. "Stand still and don't do anything silly."

Dan, Dave and Alex followed Fergus out from behind the bushes. "Can Fergus control 20 men?" whispered Dave. "I know he's a marksman, but..."

"The guards we passed will be coming," called Fergus. "See if you can stop them."

Alex and Dan looked at each other, then ran towards the main track. Each knew that the other believed that Jesus had told his followers not to fight, so what should they do? As they followed the track, they were amazed to see a host of jerking, shaking, twirling lights approaching. Turning on their own torches, they saw uniformed men running towards them.

"Police!" exclaimed Dan, then shouting, to make sure that Fergus heard him, "Police!"

The first runners were now within metres and seemed intent on pouncing upon Alex and Dan, until Dan had the brilliant idea of stepping back and pointing towards the pit. Alex immediately did the same and the policemen directed their attention towards the events near the pit, quickly flooding the area with blue coats.

Many on both sides seemed to recognise Fergus, and this probably contributed to a peaceful outcome.

"Welcome," called Fergus to the most senior policeman. "I think you're too late to capture one of the gang, but we've got most of the rest here. Did you get the guards near the truck?"

"Yes, we got them," said the senior policeman in a deep voice. "I'm Detective Les Talbot. Who are you?"

"Fergus Norton is the name."

"Ah, you're Fergus Norton? Well, well, well. So you're the one who wanted all these extra policemen available, then?"

"I am indeed. Now let's get these criminals arrested."

"OK, sir."

The police arrested and restrained Brad and all the gang members present, with the exception of Craig. Craig's lifeless body lay in the pit, having borne the full brunt of Harry's masterpiece. Apparently Harry had modified his booby-trapped toolbox after learning that Craig had murdered his brother – and warned Brad of the change.

Ignorant of those modifications, Craig had opened the lid to arm the device as instructed, only to trigger it instead. Steve Jones' stolen toolbox would never be any use as a toolbox again, but nor would Craig ever murder again.

Perhaps Brad might have warned Craig had Craig not just bullied him more brutally than normal.

The arrests were soon complete and everything seemed to be under control when Dan's phone rang. He was so un-used to having his phone ring that it took him some time to notice the noise and vibration in his pocket. Pulling it out, he checked the number but didn't recognise it, so he answered with a cautious, "Hello?"

"It's me, Belinda," said a voice. Dan didn't answer, wondering why she was ringing from another number. "I'm ringing from Miranda's phone since it works on this network," she continued. "I hope this isn't a bad time to ring." How like Belinda, thought Dan – to ring at a time when she might get him into trouble and then check if she had!

"No problem, Sis. The police have just finished arresting Brad and his gang."

"Miranda hoped it would be like that."

"How would she know?"

"A bloke named Harry rang her earlier and told her he'd set up a booby-trap for Craig – you know that brute we saw at Beehive Falls – and she could do what she wanted with the news because he wants nothing more to do with the gang. Apparently Craig's been trying to bully her into being his girlfriend and she's terrified of him. I was talking to her when Harry called, and afterwards she explained a few things to me."

"Craig said she helped him rob the mine."

"I don't know about that, but I do know she called the police and warned them of the gang's plans. Apparently Brad also rang her earlier and told her Craig had murdered Harry's brother. She says Brad never wanted her to have anything to do with Craig. Anyway, the police must've left immediately if they're there already."

"They've been here for about half-an-hour, I guess."

"They *were* quick! Well, a few minutes ago, Harry rang her again to warn her that Craig and some accomplices robbed a bank in Horsham this afternoon. One of the robbers knew Harry from the mine and rang him to boast about the robbery. They killed a guard and stole millions of dollars' worth of those new gold coins. Craig headed straight for Heatherlie, but a four-wheel drive full of his men sped away towards the South Australian border. They never really intended to go to the border, though, so after a while they left the highway and turned back towards the Grampians. The really important news is that they'll arrive at Heatherlie soon. Harry pumped all the information he could out of him, and apparently they plan to attack Brad's gang at Heatherlie and steal all the loot they've collected from other robberies."

"Not much loyalty among thieves, is there?"

"No. Now, stop talking and warn the police about Craig's men."

"Yes, Ma'am! Whatever you say!"

"Sorry, Danny-boy. I'm just worried about what those men will do."

Dan hung up and approached Fergus, who was talking to Detective Talbot. Quickly he explained the situation, adding, "I reckon they'll park down near Craig's car."

Fergus agreed. Reluctantly he asked Dan, Dave and Alex to lead him and another ten policemen to the place, while the rest stayed to make sure everything was safe. As they walked, he gave Dan and the others strict instructions to keep well out of the way of Craig's men and stay safe. They grudgingly agreed.

Not far from Craig's car, they all hid behind trees and waited in silence in the pitch black. Just ten minutes later, Dan heard a car approaching. His heart in his mouth, he heard it slow down, then pick its way carefully down the track from the Mount Zero Road. Soon, a four-wheel drive with only sidelights on parked beside Craig's car. As it did so, the surrounding police closed in, careful to remain protected by trees. After all, these men were violent criminals who would not hesitate to shoot.

The car's engine fell silent, and all four doors opened slowly. For a moment, there was complete silence as the men inside the car listened for any unexpected sound. Then, apparently satisfied, they began to climb out.

"Okay, take it easy, fellas," called Les' deep, booming voice, seeming to come from all around the car. "We've got you surrounded, and Fergus Norton is here. Your boss is dead and we know your plans. Give up now and you'll stay alive."

Chapter 30

Wrapping Up

"It was amazing," explained Dan to Belinda next morning after breakfast. "They all meekly put up their hands. It seemed to be the mention of Fergus Norton that made them give up. Apparently he's really famous as a police marksman, so every criminal of that sort would know him as a dangerous enemy."

"He doesn't look dangerous to me," said Belinda. "He's nice."

Belinda had met Fergus for the first time the previous night when the police dropped him off at the camp not long after Alex, Dan and Dave returned to report the night's events to a concerned family. The police had also asked Miranda to wait at the camp the following afternoon until they could visit to tie up loose ends.

News of the excitement at Heatherlie had spread like wildfire among the mine workers at the camp. Naturally, they were shocked to learn that some of their colleagues were involved in the theft of millions of dollars' worth of ore and gold!

Miranda was the subject of plenty of sympathetic conjecture, for although only a new employee, she was already popular.

The camp was to finish immediately after lunch, and Paul, the mine's camp coordinator, asked Dan's family and Alex to join them before the meal was served.

Once everyone was seated, including Fergus as a guest, Paul stood up and gave a short speech.

"On behalf of the campers here and mine management in Stawell, I want to express our gratitude to you all: Nathan, Tanya, Dan, Belinda and Alex. You've worked tirelessly to make this camp the most enjoyable, educational and satisfying one we've ever had."

The campers began to clap loudly and Paul paused and smiled.

"Not only so," he continued, when the clapping died down, "but you've been instrumental in overcoming the attempts of Brad's gang to set up an evil empire. Sorry to criticise your brother, Miranda, but his gang was dangerous and caused significant damage to the mine's business, threatening the jobs of everyone here.

"Our mine has great expectations of growth and prosperity in which you can all share. We have much to look forward to out here beyond the western margin – the place we all call home."

Cheers and stamps greeted his words, and he presented the family and Alex with a small gift of appreciation.

An appetising lunch followed, after which the campers left – all except Miranda.

When Les Talbot arrived an hour later with three other officers, Miranda was sitting in the mess hall with all the

Turners, Alex and Fergus. She was obviously very nervous, although Belinda was doing her best to help her relax.

Les and his men sat down and Les explained the situation. "We've got Brad and his gang in custody, including some extras from Halls Gap, but we've still got a few things to straighten out. We've spent the morning interviewing Brad and his men about their setup, and they're all cooperating except in one area – no-one will say anything about NK2. Some obviously know nothing about NK2, but a few obviously know but won't tell."

"But we already..." began Dan.

"Maybe Brad thinks NK2 will be punished severely, so he's pretending not to be him," interrupted Nathan.

Dan tried again. "We know..."

He fell silent again as Les held up his hands. "Let's start with some background questions. Firstly, how could they ring each other when nobody else can use the mobile networks?"

Dan answered, "Three weeks ago we walked up Mount Stapylton, and I saw people go into the Hollow Mountain Exchange. Glen and I visited yesterday to investigate, and he found they'd hacked the tower so that it only allowed calls from their own list of numbers. He reckons they've probably done the same to other towers around the Grampians. Glen also set the system to record calls, so you should be able to listen to any calls made last night."

"Glen," said Les, making a note. "That's good. We'll talk to him."

"I think I know who NK2 was," said Dan, and this time he wasn't interrupted.

"Tell us," invited Les.

"Brad Jessop was only second in command. NK2 was the real boss – the man called Craig. He loved robbery and violence and hated police. He masterminded the gold robbery near the margin and the bank robbery yesterday in Horsham. He arranged the ore theft, too, and hoped to kill some policemen by tricking you into digging up the ore at Heatherlie and opening a booby-trapped toolbox. He sneered at his men and thought he was very clever, but he made a few big mistakes."

"Such as?"

"Last night he told us all about how clever NK2 was, ridiculing any suggestion that it could be Brad. He talked about keeping NK2 mysteriously unknown, while dropping tantalising hints about his gang. He knew too much about NK2's plans not to be NK2 himself. Everyone who knew him saw his love of violence.

"A final hint came when you told those bank robbers about Craig's death: one said to another, 'Such is life!', a line Ned Kelly is famous for."

"You're right, Dan – Craig was NK2, and he was obsessed with Ned Kelly," said Miranda. "He often used that expression. And he really was determined to kill policemen."

"Well, I'm glad to say he never achieved that," said Les. "But he did kill Darren on Wednesday night, and a bank guard yesterday."

"I also recognised one of Craig's men last night," added Dan, "His name was Ed and he was at the Lake Burrumbeet Camping Ground when we stopped there a few weeks ago. He did his best to convince us to cross the margin later in the morning, which would have been after the convoy passed. Without the convoy for protection, I'm sure he and his cronies would have robbed us."

"We'll follow that one up too," said Les, making more notes. "And what about the ore? We took a sample to the mine from one of those barrels they were burying last night, and they say it's not the special ore they believe was stolen."

"The barrels they left on the truck are sure to be the high-grade ore," said Alex. "Craig was burying ore as a trap, just hoping to kill policemen. He would've planned to take the good stuff with him."

"Along with the twenty million dollars of gold from the bullion robbery and the two million dollars of gold coins from the robbery yesterday," said Belinda.

"That makes sense," said Les. "Okay, since you all know so much about this case, where should we start looking for all that gold?"

"Have you looked in Craig's car?" asked Dave.

"And his accomplices' car too," added Dan.

"I reckon you'll find the gold coins in those two cars," said Alex.

"And the gold bullion?" asked Les.

"Have you looked in the stone cottages?" asked Dan.

"Only a cursory glance," said Les.

"Better go back and look properly," smiled Fergus.

"Well, that ties up a lot of loose ends and I'm looking forward to getting our hands on the gold," said Les, well satisfied. "So, Miranda, what was your involvement in this?"

"I thought Brad and I were the only ones who knew the truth about Craig. Brad's probably avoiding talking about NK2 in case I really did help Craig as he claimed. Craig wanted me as his girlfriend, but I refused. Then he threatened to kill Brad if I didn't agree. I was still avoiding giving him an answer when he came up with this idea of stealing ore from the mine."

"Why didn't you tell the police?" asked Les.

"I didn't want to get Brad into trouble. Anyway, Craig wanted me to modify the shift records to hide what his men were doing, but I refused, so he threatened to plant evidence proving that I'd done it. He got his communications expert to access the admin network and change the records."

"Can you prove that?"

"It's just what Craig told me."

"Craig told us *you'd* made the changes," said Fergus.

"I'm not surprised – it's what he threatened to do."

"Don't worry," said Fergus, "we'll check it. The database auditing records should show when and how the changes were made. An expert should be able to track down who did it."

☙

"When we came here, I wanted a lazy holiday and was hoping to avoid uni," said Dan. "It's funny, but we've been busy, busy, busy ever since we arrived, and I've loved every second of it!"

"It's not even Christmas yet, but we've had all sorts of excitement, learned how to run a camp, and helped catch a bunch of crooks," said Belinda.

"And we've started giving religion a fair go," added Tanya. "We might never have done that in the city."

"It hasn't been as bad as I feared," said Belinda, straight-faced, then she smiled. "I love the singing, but I'm worried that I'm starting to pay attention to the words!"

Dan laughed. "That's not a bad thing. I sometimes get to the end of a hymn and wonder what the words were."

"Well, that's what I'm like when we read the Bible."

"I find it too interesting for that."

"Maybe you can help each other, then," said Tanya. "We've had a lovely time here so far, and I do think God has had something to do with that."

"I agree," said Nathan. "So thanks for pushing us a bit, son."

Dan flushed and looked down at his toast. He was thrilled with his family's response to God and couldn't wait to tell Alex about it. He looked up again. "He's kept us safe, too, despite the efforts of Brad and Craig."

"That's true," said Tanya.

"Have either of you had more thoughts about the reward Les mentioned?" asked Nathan. "It sounds like it could even be enough to get us back into Victoria if we wanted to."

"I liked Mum's suggestion of covering Sylvia's medical costs," said Belinda, and Dan nodded.

"Sounds like we're all agreed, then," said Nathan. "That will leave us stuck out here in God's own country!"

It was Saturday morning and the family was eating a late breakfast together, discussing the unexpected events of the last few weeks. Alex had left for Stawell earlier, intending to visit his parents and return in the evening. He had plenty to tell them! Uncle Mick and Aunty Robyn had followed him in their own car with Dave and Grandma and Grandpa Turner, intending to do some shopping in Stawell, which left Dan's family on their own for the day.

"So what do you think, kids?" continued Nathan. "Was it worth coming out here beyond the western margin?"

"Of course," chorused Dan and Belinda.

"And we've still got so much more to look forward to, with Grandma and Grandpa Turner and Uncle Mick, Aunty Robyn and Dave staying here," said Tanya.

"No more thieves trying to take over the National Park," mused Dan, "and another couple of months at the camp before we need to make any more decisions."

"You're right, Danny-boy," said Belinda.

Notes

This story is set in many real locations in the state of Victoria in south-eastern Australia.

There is an existing resort near the Beehive Falls parking area, but I have never visited it, beyond a brief look at their website.[3] The camp site described in this story may or may not bear much similarity to that resort – I don't know.

The roads, mountains, tracks and distances referred to all reflect the true locations of places in and around the Grampians in western Victoria.

For information about the National Park, see the Parks Victoria website.[4]

As a story placed a few years in the future, there are many guesses and assumptions of possible changes due to the effects of the COVID-19 pandemic and possible subsequent pandemics. These may or may not prove to be well-founded guesses: only time will tell!

The story is not intended as any sort of praise, criticism, or deep analysis of existing government policies or actions; any references to suggested future policies are simply part of the storyline imagined by the author.

Maps have been made from Open Street Map[5] data with some additional features added to fit the story. The margins drawn are completely imaginary. For a map of Victoria including the Grampians, see the link below.[6]

---

[3] https://www.rosesgap.com.au/
[4] https://www.parks.vic.gov.au/places-to-see/parks/grampians-national-park
[5] https://www.openstreetmap.org/
[6] https://www.openstreetmap.org/#map=8/-37.6/143

About the Author

Mark Morgan was born in Australia in 1963, the youngest son of Peter and Meryl Morgan. Deeply involved in religion all of his life, he has worked as a lay preacher, Sunday School teacher and missionary – trying to balance the many demands of spiritual life with those of family and paid employment.

After graduating, he worked in engineering for sever-al years before concentrating on software development. Happily married and blessed with eight children, he has spent many years reading the Bible and learning to teach its lessons.

Writing Bible-based novels now fills much of his time.

Free Download

Paul in Snippets

A 109-page PDF novelette by Mark Morgan.

The life of Paul painted from the Acts of the Apostles.

Get your free copy of *Paul in Snippets* when you sign up for the Bible Tales mailing list. As well as the eBook, you will receive a weekly email newsletter with micro tales, informative articles and special offers.

Visit **https://www.BibleTales.online/free-pins**

www.BibleTales.online

Bible Tales Online

Other books are also available from Bible Tales Online.

Terror on Every Side!
THE LIFE OF JEREMIAH by Mark Morgan

From a family of priests in the peaceful reign of good King Josiah, came a young man Jeremiah, bringing words from God to his people. It was no message for the fainthearted, either. It was a message of *Terror on Every Side!*

Volume 1 – Early Days
Volume 2 – As Good As It Gets
Volume 3 – Darkness Falling
Volume 4 – The Darkness Deepens
Volume 5 – No Remedy
Volume 6 – That Broken Reed

Available in hardcover, paperback, eBook and audio-book.

Micro-tales

Collections of short stories about Bible characters or events, available in paperback, eBook and audiobook.

Fiction Favours the Facts
Fiction Favours the Facts – Book 2
Fiction Favours the Facts – Book 3
by Mark Morgan and others

Other novels

**Joseph,
Rachel's son**

(p'back, eBook, audiobook)

**The King's
Armour-bearer**

(h'cover, p'back, eBook)

Bible Tales Online continues to publish books.
To find the list of currently available books, visit

https://www.BibleTales.online/books

Bible
Tales
www.BibleTales.online